The Elusive

John Borden was watching me, *studying* me. The idea was idiotic, but I couldn't shake it. His eyes were very sharp. Very blue . . .

There was a rattling and clanking outside, as the taxi pulled up. I followed John Borden out and climbed into the back seat of the cab, while he gave the driver directions in rapid-fire Greek. Then he stuck his head through the window on my side and said, "It's all set up. He'll take you straight to Kilithia, ninety drachmas."

Let me tell you how tired I was: we were halfway up the mountain when I realized what was wrong.

I hadn't told John Borden I was going to Kilithia.

And he had no reason to suspect I'd be going to a village so small and anonymous I have never seen it on any map . . .

ANN PARIS

GRAVEN IMAGE

PUBLISHED BY POCKET BOOKS NEW YORK

This novel is a work of fiction. Names, characters, places and incidents are either the product of the author's imagination or are used fictitiously. Any resemblance to actual events or locales or persons, living or dead, is entirely coincidental.

Another *Original* publication of POCKET BOOKS

POCKET BOOKS, a division of Simon & Schuster, Inc.
1230 Avenue of the Americas, New York, N.Y. 10020

ISBN: 0-671-62191-2

First Pocket Books printing April 1987

10 9 8 7 6 5 4 3 2 1

POCKET and colophon are registered trademarks
of Simon & Schuster, Inc.

Printed in the U.S.A.

ONE OF THE working-girl magazines my mother sends me every month runs a regular column on "How to Avoid Doing Personal Errands for Your Boss." The column, like everything else in the magazine, is written for secretaries—maybe that's the trouble. I am not a secretary. I am the editor, theoretically the *executive* editor, of a small, full-color national magazine called *Greek Time*. According to my job description, it is my responsibility to assign and schedule all articles, columns, and features; establish the particulars of the budget for editorial, art, and printing; review and pass on all layouts and illustrations; determine long-term editorial objectives and policy; and produce a "From the Editor" column once a month. Right. Job descriptions being what they are, it might be helpful to get a little real here. What I am is one of the world's most expensive gofers.

Not that I get paid well, mind you. It's not my salary that makes me expensive. It's the gofer-ing. My boss, Panyotis Sotirios Peteris (called Panos, or Pan), has very interesting ideas on what gofers should go *for*.

I was gofer-ing that day in February when I landed at Agios Constantinos, on the island of Themnos, for

1

the fifth time in four months. "Landed" may be a bit misleading. Olympic has an excellent shuttle-plane system to most of the important Greek islands, but Themnos isn't one of them. Themnos isn't a tourist island or a hub of business activity or even the kind of place where the new rich of Athens like to build summer houses. Themnos has Agios Constantinos, which has one hotel and four tavernas and the minuscule port that allows the shepherds in the mud villages up the mountain to transport raw wool to a wider world, which might be willing to pay for it. The mail boat stops there twice a week, skidding across the Aegean Sea and threatening to crash into the sheer rock face that is the edge of the island. Seen from a distance, from one of the cruise boats for foreigners that are so careful to stop only on "picturesque" islands, Themnos looks like a small, worn Alp that has been heaved, new-minted, and untouched by water erosion, from the ocean floor.

Seen close up that day in February, Themnos looked in the process of drowning, going down for the third time under an angry mass of cloud banks so thick and dark, it made the Aegean look black. Rain is always like that in Greece—silent and ominous, unrelieved by thunder or lightning, relentless. It starts in late October and goes on until April, hostile, bitter, threatening—and cold. To be caught in a storm in the Aegean is no different from being caught in a storm anywhere else. To be caught in one of those great endless weather fronts, however, is to test your ability to stay cool in a crisis. The clouds begin to sound like the secret voices of the mud villages on the mountain —no, Themnos is not a tourist island; and no, they don't want you there. You or anybody else.

We bounced off the line of thick wooden pilings that had been driven into the sea to act as a break with all the finesse of Jerry Lewis doing a pratfall, shuddered until the water slopped over the deck, and came to a sighing stop, like a dog settling in front of a fireplace. The woman next to me stopped crossing herself and released the sheep she had been strangling the entire half hour we'd been coming into port. The sheep was in even worse shape than the rest of us, wet and dirty and miserable, and I felt a little guilty about feeling so much better when I looked at it. Unfortunately, although I knew the animal was suffering, I needed to laugh at it—needed to desperately, with a kind of elemental manicness I hoped was the result of lack of sleep and lack of food and seventeen hours on a pitching, leaky mail boat in a sly and violent sea. The sight of Agios Constantinos, a travel-poster anomaly of whitewashed walls and red tile roofs huddled at the edge of the water, did nothing to improve my mood. Themnos was getting to me in a way it never had before. It looked dangerous. It made me want to cut and run.

I shook the water out of my hair and headed toward the flat wooden plank that had been laid from the gap in the rail to the wharf. I was being ridiculous, and I knew it. I was tired—getting to Themnos meant a ten-hour plane ride from New York to Athens, an hour-and-a-half plane ride from Athens to Rhodes, and that interminable mail boat—and I was more than a little upset with myself and Pan and my brother and my father and everybody else I knew. Events, as they said in the books I sometimes borrowed from my next-door neighbor when I had nothing to do on Saturday night, were conspiring against me. Two years ago, when my brother, Chas, had first put me on to Pan Peteris and *Greek Time,* I thought I'd found the Holy Grail. Being the stubborn sort—all Hansens are the stubborn sort, especially my father, even though he won't admit it—it had taken me nearly twenty-four months to accept that seventeen-five a year and the title "executive editor" could not make up for what I was being put through. Even that would have been all right—better late than never—except that I knew perfectly well I wasn't going to do anything about it. There was nothing I could do about it. I lived from paycheck to paycheck, Chas was starving as a doctoral candidate at Columbia, and our father (who, if the last two years had been anything like the twenty preceding, could probably buy and sell several small national corporations) was talking to neither of us.

I pushed my two large, impossibly heavy suitcases down the ramp and followed them on foot. I think I was hoping they'd fall into the sea. They weighed fifty pounds—I'd had to pay the overweight twice, in New York and Athens, out of my own pocket—and only half a pound of it was mine. The rest was paraphernalia for Pan's brand-new, conspicuous-consumption house, that squatter's palace he was building on the mountain above the mud village where he'd been born and raised to the age of twelve, when his mother, finally sick of being a good Greek wife, had packed herself and her children into the island's single bus and started out on the long journey to New York.

I landed on the wharf, picked up the suitcases, and began to drag them to the first, and largest, of Agios Constantinos's four tavernas. The taxi stand out front was empty. I would have to wait in the taverna, which would not be comfortable. The man who owned it, although perfectly willing to serve anyone who would pay him in hard cash, was not partial to women. It would have been enough to make me want to lie down and die, but I had something to hang on to: Chas was on Themnos. He was doing his doctorate in anthropology, with a dissertation on Greek island folk

4

customs, and he had a grant. It was a very small grant, but that was beside the point. He was on Themnos, I was on Themnos, and we hadn't seen each other in months. At least *something* about this trip was going to be bliss.

I was thinking about bliss when I ducked under the taverna's green canvas awning, swung my suitcases blindly in front of me, and ran straight into the man in the black leather jacket.

I am a small woman (five-four and a hundred and six), and dark. My hair, which is almost black, has a tendency to disappear in unlit rooms. So do my clothes. I have been addicted since college to black turtlenecks and maroon Baxter State parkas, making me exactly the kind of person most likely to be run over in the night while walking on some godforsaken country road. The man in the black leather jacket didn't even see me coming. He went over like a boxer's dummy, landed on bare wooden boards so hard it sounded as if he'd cracked them, and started swearing more fiercely than anyone I'd heard since I'd seen George C. Scott in *Patton*.

I knew even before he got up that I'd interrupted something I shouldn't have been anywhere near. I could see it on the face of the man who owned the taverna, a black, surly Greek who looked more Arab than anything else and whose face was covered with scars that ended in deep, round points. The taverna owner and I knew each other by sight, if not by name, and hated each other on principle, but the way he was looking at me now was more than that. He made no move to help the man on the floor. He just stared at me, minute after minute, as if I were responsible for opening Pandora's box and calling the devil out of hell and bringing all these tourists into Greece.

I looked down and saw a strong, long-fingered hand running through a patch of golden hair. The hair was very thick, even thicker than mine, but also very straight. Then he put his head back to look at me, and I saw that his face was as fine and strong and well defined as his hands—a sculptor's face, with every plane polished smooth and every angle chiseled into certainty.

He got to his knees, shook his head twice, and said, "Jesus *Christ.*"

I nearly said the same thing myself. You do not put a man like that one down on a remote island in Greece—not alone and unprotected, anyway. Every woman in screaming distance was going to follow him as blindly as the children followed the Pied Piper. Their men weren't going to like it one bit, and the local Greek Orthodox priests were going to like it even less. Someone was going to murder him in his sleep.

He got to his feet, brushed off his pants, shoved his hands in the pockets of his jacket, and said, "What the *hell* did you think you were doing?"

Maybe it was because I was tired or because I'd finally had enough of men ordering me around—between my father and Pan Peteris, my life was practically nothing *but* men ordering me around—but I just couldn't force myself to be polite to him.

I dropped into the nearest chair, reached into my parka for the cigarettes I'd been trying to give up for six months, and said, "How do you expect anyone to see you, dressed up like an undertaker like that?"

He blinked, and I blushed. The fact was, he was dressed nothing like an undertaker. He was dressed like a spy in a Robert Ludlum novel, and he looked *wonderful.*

To be precise, he looked entirely too wonderful.

I fumbled around with a box of Greek government-issue matches until I managed to get my cigarette lit. It was better than having to look at him or the man who owned the taverna, and it gave me something to do. That's the real problem with giving up cigarettes —they provide you with something to do when the only other alternative is to sit there looking ashamed of yourself.

He sat down in a seat on the far side of the aisle, put his hands on his knees, and stared into my face. "All right," he said. "Who *are* you?"

I said, "My name is Kerry Hansen," and coughed. I had smoke in my eyes. It made my eyelids feel full of sand and tears run down my face. I rubbed them ineffectually, trying to regain something like sight. I'd almost managed it when I caught the way he was looking at me. It was one of the strangest moments of my life. It was as if my name had done something . . . peculiar to his face: made his eyes wider and his cheeks more indrawn, made his mind more alert.

The idea was so patently absurd, I got rid of it right away. I'd never seen the man before—I'd have remembered if I had—and my father, though better than well off, was not famous. I waited patiently for him to tell me I didn't look Scandinavian—which everybody does, since Hansen is the shortened form of something ethnic my father got rid of the day he got a scholarship to Harvard Law School.

Instead, he took the cigarette out of my hand and killed it in the nearest excuse for an ashtray. "Why smoke the damn things if you don't even like them?" he said. "I mean, for God's sake—" He stopped in the middle of his sentence, turned to the taverna owner, and started spewing out something in rapid-fire Greek. It surprised me. Chas, who has been studying modern Greek since college, can manage no more

7

than halting, overly formal polite phrases. From the rhythm of this man's conversation, I could tell he was more than familiar with the language. He knew the idiom, and his talent at casual obscenity was undoubtedly bilingual.

Whatever he was saying, the taverna owner didn't like it. He did, however, accept it. When the black-leather-jacket man was finished spewing orders, the taverna owner turned on his heel and stomped away toward the back of the shop—out of sight and, I hoped, out of mind. I would have been overjoyed never to lay eyes on that monster again as long as I lived.

The black-leather-jacket man took out his own cigarettes, lit up with a shiny new American Zippo, and said, "John Borden."

I said, "How do you do."

He sighed. Now that I was getting used to the dimness under the canvas, I could see more details in his face. He looked even more tired than I felt. There were bags under his eyes big enough to hold acorns, and deep lines on the sides of his face. I had registered these at first as signs of age. Without thinking about it, I had assumed him to be in his late thirties or even early forties. Now I realized he was much younger than that, in his late twenties at best, not much older than I. I wondered idly if I looked like that, too—baggy and lined and brutalized by exhaustion. I hoped not.

The taverna owner came back carrying a small, round tray with two palm-sized cups of thick Greek coffee and a plate of *loukoumia* on it. He put it down on the table near John Borden's elbow—he didn't seem to want to get any nearer to me than he had to—and marched away again.

John Borden handed me one of the cups of coffee

and the *loukoumia*. Then he sat back in his chair and tried to look comfortable.

"Kerry Hansen," he said affably.

I like *loukoumia,* which is a kind of jellied fruit candy covered with powdered sugar, so I took four pieces of it and started stuffing them in my mouth. "Katherine," I told him, letting the words come out muffled by the food.

He looked blank for a minute, then nodded. "Katherine," he said. "Kerry is short for Katherine."

"Is John short for Jonathan?"

"No, John is just John."

The conversation was getting so inane, neither one of us could stand it. I put away the *loukoumia*—if I don't watch it, I don't stay at a hundred six pounds for long—and dived for the Greek coffee.

On the other side of the narrow aisle, John Borden was watching me, *studying* me. That idea was as idiotic as the one I'd had about his recognizing my name, but this one I couldn't shake. He *was* studying me, following every move I made, and I began to wish he'd gone whole hog on the spy costume and fitted himself with a pair of dark glasses. His eyes were very blue and very sharp.

I got out another cigarette, braving his disapproval, and realized I felt like a fool. The man had me wound up like a watch spring, and I'd hardly said a sensible English sentence to him. He hadn't said one to me, either. We were just sitting there, on either side of a narrow aisle in an overfurnished taverna at the edge of an empty sea, making each other uncomfortable.

There was a rattling and clanking outside and the taxi pulled up to the bent and rusted metal pole that marked its stand. I nearly leaped to my feet.

I wasn't fast enough. By the time I started reaching for my suitcases, John Borden already had them in his

9

hands and was heading down the aisle for the street, as relieved as a condemned man who has just received a reprieve from the governor.

I followed him in a state of some dejection. God only knew I was glad to get rid of him—I'd never spent a less congenial fifteen minutes in my life—but I wasn't so happy to see him so glad to be rid of me. It was the kind of thing that never happened to the working girls in those magazines my mother sent me.

I got to the curb to find my bags already deposited in the taxi's trunk and John Borden giving directions to the driver in more rapid-fire Greek, gesturing and enunciating with curious exaggeration. The driver seemed to be objecting to something, but I couldn't think what. He'd taken me up the mountain enough times to know where I was going without having to ask. I'd ridden with him enough times to know I didn't want to—you may not think it's possible to get an ill-used 1957 Ford up to 95, but it is—but since there was no other choice but a long walk, I knew I was going to have to. Kerry Hansen Goes to Greece. With the exception of meeting John Borden, it was a day like any other day when Pan had decided he *had* to have somebody take care of a few things on Themnos.

I jerked open the back door and collapsed on the lumpy seat, leaving the men to engage in stupidities by themselves. Now that I thought of it, I was not only going to be glad to be rid of John Borden, I was going to be overjoyed to get to Pan's monstrosity of a house—anything, as long as there was a bed at the end of it, where I could collapse and sleep for a week.

John Borden and the driver finished their interminable discussion. The driver sprinted around the front of the car, climbed in behind the wheel, and slammed the door shut. The motor coughed and hissed and jumped and bucked, sounding for all the world like a dying sea monster.

At the last minute, John Borden stuck his head through the window on my side and said, "It's all set up. He'll take you straight to Kilithia, ninety drachmas, no stops along the way."

Let me tell you how tired I was: we were halfway up the mountain, a good fifteen minutes from the outskirts of Agios Constantinos, when I realized what was wrong with that picture.

Like the fact that I had not told John Borden I was going to Kilithia.

Like the fact that he had no reason to suspect I'd be going there or to have heard of the village at all. Kilithia is a shepherd's outpost built into the mud and the rock, so small and anonymous, I have never seen it on any map.

I twisted around in my seat, trying to see out the dirt-encrusted back window, trying to see Agios Constantinos and John Borden and the scene in front of the taverna, where everything had gone so terribly strange at the last minute. I couldn't see anything, of course. There was just a rutted dirt road turning to mud and the sparse scrub that covered the mountain like a five o'clock shadow and that weather front coming in from the east, a dark wall of churning black clouds, shutting out the sun.

IN KILITHIA, THE house had been finished, but the driveway had not. This made a certain amount of sense—I won't go into an involved explanation of Greek labor union regulations, which by now may be inexplicable, but I will say this: every major paved road in the country was built by one American corporation or another—but it also caused a certain amount of trouble. One of the eternal problems of gofers is that they lack the authority of the people they gofer for. Pan, having returned to Greece after getting rich in America, would have commanded a certain amount of respect. I, being a mere employee, and female and American in the bargain, encountered mostly resistance. The driver didn't want to take his precious rattletrap up the last of the hill, over scrub and rock and broken pieces of wood and plaster. Coaxed to the front door, he absolutely refused to take my bags out of the trunk and haul them inside. I struggled away on my own, proving once more Hansen's law of international travel: suitcases get heavier the longer you have to carry them. Then I came back out of the house to pay the man and was treated to five minutes of abuse because I, a rich American (all Americans are rich—ask any Greek), had had the unmitigated arrogance to tender no better than a ten percent tip. Or words to that effect. Fortunately for me, the driver was not only Greek but both provincial and uneducated. He spoke a dialect I understood only two or three words of, and even my "understanding" of those was mostly guess.

I let myself into Pan's marble-floored foyer and locked the door behind me. In its way, it was out of the frying pan into the fire. God only knows, Pan's taste in furniture would have been bad enough—you should have seen his taste in New York women—but the house in Kilithia didn't have the benefit even of his scant acquaintance with Anglo-Saxon understatement. The whole thing—heart-shaped bathroom off the master bedroom, mirrored ceilings in the master bedroom, room after room of wall after wall of niches stuffed with plaster reproductions of Greek statues—had been put together by the Athenian architect of the moment, a man guaranteed to spend more money than any of his competitors. Pan had never seen the place. Neither had his mother, Marina, or his sister, Caliope. In fact, the Peterises never came to Greece at all. They had not come a year ago, when Pan's father died. They had not come six months after that, when Marina, a village Greek to her bones, chose the village girl Pan was going to marry. They had certainly never come to see to the export end of the import/export souvenir business they had started the year before I went to work for them, but that was less strange. That was what they had *me* for.

I wandered into the living room—it was the size of the Starlight Room at the Waldorf, with Doric columns scattered throughout, holding up nothing—and threw myself into a comfortable if slightly bizarre-looking chair, thinking all the time about Pan and Marina and that strange man at the wharf, John Borden. If I thought about it long enough, I knew the

Peterises were strange. I hadn't known any immigrant Greeks before I took the job at *Greek Time,* but after two years I'd met quite a few, and they tended to run to pattern: three jobs, house in Astoria, trip home every Christmas. The trip home was as important as the house in Astoria. It was a way to refuel, to remember what they had to prove and to whom. Sometimes this was easy—there are still many remote villages in Greece where indoor plumbing has yet to make an appearance—and sometimes hard, but nothing is as hard as doing eighteen hours of menial labor a day. Especially when you're doing it to keep a house you can't quite afford and send your children to private school in Manhattan.

Of course, the Peterises were well beyond menial labor by the time I met them. That had been Marina's job, and she must have done it well. Pan had had to settle for Queens College, but he'd taken his business degree at Columbia, and even fifteen years ago that must have been expensive. What must have been even more expensive was buying the business—not *Greek Time* or the souvenir thing but the core business, a national Greek-language daily called *The Banner.* The idea of a Greek-language daily newspaper operating in the United States may seem lame, but it isn't. *The Banner* has over seventy thousand subscribers, and it isn't the only or even the largest in the country. The *Ethniko Kirix* has more subscribers. So does *Proini.* And they're only the beginning.

What distinguished Pan from his competitors wasn't journalistic competence or journalistic integrity—none of the Greeks who run these papers would know what the words mean or see the point in them if they did—but sheer unmitigated gall. Maybe I should say unmitigated gall and blatant amorality. Pan really didn't care what he did or how he did it as

14

long as he got where he was going. At the same time, he wasn't exactly Cesare Borgia. It would never have occurred to him to poison Fanny Pestilides's coffee or have Tony Diamataris kidnapped. Pan simply had an unshakable conviction that the character of all Greek-born people, not excluding his mother and sister, was of the cesspool. He treated them accordingly.

What I had going for me, of course, was the fact that I was "American." I was born in Connecticut. My father was born in Massachusetts. My grandparents were born somewhere else, but Pan never went back that far. He was perfectly happy to have my assistant, George Kalimaris, who had been born in Manhattan of parents born in Thessalonika. Anything, as long as you yourself could legally run for president.

On the other hand, Pan never let himself get too far away from what all the other transplanted Greeks thought of as normal behavior. He might not have gone home for his father's funeral, but he made a sacrifice big enough to impress even Iakovos, Greek Orthodox archbishop of North and South America—he bumped part three of the Greek press story of the year, the high-speed chase for the five men who had robbed the National Bank of Greece of six million dollars in gold bullion, to put his father's obituary on the front page of *The Banner*.

I got out of my chair and began to make my unsteady way in the direction of the kitchen. Thinking about Pan was one thing—I couldn't stop thinking about Pan, because on the days I didn't want to quit, I wanted to kill him—but once I got started, I always found myself contemplating Marina and Caliope and that wild woman of the Greek islands, Agapé Constantinos Papageorgiou. Agapé was Pan's mother-picked, sight-unseen fiancée, a fate I was convinced he deserved. As for Marina and Caliope—well, Marina

15

could make anyone believe that the homicidal women of Greek tragedy, like Medea and Clytemnestra, were real; and Caliope was a chorus girl. I mean that figuratively, of course. Caliope was fat, dark, pockmarked, and forty. She also had the brains of the stereotypical dumb blonde in a thirties movie and the piercing screech of a silent screen vamp whose career was ruined by talking pictures. She was also downdirty furious, on principle, every waking moment of her life.

I pushed the whole lot of them out of my head and forced my way down the narrow passage that connected the main part of the house with the kitchen—proof positive that none of the Peterises had to do the cooking, since if the mistress of the house had been responsible for the housework, the kitchen would have been made much more easily accessible.

I had almost managed to focus on something half pleasant, like how I was going to convince Pan that turning *Greek Time*'s September cover over to the Cyprus problem was sheer idiocy, when I saw them: the wild woman of the Greek islands and Frankenstein's monster, Agapé and her father, Costa.

Agapé was unpacking crates of crystal glassware.

Costa was flexing his jaw and clenching his fists, as if he were getting ready to kill her.

If I have given the impression that Costa Papageorgiou is a comic-opera villain, I'm sorry. He is nothing of the kind. My father would have called him a serious man, by which he means a man you have to take seriously. I had always taken Costa seriously enough to stay out of his way, even in the early days of the marriage negotiations, when my primary job had been to take letters back and forth between him and Marina. The ordinary island Greek male is surly, resentful that Greece is no longer the great power he thinks it deserves to be, bitter that he has had to learn a few words of English just to keep his business going. Costa was always one step away from violence, and a very short step at that. People in Kilithia said he had beaten his wife to death, just after Agapé was born, because the child was a girl and therefore an insult to his manhood. They also thought he was smuggling things to Albania or Turkey. He disappeared for weeks at a time (probably to Agapé's unconditional relief) and came back covered with scars and welts and bruises. And money. Costa Papageorgiou, who had lived his whole life in little better than a mud hut carved into Themnos's single mountain, always had money.

He also had a remarkable command of American English.

I considered turning right around and running for the living room and the stairs to the second floor. There was a lock on the door of the room I had been assigned to, and it seemed like the right time to start using it. Then I thought of the annoyingly mysterious Mr. John Borden. If he had to have occult knowledge of my movements, the least he could do was come to the rescue when needed.

Agapé wiped her hands on her skirt and smiled at me—charmingly, because I had been the messenger in the marriage negotiations and therefore might be important. I wondered for the five-millionth time why Marina wanted this girl to marry her son. Agapé was pretty enough—dark and small and sultry-sexy the way only southern European girls can afford to be, because they are protected by threat of blood feud from what my mother would call "importunities"— but she was sly rather than intelligent and militantly peasant. Marina and Pan had put together enough

17

real property to do better, even if Marina insisted on confining her search to the village of Kilithia. Both the mayor and the local Greek Orthodox priest had daughters Agapé's age but with twice her sophistication. The other girls had been sent to the grammar school in Agios Constantinos, and the mayor's had had a further year, at a finishing school in Athens. I doubted if Agapé could read. Her English was confined to the pleasantries required to sell badly woven blankets to buyers from American crafts stores, off the beaten track and foraging in out-of-the-way places in search of "authenticity." Her taste in clothes, now that Pan had sent her money to mail-order a few things from Athens, ran to synthetic satin and shiny metal spangles.

She held out her hand to me, smiled when I took it, then curtsied in the middle of the operation, as if she'd got her signals switched.

Costa said, "You're here. That means he's coming."

I sighed. Pan was coming, with Marina and Caliope, but I wasn't happy about it. According to Marina, they had to be in Kilithia for some inexplicable Greek ceremony that took place on the first anniversary of a burial, and it was "only right" to have Pan and Agapé married "at home." All of that was undoubtedly true, but the childish part of me rejected it. The childish part of me didn't understand why, since they had consistently refused to go home for over twenty-five years, they couldn't just stay in New York and make me do all the work, as usual. I wasn't fond of having to do all the work, but I was less fond of having to do it with Pan's interference, and near phobic on the subject of Caliope.

I grabbed a footstool and sat down on it. Exhaustion was destroying me. I was weak in the knees.

"He'll be here day after tomorrow," I said. "Also

18

Mrs. Peteris and Caliope. Also probably somebody from the newspaper. If you can wait that long."

Costa smiled at me. It wasn't a pleasant smile. If I had seen it on the streets of New York, I'd have headed for the nearest police officer.

Agapé grabbed her father's sleeve and pulled at it, the charming smile melting into a petulant grimace. Agapé always hated not being in the middle of whatever was going on. She hated not being able to *control* it.

Costa shook her off. "You are going to arrange the wedding?"

"Don't be ridiculous," I said.

Costa made what I knew he thought was a James Cagney face. There is television in Themnos, three hours on both Friday evenings and Saturday afternoons, and most of what appears are James Cagney movies dubbed into Greek.

"What are you doing here, then? You have come just for the party?"

"I've come to look over the shipment," I said. "You may be getting married, but there's a shipment of those—things—going out in two weeks. I'm probably supposed to count boxes."

Agapé crossed her arms over her breasts, stamped her foot, and let out a stream of poisonous-sounding Greek. She didn't even get Costa's attention. The violence had come back into his face, making his nose red and his eyes darker.

"I don't see what you're so upset about," I said. "I haven't asked you to do anything."

"No?"

"Trust me, this whole thing will go much faster if I'm left alone to do it myself. I keep saying that, but nobody ever seems to believe me."

"You don't see the insult?"

19

"What insult?"

"Do you think he'd do this to a *kiri* from Athens?"

"Do what, for God's sake?"

"Use his own wedding as an occasion for business."

I brushed hair out of my face. Themnos has electricity only six hours a day, from nine in the morning until three in the afternoon, to facilitate the work at the government offices in Agios Constantinos. We were talking to each other in the light of one kerosene lamp and two tallow candles, a circumstance that made the scene not only eerie, but vague. Costa's face hung in front of me, a disembodied globe, angry and dangerous and threatening. Somehow, a simple conversation in a kitchen full of appliances that would be useless most of the time had metamorphosed into a scene from *Daughter of Dracula*.

I got off my stool and headed for the candles, hoping to find more. It was all too much. I couldn't cope with Costa's craziness or Agapé's pouting willfulness or the unwanted memory of that last, strange conversation with John Borden, which kept sneaking up on me whenever I wasn't looking. I wanted a candle and some food and a nice long sleep. I wanted *out* of there.

I found candles in a box near the sink—the sink had a tap, but Kilithia had no running water, so I didn't know what all that was about—and boxes of matches next to them. I grabbed one of each and whirled, meaning to make an end run around Costa and escape, as quickly and cleanly as possible, to my room.

"Look," I said. "If you've got a problem with Pan, talk it over with Pan, all right? I've been traveling for over twenty-four hours, I'm starving to death, I'm cold, I'm wet, I'm tired, and as you know perfectly well—"

"Shut up," Costa said.

"What?"

"Shut up," Costa said again. "American women talk too much."

At that moment, Agapé let out with another stream of nagging Greek, which was just as well. My instinct was to let Costa have it, on the peasant-ignorant male chauvinism of Greek men, the general unfriendliness of remote Greek islands, and his personal bathing habits. Instead, I had time enough to reflect on just how idiotic that would be and to scare myself silly. Costa Papageorgiou may or may not have beaten his wife to death for presenting him with a girl child. That was conjecture. What was not conjecture was just how much pleasure he would take in teaching one of those American women who talked too much a lesson in the relative muscle-to-fat ratio of the two genders. He would love it.

I grabbed a hunk of cheese and some indeterminate kind of bun from the basket Agapé had left on the counter and bolted. I made it past Costa and into the hall before he even realized I was moving, but not through the dining-room door. I had my hand on the knob when Costa started shouting.

"Don't let him think he's going to get away with it," Costa screamed at me. "Don't let him think I won't have his balls in my pocket first time he pulls any shit."

I plunged into the dining room, slammed the door behind me, and headed for the stairs.

It was dark and I was frightened and I'd never managed to get my candle lit. I kept stumbling over things, knocking my knees into furniture, slamming into walls. By the time I got to the second floor, I felt—and probably looked—as if I'd been through a war.

It did something to my appetite. I locked the door of my room behind me, stared at the food in my hands, and ate it—fast, like a neurotic gobbling tranquilizers. Then I got my last-minute supply of dried fruit—two pounds of leathery apricots and sugar-encrusted bananas—out of the bag I'd been carrying unconsciously through that entire scene downstairs, and ate that, too. Then I ate all the bags of dry-roasted peanuts and the plastic packages of peanut butter and crackers I'd stuffed into my pockets on the plane. I made myself thoroughly ill.

Then I threw myself on the honeymoon hotel bed that took up three quarters of what was hardly better than a cubicle and passed out.

3

I MIGHT HAVE slept forever, caught in a dream where I was doing a round-robin panel for *Greek Time,* interviewing Pan and Chas and my father and Costa Papageorgiou and even John Borden on the exact nature of my inadequacies.

This is the kind of thing that happens a great deal if you are not a reflective person, and I'm not. I like flowers on Valentine's Day and Joni Mitchell records and Agatha Christie novels and even Greece when the weather is fine, but I do not like thinking about myself or even thinking about the possibility that thinking about myself might be a good idea. That probably has a lot to do with how I end up in the messes I so often end up in—the situation with my father, for instance, had been going on for several years before that late February evening, and I was no closer to resolving it, or even to understanding it, than I had been when it started. I was vaguely aware that Pan and my father were a lot alike. They were both large men, sons of immigrant mothers, and self-made. They were both, essentially, bullies: Pan because he was too good-looking (in a reformed-greaser, bookie-hustler way) for his own good and didn't have the brains to know better; and my father because the trip from a working-

23

class neighborhood in a Massachusetts mill town to a fourteen-room duplex on Sutton Place is considerably longer than the five hundred miles the road maps say it is. In a mellow mood, or on three double Drambuies with ice, I could not only sympathize with them, but also sympathize with their impatience with me. I am, after all, the daughter of a man with money. Twenty-three years of never having had to worry about a thing—until the final argument threw me out on my own to feed myself—has left me a little flaky. Two years of having to pay my own bills and wonder where the money was going to come from hadn't done much to correct the situation. I am capable of doing a better than competent job and of earning my own keep. I am not capable of taking it all deadly seriously, which is how my father thinks you have to take things if you're going to get anywhere in the world.

My father wanted me to go to law school. I would have swallowed hemlock first.

On the other hand, lawyers in white-shoe Wall Street firms start at forty-five thousand a year, even before they pass the bar.

I tossed and turned on that honeymoon hotel bed, awake half the time, asleep half the time, lost in confusion and rancor. I had no doubt Pan had spent an arm and a leg to furnish his house, but he had paid for appearances, not comfort. The bed was lumpy and hard and creaked complainingly on unoiled springs. I tossed and turned and woke myself up every five minutes. Every time I surfaced into consciousness, I found myself thinking about one man or the other, every last damn one of them giving me a little advice for my own good.

"Listen," my father said. "Everybody has to make their way in the world. Everybody. If you think you're going to fart around with a lot of literary nonsense on my money, you're out of your mind."

"Listen," Pan said. "I'm not asking you to lie. I'm asking you to slant. We're never going to go broke sticking it to the archdiocese."

"You've got to learn to be practical," my father said.

"You've got to learn to be aggressive," Pan said.

Impractical, nonaggressive me had answers for them in my sleep, the answers I could never think of when I was wide-awake and caught in the arguments that would later give me the nightmares.

Like: law bores me, lawyers bore me, and according to the *Columbia Law Review,* there's getting to be a glut in the profession anyway.

Like: sticking it to the archdiocese *is* lying and aggressive people give me headaches and we're going broke as it is.

I sat up in bed and swung my legs over the side. Outside, the rain had changed from a steady, depressing drizzle to a full-blown storm, all wind and lightning and hard pellets of water against the window glass. I felt myself relax a little. Those weather fronts can get you crazy—according to the statistics, acts of violence rise forty percent during the season—but fear of a thunderstorm is just a vestige of childhood, not to be taken seriously.

I fumbled in my bag until I found the proofs for the next issue of *Greek Time* and my flashlight, and went back to bed to get some real work done. I was just settled under the blankets when I realized the flashlight was without batteries. Of course it was. If it had been working, I'd have used it downstairs instead of dodging Costa and Agapé for tallow candles.

I got out of bed again, found the candle and

matches I'd brought up, got some light going, and got back into bed. I was just settling against the pillows, wondering how I was going to manage to get anything done in such dim light, when I heard the first noise.

"Cats," I said to myself, trying to sound positive. What I'd heard had sounded like furniture toppling, a heavy piece hitting a hard stone floor, except that it was too far away, much farther than the first floor. I held my breath, waiting for a noise to follow the noise, for a clue to what was happening. There was nothing. The candle flickered and sank and rose again in a draft. The papers on my knees started sliding down the smooth surface of the comforter toward the floor. I caught them and listened again. Still nothing.

I thought, half seriously, about getting out of bed and going downstairs to see if something was wrong. Then I thought about Costa, who could still be lurking downstairs, and about the papers on my knees, which represented work that really had to be done. I wriggled into the lumpy mattress and tried to concentrate on Penny Hadzipetros's profile of the Greek-American community of Dallas.

I was considering the exact financial status of *Greek Time* when the second noise came. The fact was, although I always wanted to tell Pan we were going broke, we weren't. Heaven only knew how we were managing to avoid it—we had five thousand subscribers and almost no ads—but I had seen the profit-and-loss statements once on a trip to the comptroller's office, and we were actually doing quite well. It offended my sense of the fitness of things. Granted, our subscription rate was high and our payment schedule for artists and writers nearly nonexistent—and forked over on publication, at that—but how many people could there be in the world willing to put out forty-five dollars a year for interviews with the Greek-American mayors of small midwestern cities and twelve-page four-color extravaganzas on Greek festivals in Oregon? Besides, we had competition. Diamataris's *Greek Accent* was better run, better looking, better written, and cheaper, and the *Hellenic Chronicle* had more to say than anybody wanted to hear on the Greek Orthodox Church in America.

The second noise was a clang, like a bell going off. It nearly sent me leaping out of my bed.

When I had calmed down enough to think straight, I put the *Greek Time* galleys to one side and swung my legs off the bed again, waiting. I told myself I had nothing to worry about, really. Costa was rummaging around in the living room or Agapé was breaking glasses in the kitchen or there really were cats. Any minute now I would hear a definitive noise, something I could recognize, and everything would be explained. Then all the rest of it—my heart pounding so hard the beat was being echoed by my eardrums, my back beginning to run with sweat, my head beginning to run with fantasies of dark and stormy nights and vampire castles and the Hound of the Baskervilles hunting fox in the bushes—would seem like so much idiocy concocted out of whole cloth by an overactive imagination.

The silence went on and on and on, broken only by the sound of rain on the window. Even the thunder seemed to have backed off. The lightning, which I would have welcomed, if only because it would have helped light my dark bedroom, went off too far away to do me any good.

I pulled my feet up and buried them under the blankets again, slowly, slowly. I slid down until the great square pillow towered over me like a canopy. I reached for the *Greek Time* galleys.

And then all hell broke loose.

It was like listening to a wrecking ball destroy a wall. There was no way to explain it away as cats or even Costa or Agapé clumsily doing something ordinary. Somewhere underneath me, not on the first floor but in the basement, someone or something was taking the place apart.

This time, I got out of bed and got my feet on the floor and took up the candle. It had nothing to do with bravery. As far as I knew, whatever was down there was just starting. After he or she or it finished with the basement, it might very well just keep going until it got to me. I was not very far from the ground. I supposed I could escape out the window, but I didn't like the idea. It didn't feel very safe or very sure. The storm was revving up again, battering and rattling against the outer wall. I could fall the wrong way and break my arms or my legs or my neck. I could land safely, only to find myself confronted by whatever it was, craftily emerging from the front door as I landed in its path. There were a hundred worse alternatives to going down to find out what was going on, and I didn't want to take any of them.

At the last minute, I lit a cigarette. I didn't want to smoke it. I don't actually like smoking when I'm not drinking liqueur, and I've never been able to smoke when I'm nervous. What I wanted the lit cigarette for was protection. Part of me had some crazy idea that if attacked, I could jab the burning tip into some physically sensitive place on the attacker's body and make my escape.

I made my way into the hall first, moving too cautiously to make good time. The noise below me had stopped. I wondered briefly if I should call out, and decided it was worse than useless. Someone who could hear me—someone on my side—would already have gone to the basement to look. Anyone else would hardly be friendly.

I edged to the top of the stairs, stopped, listened, waited. Below me, the house lay in absolute silence, its only soundtrack provided by Mother Nature. Thunder rolled and clapped and bellowed. Lightning lit up the windows at the end of the hall and subsided. Bulwer-Lytton could not have asked for a better setting.

I made my way to the first floor, stopping a full minute on every step, wishing Pan had had the good taste to build a smaller and less elaborate house. Not for Pan charming, graceful rooms in human scale. Not for Pan great sweeping open rooms, either. Pan's squatter's palace was a monstrosity of the worst sort, the rooms tortured into eccentric shapes, the walls thick not only with niches and statues, but bad modern art, hideous and expensive. All that nonsense did weird things to the acoustics. I *knew* it did.

I stopped one last time, in the living room, just to make sure. For a single, disorienting second I thought I could hear something or someone. There was a sound like wash on a line in a breeze and another like a sigh. Then it was gone. I was left alone with my candle sputtering in the sucking air currents caused by the badly fitted wall of windows that made up the east side of the house.

There was another sound, like a grunt, which might have come from the basement. I couldn't be sure. The storm gave a final, heaving crash and seemed to subside altogether. Then it really was quiet, as only a remote island village can be in dead of night after a storm.

I made myself move to the basement door. Unless I wanted to start believing in ghosts—and I didn't—whatever had been there had to be gone.

In the end, I ran down those stairs as fast as I could, because running was the only way I was going to be able to get myself to the basement before I panicked so badly I gave up the whole enterprise. With silence had come common sense. Common sense dictated a hasty and well-considered retreat behind a locked bedroom door, said door to remain locked until the sun rose. Assuming the sun ever rose, this being Greece in February. Under the circumstances, I might not have minded a few days of stormy blackness as an excuse to stay barricaded on the second floor until other people came to exorcise this insanity.

My candle went out almost as soon as I stepped off the stairs, through my own fault, since I took a nervous plunge meant to get me over the last of my fear. It didn't work. I stood paralyzed for what seemed like forever on a cold marble floor, realizing for the first time that I was wandering around in a thin cotton nightgown and bare feet. The basement must have been completed unheated. It was freezing down there. I rubbed my hands against my upper arms and wished for rescue or slippers or *something*.

Finally, I made myself move. I inched carefully forward, poking my toes into the air to catch any obstruction before I fell over it. There were no obstructions. I had maneuvered myself into what felt like a vast open space, so far from walls and doors and the other limitations of a house, I felt almost as if I were alone on an open plain. It was a distinctly uncomfortable feeling. It was too exposed and too vulnerable. It was also too dark. I whirled sideways and speeded up, moving toward what I hoped would be the infamous pine paneling of Pan's conceit. Pine paneling might rot in the humid air of Greece, but I was too frightened to stick at a little rotting softwood. I needed something to hold on to.

I forgot to stick my toes out to check for obstructions. I fell over the splintered remains of a chair, turning my ankle and pitching backward onto the scattered cushions. I screamed, the first time, more from surprise than fright—one moment I was standing, the next I was in the air, the next I was drowning in an ocean of shredded foam rubber. Someone had taken a knife or a razor to all that fluffy chair padding, leaving a heap of spongy confetti on the floor.

I screamed the second time from pain. Someone had taken what must have been an ax to the chair frame. There were needle-size pieces of wood everywhere. Some of them were stuck into my skin, like porcupine quills.

I screamed the third time with damn good reason—such good reason, it was a long time before I stopped.

I had put my hand out to steady myself on the floor. I had plunged my fingers into something thick and sticky and wet.

Moving away, I had found something cold and slick and dry and hard and stiff and pliable and unmistakable.

The fingers of somebody's hand.

4

THEY CAME THEN, of course—from the small triangle
of whitewashed two-story buildings that was Kilithia
proper and from Agios Constantinos, even from the
American consulate in Malina on the island of Konos,
although that was later. In the first hour, I had only
the thin, nervous man who served as police constable
for Kilithia and two neighboring villages and his fat,
blustery cousin, the prefect of police from Agios
Constantinos. I also had a headache as big and
intractable as a boulder. There were so many things I
couldn't remember, like who had called all these
people and what I had done when I first came into the
basement. I remembered leaving the basement, because it was almost as traumatic as finding that hand,
but the police didn't need me for that. They had Costa
Papageorgiou to testify that he had heard me screaming and found me hysterical and carried me into the
light. I could have told them he was none too gracious
about it and none too comforting, but it probably
didn't make any difference.

The prefect of police spoke English. As far as I
could figure out, he had once been head of the tourist
police in these islands and had only recently been
promoted to the regular force. It did not bode well.
The tourist police are supposed to take care of things

32

like lost passports and currency-changing scams and hotels that charge more than their government classification allows. They liaised with foreigners. They do not handle, and are not trained to handle, real crime or real criminals.

I sat on a chair in the living room and tried, without success, to smoke cigarettes. The "crime team" from Agios Constantinos was busy taking the body out of the basement and doing a hundred other things the boys on "Miami Vice" would have been appalled even to have heard suggested. I didn't really blame them. Murder on the mountain islands is mostly a matter of blood feud or drunkenness or what is euphemistically known as family violence, things everyone knows about and can see coming. I knew that what had gone on in that basement was something worse than that, something more twisted, but there was no reason for the prefect of police to know it.

When he came to talk to me, he brought me a glass of Metaxas Seven Star from the stock in the bar and patted my hand. It made me feel instantly better. I almost giggled. After all, I was the one who'd ordered all the liquor for Pan's private stock. I knew perfectly well that Metaxas Seven Star was the most expensive stuff he had. I took a long hard swallow, grimaced, and lit another cigarette to cover the taste. This time, I actually managed to get smoke in my mouth. Liquor is the main reason I smoke cigarettes. I don't like the taste of either, so they cancel each other out.

The prefect pulled a chair up beside me, repositioned the tallow candles on the table between us so he could better see my face, and said, "So. You want to tell me exactly what happened?"

I shook my head. "I don't know what happened," I said. "Not exactly. Except I heard a noise in the

33

basement and I went to look and it was dark and I fell over a chair and then—and then—"

"And then you found the body," he said reasonably.

"I didn't find the body," I said. "I found part of the body. I found . . . the hand."

"The hand." He said it the way a history professor would say, "And then, the invasion of Poland . . ." as if it were something that changed the world. He looked distinctly uncomfortable. He bummed a cigarette from a passing technician—one of those cardboard and unidentified-weed, Greek-manufactured cigarettes that, in sophisticated places like Athens, even the Greeks won't buy—and resettled himself in his chair.

"Now, dear," he said. "The hand—we do not have a—the word?—a hand by itself."

"Detached," I said, feeling a little sick. "A detached hand."

"Exactly. We have only the hands on the body. You see?"

"Yes," I said. "I see." I wriggled around uncomfortably in my chair. Neither of us had enough of the other's language for me to explain what was happening to me. It wasn't just fear or sickness, although both of those were operating. Those I thought of as "real" emotions. I could handle them. It was the unreal ones—the persistent feeling that none of this was actually happening, or that it was happening, but not to me—that were throwing me off balance. The kerosene lamps and tallow candles had been joined by battery-powered arc lamps brought in by the crime team, but instead of brightening up the room and making the scene seem modern and scientific, they only added to my unshakable intuition that I had somehow stumbled onto the set of a horror movie.

Two horror movies. On one side, with the kerosene lamps and the tallow candles, we had something in the haunted house vein: *The House on Haunted Hill,* perhaps. On the other, we had the Hollywood version of *Frankenstein,* complete with spiders of electricity shooting out from odd places on the walls. (The battery-powered arc lamps were not well wired, and caused sparks.) The fact that the prefect of police looked remarkably like a somber Captain Kangaroo did not help matters.

I was in shock and I knew it, but I didn't know what to do about it. Captain Kangaroo was waiting for me. He had the face of a man with infinite patience.

I took a deep breath and gave it my best shot. "It was very dark," I said, "and my light had gone out. I fell. It was when I fell that I touched it, the hand, I mean." I swallowed hard. Just thinking about it made me want to scream or cry or be sick, anything to uncork the emotions I had crammed into the deepest part of me. Dear God in heaven, that hand. Every time I thought about it, I could *feel* it, feel the warm and yet somehow clammy surface of it sliding across my fingers, like a reptile crossing a body it thinks is unaware. I folded myself even more compactly into that chair and tried to shudder privately, without anyone noticing.

"Anyway," I said, staring straight into one of the arc lamps, as if I were trying to hypnotize myself. "The hand was all I saw. I knew somebody'd been at the chair because I could feel the foam rubber—the stuff inside it—strewn all over, but I couldn't actually see the chair, either, and then I fell over it and when I did, I reached out and there was this—"

"Hand," he said. He didn't mention the fact that I was repeating myself, but I supposed he was used to that. He shook his head. "Yes," he said. "Yes."

"I don't even know who it was," I said. I felt very proud of my restraint. Not only didn't I know who it was, I didn't know what it was—male or female, young or old. Part of me didn't want to know.

The prefect looked me up and down very carefully, very solemnly, making me squirm. It suddenly occurred to me that I knew absolutely nothing about the Greek criminal code. Did they use the American system or the French? Was I innocent until proven guilty or guilty until proven innocent? Did it matter? Did the prefect suspect me of anything? I told myself I was being nonsensical. I had only arrived in Kilithia a few hours before, and although I knew most of the people in the village—I had to, since I hired and fired for Pan—I didn't know them well. Why would anyone think I'd killed one of them?

"Let me see," the prefect of police said. "You found this . . . hand. And then you screamed. From what I have been told, you screamed very loudly for a long time. And then someone came, Kiriou Papageorgiou. And then?"

He waited, looking helpful. I blushed.

"I don't know," I said. "I remember screaming. The next thing I remember after that is being up here and Agapé saying Costa had gone into town for the police. And the next thing I remember after that is all the police coming. The constable first, and then you."

"You don't remember." I couldn't decide if that look on his face meant he didn't believe me or that he did, because disrupted memory was a symptom of exactly what he'd suspected me of all along: homicidal mania.

"I thought it was Costa," I said quickly, sitting up as straight as I could, so I looked erect and alert and, I thought, very sane. I sent up a silent prayer that someone would come by with more Metaxas. Metaxas, bitter as it was on the back of my tongue, would be better than this.

"When I first found the hand," I repeated (slowly, slowly—don't get sick), "I thought it was Costa. But then Agapé kept talking about sending Costa into town for the police, so I knew it wasn't him."

"Costa?"

"Kiriou Papageorgiou."

"Ah."

"And I knew it couldn't be Agapé, because Agapé was there with me. And besides, it was too . . . big."

"Yes," the prefect said. "Precisely." He shook his head again. It seemed to be his one expressive gesture. "You did not ask the priest to visit you. To bless the house, perhaps?"

"Priest?" I was used to the strange digressions of Greek conversation, but this was a bit much. "Why would I want to call a priest?"

"To bless the house," the prefect repeated.

"It didn't even occur to me," I said honestly.

"You are not Orthodox?"

"I'm Episcopalian. Or I was brought up that way, anyway." There was no use explaining to this man that religion in America was not quite what it was in Greece, where almost everybody belongs to the same church and that church had, for millennia, government support. Besides, why would he want to know?

He was looking very grave. "But you are Greek," he insisted. He rummaged in his pockets until he came up with a sodden wad of papers and then thumbed through them. "Your mother's mother was Greek?"

Where had he got *that* information? It was true— the way it was true that my father's father had been Lithuanian—but it wasn't the kind of thing I tell casual acquaintances or even think about much. And how *had* he got hold of it? Did the consulate supply the police with information on Americans traveling in Greece? Would the consulate have known?

"I hardly knew my mother's mother," I said. "She died when I was six."

"Your grandmother or your mother, they went to their husband's church? They abandoned the Christian religion for heresy?"

"I guess," I said, trying not to wince. Like most Americans (and western Europeans, for that matter) what knowledge I had of the history of religion boiled down to a vague notion that it had all started with the Roman Catholic Church, from which various Protestant sects had defected. As far as the Eastern Orthodox Church is concerned—and it's larger than anyone thinks, taking in not only Greeks and Russians, but Lithuanians and Albanians and Armenians and Egyptians and most of the Christianized Middle East—the Roman Catholics broke off from *them,* and have been busy making dangerous and heretical innovations ever since. I did not, thank heaven, know enough about it to argue. This man was trying, and it was better to have him trying than to face a police officer with no English and no patience and that curious Greek conviction that the CIA is responsible for every terrible thing that happens in Greece, including earthquakes. On the other hand, I didn't see any reason to give him the complicated religious history of my family. Like the fact that my father, who had started out a Lithuanian Uniate Roman Catholic, had eventually converted to the Episcopalians because it was a more "American" religion.

"Look," I said. "Pan—Kiriou Peteris—will probably have all that done when he gets here, the priest coming to the house, I mean, or his mother will, but all I was supposed to do was—"

"The *tiri,*" he said with some satisfaction.

For what must have been the fiftieth time, I looked blank.

"That was why I thought you might be Orthodox," he explained patiently. "The *tiri*. You come here several times a year and oversee the packing and the shipping of *tiri* to America. No?"

"Oh," I said. "The offerings. In America we call them offerings. And not exactly. I mean, usually it isn't offerings. It's worry beads, that's the big thing, and replicas of icons, and statues. We get the statues in Athens. The rest we have made in Kilithia. Pan thinks it's good for the village. To have employment here."

"I see." He nodded. "But now there are *tiri*, yes? You will ship a great many *tiri* to America. The people in this village have been making these *tiri* for months. And you are the one who comes to watch them do it."

"Right," I said. Actually, I didn't do much watching. People in Kilithia were not fond of letting strangers into their homes, especially American strangers, and I didn't like to push. "Pan got a huge order for them," I said. "But they're replicas, too. In tin. Not the gold and silver ones you use in the churches here."

"Of course not," the prefect agreed. "But you know what these *tiri* are for?"

"Oh yes." Pan had explained at length. *Tiri*, or offerings, are small, flat gold and silver models of various parts of the body (hand, arm, eye) or symbols of Christ (fish) that are left against the walls of icons concealing the altar in an Orthodox church to "repay" a saint for intervening in your behalf. A man who has asked a saint to petition God to return sight to his sightless eye will, when the sight has returned, leave an offering in the shape of an eye, or a square one engraved with an eye, against the altar. Churches in Greece sell the gold and silver offerings to pay their priests and tend their buildings and do their charitable work. In America, the offerings are replicas in plated tin, and the churches accept checks or envelopes of cash. There was usually very little call for them in the States. Non-Greek-American tourists in Greek Town Detroit or Tarpon Springs didn't know what they were or what they were for, and American Orthodox had been educated away from the custom. Then, a little less than a year ago, Pan had received a huge order for the things, the largest order for any single item his import/export line had ever been asked to handle. We were due to ship three hundred boxes of five hundred replica *tiri* each in less than two weeks. The project was a veritable nightmare of large-scale cottage production, shipping, and distribution that ate away my days like a high fever.

"I don't understand," I said. "What's all this got to do with anything? You can't mean to tell me that because I slept in the house before it was blessed or something, some ghost body got in or—well, it wasn't a ghost body, you can see that, and—"

"No, no," the prefect of police said. "No ghost body. And no—curse? Is that the word?—because as a heretic you touched the *tiri.*"

I was going to tell him I hadn't touched the *tiri*— the native hostility of the people of Kilithia had reached pathological proportions over the past year, so although they let me look at the *tiri* (they had to), they wouldn't let me touch them, and they made their resentment plain anytime I came to check their progress—but the man was smiling, and I had sense enough to smile back. After all, a smiling policeman is not likely to be ready to arrest you.

"All right," I said. "So I'm not Orthodox and I didn't have the priest in to bless the house. What does it matter?"

40

"That the priest didn't bless the house? Nothing at all—to you. It's not the blessing, it's the priest."

"I don't understand."

"The priest," the prefect said. "It was the priest. Downstairs. It was the priest who died."

I started to say "oh," but I was cut off. There was a great commotion at the door, people shouting in Greek and other people shouting in English and everybody banging the doors and the walls the way they do in any Mediterranean argument. Only the English got my attention. The rest of it had been going on most of the night, between the technicians and the photographers and the locals and the professionals and the officers and the men. The Greeks do not believe in welding themselves into efficient crime-fighting machines, or any kind of machines at all. They have made anarchy a fine art.

I turned my head and craned my neck to get a look at the door, but I couldn't make anything out. There were a lot of people, all male, pushed together in what looked like a soccer riot. They were pushing each other. They were screaming into each other's ears. They were jumping up and down, protesting, remonstrating, cursing, denying, and swearing their reliability on everything from their mother's grave to the flag. I couldn't keep my eye on anyone long enough to identify him.

The prefect of police was having much better luck. He got to his feet, stared into the crowd, and smiled. Then he looked down at me, clapped his hands together, and spread his arms as if everything had been solved.

"There," he said. "Help has come."

"The marines have landed," I suggested helpfully.

"No, no," the prefect of police said. "Not the military. The consulate."

"The consulate," I repeated.

"Of course," the prefect of police said. "The American consul. Or perhaps the vice-consul? It doesn't matter. Someone from your consulate has come."

I looked at the door again. This time I saw a tall, thin middle-aged man in a straighter-than-straight Brooks Brothers suit—white Oxford shirt, rep tie—emerging from the melee, briefcase held before him like a battering ram. He was not, however, the man who interested me most.

The man who interested me most was the one coming up behind him, the one in the black leather jacket, with the golden hair.

John Borden.

42

5

I SHOULD HAVE been glad to see him. He was, after all, the only American I'd ever spoken to on Themnos. And he'd been kind to me. He'd handled my bags and dealt with the driver and even lectured me about smoking. I tend to think anyone who lectures me about smoking has my best interests at heart.

Then I thought about the driver and the directions John Borden had given him to Kilithia. I don't speak Greek, but I can recognize the word *Kilithia*. Neither John Borden nor the driver had used it once.

I sat back in my chair and held out my glass to Agapé, who was coming through the crowd with another bottle of Metaxas. First, John Borden was at the wharf, with complete knowledge of my itinerary. Now he was here, hot on the heels of the American consul, right in the middle of a murder investigation. I didn't like it. I didn't like it at all.

The prefect of police loved it. He held out his hand to the middle-aged man in the Brooks Brothers suit and pumped away at the handshake until I thought my compatriot's arm was going to fall off. He blabbered away in Greek, praising this, that, and the other thing, using the word *America* every other half second. The American consul smiled back and didn't even try to get a word in.

John Borden stood to the side, hands in the pockets of his jacket, one eyebrow raised. He was staring at me.

Finally, the American consul extricated himself from the prefect of police and turned to me, trying to look like a kindly old uncle who will forgive anything. I didn't believe it, but I wanted to. I wanted to believe anything that would put a little space between me and John Borden.

"I'm Robert Hobart, Miss Hansen." He held his hand out, and I took it awkwardly, not sure what I was supposed to do with my cigarette. "I knew your father, you know, years ago, at Harvard."

"Oh," I said. What I wanted to say was, "How lovely for you," but I didn't dare try it. My stomach had started to roll. I was dangerously close to being sick. "Does my father—have you talked to him?"

"Lately?" Robert Hobart said. "Oh no. Not in years. Of course, I'll call him in the morning and tell him what the situation is. And that you're all right."

"I'm fine," I said.

"I'm sure you are," he said. He moved back a little. "You've met Mr. Borden?"

"Yes," I said. "Yes, I have."

"That's fine," Robert Hobart said.

I sighed. It was going to be another one of those conversations, and I'd already had too many of them today. I looked around for the prefect of police, but he had disappeared into the crowd.

John Borden tapped Robert Hobart on the shoulder and whispered in his ear. Hobart frowned.

"If you're sure," he said. "It would be a big help."

"I'm positive."

"Go do it, then."

"Back in a minute."

Borden nodded to me, turned on his heel, and walked out. I watched him go. He moved like a mountain climber, or Baryshnikov.

"Do you know him?" I asked Robert Hobart. "I mean, know him well?"

"Know him? I've met him, of course, several times."

"Do you think he's dangerous?"

"Dangerous?" Robert Hobart blinked. "I don't know what you mean."

"What does he do? I mean, for a living?"

Robert Hobart cleared his throat. "Really, Miss Hansen, this is an emergency situation and—"

"Never mind," I said. I turned to face him. "I suppose I ought to be worrying about whether or not they're going to arrest me for this, but if you don't mind my saying so, I can't seem to take it seriously."

"Well, there's no reason to take it that seriously, anyway. They're not going to arrest you. Whatever gave you the idea they were?"

"Why not? Practically everything that's going on here is going on in Greek. The prefect of police keeps referring to it as my house, there's a dead person in the basement. Why not?"

Robert Hobart cleared his throat again. "Well," he said. "You see, I don't mean to alarm you, of course, I wouldn't want to do anything like that, but—"

"But?"

"Well," Robert Hobart said. "You see. It isn't the first time."

Agapé was coming through again with the bottle. I stuck my glass out, chagrined to realize it was bone dry. I seemed to be inhaling the stuff.

"It happened about a year ago," Robert Hobart was saying. "Not quite a year, but about. Anyway, it was a priest that time, too. Only they found him in the cemetery, behind the church."

"Oh fine," I said. "Someone's doing in the local clergy."

"Yes," Robert Hobart said. "Well. You see. You weren't here the last time."

"I was here about a year ago," I said. "For a funeral. My boss's father died. Pan Peteris's father. I came to see to the arrangements."

"A big funeral?"

"Huge, I think, for this part of the world, anyway. Casket and flowers flown in from Athens. Food for the wake brought in from Agios Constantinos."

"Your boss didn't come?"

"No."

"Well, that's odd enough. He should have seen to it himself. Of course, it doesn't change anything here. I remember hearing about a big funeral. If I'd known it was you, I'd have come over and given you some assistance. Anyway, that was several weeks before Papa Papanicolau was—"

"Cut up?"

"Yes."

"It was a knife that time, too?"

"Oh yes. Much worse than this, from what I hear. Vicious. And outside, in the cemetery, so nobody found him for several days. And the rain . . ." His voice trailed off, and I felt my first twinge of sympathy for him. The thought of a Greek Orthodox priest in all those robes, dead and rotting outside in the rain, didn't do much for my stomach, either.

I got out another cigarette, lit it, and began to sip at my Metaxas. The Metaxas was definitely beginning to taste better. So were the cigarettes.

"They think it's some kind of religious psychopath,

46

of course," Robert Hobart said. "Not that they'd use those words here, you know, but it comes to the same thing. Some man with a great hatred of the church."

"If they pay any attention to casual conversation, they'll have to arrest half the country. The only Greek men I've ever heard speak well of priests have been priests."

"Yes," Robert Hobart said. "Well. They won't have to go that far afield, will they? After all, it's all happening here."

"But since I'm mostly not here, I have nothing to worry about."

"Right."

"And since I'm not a priest, I have nothing to worry about."

"Right again."

"Fine, now tell me this: what am I so worried about?"

Robert Hobart looked nonplussed. I took pity on him. I sank into my chair, cigarette abandoned, sucking on my Metaxas like a baby on a bottle, eyes closed. The closed eyes were the key thing. There was still too much going on for me to handle, too much noise and movement and color. I wanted to blot it all out.

I was busy trying to psych myself into a dream of a New England autumn when I felt movement beside me and looked up. There stood John Borden, jacket open on a white Irish fisherman's sweater, one hand on the switch of a big brass lamp Pan had had me order from Bloomingdale's.

"No use," I told him sleepily. "No electricity until nine."

"Ah," he said. "But I've got a secret."

"I'll bet you do," I said.

47

He fiddled with the switch again, then tried it with two hands. Light flickered, died, flickered again, and finally began to glow strongly under the opaque lavender shade.

"There we go," he said. "There's a generator in a little shed outside."

6

THE ELECTRICITY MADE everything better, as long as it lasted. It didn't last long. It had to have fuel oil to run, and there wasn't much of that. For about an hour, while the police did the last of their work in the basement and Agapé fed everyone in sight enough liquor to put them away for a week, lights burned all over the house, upstairs as well as down. I would have loved it unconditionally, except that it gave me more time to look at John Borden, and that was disturbing. More than disturbing. He really did look dangerous when you looked at him long enough, like one of those very sensitive professional killers in the Trevanian books. Worse, after talking to Robert Hobart for another half hour, I began to get the feeling he didn't know much more about John Borden than I did. He said something about John being a "student" and something else about his being a "professor," but it was all a terrible hash. Of course, Robert Hobart's mind was a terrible hash, but knowing it didn't make me feel any better. I wanted to do something about John Borden—nail him down—but I couldn't think of anything that would work.

At about six in the morning, the storm began to let up. Half an hour later, it was dawn. By then, most of the police had already gone. Only the prefect and the town constable were left in Pan's living room, drinking Pan's liquor and keeping Robert Hobart and John Borden company. Nobody was keeping me company. I could have been dead.

Untrue: if I had been dead, they wouldn't have been able to stay away from me.

I picked up dirty glasses and empty bottles and overflowing ashtrays from the odd corners of the room where people had left them—as if this had been a BYO party in a small college town instead of a murder. Agapé had her priorities. She enjoyed serving drinks, twitching through the crowd, collecting admiration and attention. She had no desire to burden herself with the kind of dirty work that is done, out of the sight of men, in a dark kitchen. Besides, Costa had been insistent. So insistent, in fact, I had begun to worry about the girl. God only knew she was useless, feline-female, but I didn't want to see her beaten into unconsciousness or accidentally dead. I didn't think her habit of giving Costa what-for would be a help, either. He was not the kind of man to admire "spunk" in a woman.

I put everything I could on a cork-lined drinks tray and headed down through the dining room and down the narrow annex hall to the kitchen, thinking all the time about Agapé in that crowd, smiling and swaying and treating everything in pants to great liquid stares that made her eyes seem even larger and darker than they were. Maybe Costa had had to lever her into this marriage the way Marina had had to lever Pan. Maybe Agapé would have preferred one of the boys from the village, someone her own age and nationality. Then again, maybe not. Pan was, after all, a relatively rich man. In a place like Kilithia, what he had and what he could buy must seem like a legendary fortune. No matter how pretty it looked on a fine sunny day, Kilithia was still a mountain village. There was no central heating or hot water, no vacuum cleaners or dishwashers. Women got old quickly here.

And Agapé liked to spend money. That much I knew from servicing Pan's bank account in Athens. Agapé *loved* to spend money.

I put the dishes in the sink, got a fire going in the stove, and started drawing water from the hand pump. Most island houses with modern kitchens had a hand pump next to the sink, for convenience in the hours the electricity was out. Pan had had his hidden in a dark corner near the stove, as if he were ashamed of it. I wondered what he'd think of it when he saw it, an expensive reality built from an architect's conception, all chrome and steel and gleaming brass.

I was dragging the pot of water to the stove when I heard somebody behind me. I put it down and turned, wishing I'd lit more candles or the kerosene lamp. I could hardly see what I was doing, never mind what was going on on the other side of the room.

The figure in the shadows let out an expletive and started moving toward me: John Borden, looking disgusted.

"Here," he said, bending down to take the pot. "Let me handle that."

"Go right ahead." I stood up and brushed off the frayed jeans I had changed into soon after the police had been summoned. "They do this every day, you know, the women in the village. They drag big pots of water from one end of town to the other. To wash clothes. And cook."

"Which is why they look ready for the grave at thirty." He heaved the pot onto the stove and stepped back. "Is that what you were thinking of, the village women getting water?"

51

"I wasn't thinking of bodies in the basement," I said irritably. "What do you take me for?"

"I think it would be perfectly natural to think about bodies in the basement. Under the circumstances."

"Under the circumstances, I'm not going to get to sleep as it is." I dropped into a chair at the kitchen table. "I've seen him, that Greek priest. A poor old man without a wife to pick up after him, too thin, too tired, too—I don't know. Overworked, maybe. I don't know."

"According to the local constable, he was a foul-minded, nasty man." John Borden took the chair facing me. "And his predecessor wasn't much better."

"How can he say that about a priest?"

John shrugged. "It's not the same here. A lot of boys go into the priesthood because they're poor and it's a way to get an education. And a living. They're not necessarily . . . religious when they start."

"And some of them never get religion at all, no matter how long they stay at it?" I moved the candle back and forth between us. John Borden was very still, watching me, as if he expected to see something significant in my face. It made me jumpy. "I think it's terrible the way everybody goes on and on about the Greek Orthodox clergy. And that poor man is dead. All cut up." I rubbed my hands over my face. "Why don't we just talk about something else?"

"I was just trying to help. I thought you might be sitting in here worrying over the demise of a poor holy man."

"And it doesn't matter that he's dead, because he might not have been so holy?" I got out of my chair and headed for the stove. The water in the pot had started a slow simmer, making it as hot as I would be able to stand it for the purpose of washing dishes. I wanted to get away from John Borden. I didn't like the way he was looking at me and the way he seemed to be able to do it minute after minute without blinking. I didn't like his face in candlelight, either. It had too much in common with Jekyll and Hyde.

I poured the water over the dishes into the stoppered sink. Then I saw the kerosene lamp. Someone had pushed it aside, so that it was nearly hidden by a state-of-the-art Hamilton Beach blender. I pulled it toward me and lit it.

"You know what gets me about this house?" I said. Since I could think of no polite way to get John Borden out of there, I was determined to change the subject. "It cost half a million dollars to build and outfit this thing. It's got every modern convenience, including some I'd never heard of before I started dealing with Pan's man in Athens. And I don't think Pan intends to spend two weeks a year here."

Behind me, John Borden lit a cigarette. "Did he tell you that? That it cost half a million dollars?"

"He didn't have to. I've spent half my life for the past year seeing to this house. I've talked to the architect. I've ordered appliances and furniture and chandeliers, for God's sake, and run the checks through Pan's Athens account. Half a million is probably a conservative estimate."

"Why didn't he do it himself?"

"He never comes to Greece. And I mean never. His mother brought him to the States when he was twelve years old and he hasn't been back yet."

"Not even for the funeral?"

"Not even for the funeral."

"Then why keep an account in Athens?"

I shrugged. "For Agapé, in the beginning," I told him. "He opened it right around the time his mother

53

started nattering about getting him married. And then for the house. Agapé runs up bills, and the house runs up bills. He needs that account."

"Why build a house you aren't going to live in?"

"Because," I said, turning to look at him, "you don't get an island girl to marry you—and Marina was going to have a Kilithia girl or die trying—unless you can convince her she's going to see enough of her family. And of course, if you want to get what you want the way you want it, you have to convince her you're rich. Or convince her father. This place is a monument to marriage negotiations."

"Some monument."

"My sentiments exactly." I turned back to the dishes. "Before all that . . . awfulness happened in the basement, I was amusing myself thinking about what it was going to be like when they finally met. You realize they've never met."

"If he's never been back to Greece and she's never been out of Kilithia, it would make sense."

"Yes, it would. And she's only seventeen. She wasn't even born when Pan left the island. They've exchanged pictures, but it's hardly the same thing. So day after tomorrow—or maybe it's tomorrow, I've got the time all messed up with everything that's been going on tonight—anyway, sometime in the next twenty-four to forty-eight hours, Pan's going to drive up to the door of this place in something expensive he's picked up in Athens, and they're going to see each other face-to-face for the first time." I swung around and waved the scrubbing stick playfully in his direction. "I like to think she's got more taste than she seems to," I said playfully, "and she'll take one look at him and say, '*Yecch.*'"

But John Borden wasn't listening to me. He was on his feet, and unless I was completely crazy, he'd started to sweat. The candlelight made his face look like a bright wet mask.

"Here?" he said. "Pan Peteris is coming here? Tomorrow?"

I gaped at him in bewilderment. "The fourteenth," I said. "It's the anniversary of his father's death—no, the burial, I think. There's some kind of ceremony and Marina said—"

"Yes, yes," he said impatiently. "Of course there's some kind of ceremony. I know all about that."

"Well, I'm glad you do," I said, "because I don't and—"

I stopped talking. There was no point. He was on his feet, pacing the far side of the room. He wasn't listening to me. I leaned against the sink and watched him. I was no longer bewildered. I was *angry.*

"Look," I told him. "You keep popping into my life, acting like some kind of clairvoyant lunatic, and I'm getting damn sick of it. I don't *need* this."

"What?" he said. "Oh. No, no. Of course you don't. Excuse me."

"I don't want to excuse you," I said furiously. "I want to hear you explain yourself."

"Of course," he said. "Uh, look. I don't want to run off, but I've got a phone call to make and I—*damn.*"

"There isn't any phone in this house," I said.

"Of course not. No phone service in Kilithia at all. I remember."

Then he gave me a sickly smile and a halfhearted salute, turned on his heel, and practically ran out the kitchen door into the annex hall.

I followed him, of course. No matter how tired I was, I couldn't make myself not do it. The narrowness of the hall slowed him down sufficiently so I could keep him in sight, and I trailed behind him through the dining room to the small cluster of men now standing in Pan's foyer. I might as well not have bothered. The men were speaking Greek—Robert Hobart badly, the way he did everything badly—and were so calm and congenial, they could have been talking about the weather.

Worse, by the time John Borden reached them, *he* was calm and congenial too. It was as if nothing odd had happened in the kitchen, as if he'd walked instead of run into the first shards of morning light forcing their way through Pan's stained-glass foyer windows. If I'd gone to Robert Hobart and told him about John Borden's behavior only moments before, he'd have thought I was having hallucinations.

I paused at the foyer door and waited, half fascinated, while the men joked and murmured, giving a perfect imitation of English country gentlemen at the start of a hunt weekend. I was impressed and disgusted at once. How could they be like that, after all that blood in the basement?

The prefect of police caught sight of me and waved me over. "Here she is," he said to the others, patting his soft fat hands together like Sydney Greenstreet gloating over the possibilities of the Maltese falcon. "We've kept her up beyond her bedtime."

"I've been up past my bedtime for three days," I said. "I don't suppose one more is going to make much difference."

The prefect smiled broadly. "Very gracious," he said. "You see how it is? American women are always so very gracious."

His local, non-English-speaking colleague scowled. Robert Hobart rubbed his weak chin fretfully.

"Sorry to keep you up so late," he said. "We were just blowing off a little steam. Unwinding, you know. After all this mess."

"Right," I said. "Of course. We all need a little of that."

"But we'll be going now." Robert Hobart gave me the smile he had probably once thought would turn him into a politician, the kind of smile that might have looked good on television but would always look phony in person. "Have to let you get your beauty sleep, you know."

"I think," John Borden said, "we ought to make it perfectly clear we don't think Miss Hansen is in any danger from our . . . friend."

"Why don't you do me a bigger favor," I said. "Why don't you tell me exactly what you're doing here."

The words were loud enough to be heard in Agios Constantinos, but they were directed at John Borden, and everyone knew it. There was a short, embarrassed silence. Unfortunately, I couldn't tell if the embarrassment was caused by the fact that I'd boiled over in public—my anger was as unavoidable as the vast Grecian urn that took up the center of the foyer—or because I'd asked the Forbidden Question.

Robert Hobart returned to the fray, ruining any chance I would ever have to find out.

"But, Miss Hansen," he shrilled. "You know what we're doing here! We're investigating a murder! We're protecting your interests! We're seeing to the safety of the island!"

I have always hated people who talk in exclamation points.

I opened the door to the drive and waved them out, happy beyond my ability to tell them to see them go. I was so happy, in fact, that I was even able to make polite conversation with the prefect of police on how enjoyable I hoped the rest of my stay would be and how the weather would surely get better.

I didn't say good-bye to John Borden at all. I just watched him.

When he thought he was out of sight, he pulled up beside Robert Hobart, leaned over, and began talking rapidly in his ear.

I went back and did the dishes, as a kind of therapy. I cleaned all the glasses and the three plates Agapé had used to pass cheese and olives and even the pot I'd boiled the water in. The water in Kilithia is metallic. It leaves white scaly ridges on cast iron. I got them off with a piece of mesh, then put the pot away.

It had to have taken me half an hour, but it was worth it. The sun had come out by the time I started upstairs, making the house look as bright and cheerful and ordinary as a subdivision ranch in Shaker Heights, if larger. All that work had made me the good kind of tired—not nervous and exhausted, but ready for sleep. I locked myself in my bedroom, changed into a clean nightgown, and brushed my hair a hundred strokes to keep it well oiled and shiny.

I went to the window because I thought it might be nice to see Kilithia in good weather. I'd seen it much too often in bad. I pulled back the curtains and looked down at the collection of white, almost windowless two-story buildings that made up the town, shining and shimmering in the sun like the enchanted villages of Greek travel posters. The cross on the Greek Orthodox church looked washed by the rain. It shone like gold in the newness of morning.

I turned away. I didn't want anything to remind me of the priest or of how he died or of how I found him. I let my eyes travel up the rocky, uneven surface of the mountain. I was glad I had a room on this side of the house. On the other, the views would all be of the jagged wildness of the top, the violence of geological foundations and the barrenness of sand.

I was just about to let the curtain fall when I saw them, standing at the edge of the muddy drive: John Borden and Costa Papageorgiou.

I pushed closer to the window, straining to see something important. I didn't know what. They weren't stamping their feet at each other or gesturing or even shouting, as far as I could tell. Still, they didn't like each other. I could feel, all the way from my window, just how little they liked each other.

I knelt on the floor with my forehead pushed against the glass, staring. It was all violence, tremendous pent-up violence, though I couldn't have said why I thought that.

Any more than I could have explained why it should be happening.

7

"OH MY *GOD*," Caliope said. "It's *pink*."

"*Pithakim*," Marina tut-tutted. "*Pithakim, pithakim*."

"Of course it's pink," Pan said. "It's a woman's house. Women like pink."

I tumbled out of bed, not happy to be awake, in desperate need of coffee, and in no mood to see any of these people. There was no help for it. I drew the curtains and looked down on the drive. They were standing there—two of the three witches from *Macbeth* and a bad imitation of a Mississippi riverboat gambler—staring up at the house, waiting for someone to burst through the door and greet them.

I had been right about the car. It was indeed something expensive Pan had picked up in Athens. Never in my wildest dreams, however, could I have imagined the sheer outrageousness of his bad taste. The vehicle was a convertible, which was bad enough. It had bright orange fake-leather upholstery, which was worse. And it was pink. I felt a stab of sympathy for Caliope. Obviously, she had been pinked out for the duration.

There was movement on the far side of the drive, and Agapé came into view, her jaw jutting out ahead of her and her hips swaying like a fandango dancer's

60

in a Vegas act. Caliope saw her right away, and it was anything but love at first sight. Caliope had one of those thick-skinned, pockmarked, mottled faces that look somehow diseased when flushed, and she was very flushed now. She followed every movement of Agapé's hips the whole five minutes it took the girl to walk up the drive.

Pan was enchanted. I could tell from the look on his face that he'd never expected his mother to come up with anything so wonderful.

I had a painful memory of Pan in New York, unattached and overly proud of his money, showering on Caliope the kind of expensive gifts most men reserve for their wives. The situation was looking worse by the second.

"Well," Caliope said in a loud, shrill, carrying voice. "If it isn't *Never on Sunday* played as kiddie porn."

I let the curtain drop and began rummaging frantically in the mess on the floor for my clothes, wondering if the walls of Pan's house were made of paper. I could hear everything they were saying down there, and none of it was the sort of thing to cheer the heart of an exhausted, sane person.

"Look at her," Caliope was screeching. "Look at her! Look at her! She doesn't know what toilet paper is. She wipes her ass on stones, for God's sake."

Agapé let out with a string of Greek, most of which I didn't understand, but some of which I did. Like the word for *witch.* And the word for *toad.* And the word for *bitch.*

"She *stinks,"* Caliope screamed. "She smells. You could pick up the scent in New York."

Agapé spat.

Caliope let out a noise that would have been a fitting response to gang rape.

Agapé spat again.

There was the sound of buckling metal.

"What the hell do you think you're doing?" Pan shouted. "That's my car. You put a dent in my car."

"I'll put a dent in your head," Caliope shouted back. "I'm not spending one minute under the same roof with that—that underaged hooker."

"Would you shut up?" Pan yelled over the sound of Agapé spewing Greek again. "This is Greece, not Astoria, you can't go saying things—"

"She thinks she's going to put me in the street," Caliope said, probably answering whatever Agapé had said that I hadn't been able to hear. "I'll tell her who's going to end up on the street, that little—"

I grabbed my clothes and headed for the bathroom. If Pan thought I was going to referee this one, he was out of his mind.

By the time I got downstairs, they were in the living room. Costa had disappeared. The women were sitting on chairs, looking excessively polite. Pan was pacing, running a hand through his thick black hair. Every once in a while, he sent Agapé a look of unadulterated lust. The rest of the time, he just looked pained.

When he saw me come in, he broke into a broad smile, like a climber, half dead in the snow, at his first sight of the safety patrol. I wasn't having any. I leaned against the doorjamb, folded my arms across my chest, smiled at Marina—it's the height of stupidity to be rude to one's boss's mother—and waited.

Pan waited too, but not for long. There was always the possibility that any extended silence would give Caliope and Agapé the idea that they ought to think of something to say.

"Ker-ree." Pan held out his arms to me. "I thought you hadn't made it. I had no idea you were here."

"I was upstairs," I said sourly. "You woke me up."

Pan looked uneasily around him. "Yes," he said. "Well. As usual, Mama has all the answers. All the answers. Everything's all straightened out now."

"Really."

"Of course, of course." He turned to Caliope and Agapé and held out his hands again. He did not, however, look at them. "We'll have a big wedding in the village next week. My sister will be matron of honor to my bride."

"You've got to be joking," I said.

"You don't think it's a good idea?" Marina said.

"I think they're going to kill each other before Pan ever sees the inside of a church."

Agapé said something in Greek again. Caliope stared at her in absolute horror, leaped from her seat, and started tearing at her hair.

"Five bridesmaids," she ranted. "Five bridesmaids. She isn't even married yet and already she's spending him into the poorhouse, that—"

"That's enough," Marina said.

Caliope quieted immediately, her sentence cut off cleanly, mid-stride. She sent her mother a sullen, angry look—an accusation of betrayal—and sat down again, pulling the hem of her skirt over her knees like a prim secretary in the boss's office.

Marina smiled faintly, mission accomplished, harmony restored. "Sometimes," she said, "it takes more than a little self-discipline to make things come out the way you want them to."

"Maybe." I thought she probably knew everything there was to know about self-discipline. Nobody immigrates to the United States, without skills or education, and puts two children through college without it. On the other hand, all the self-discipline in the world couldn't solve the problems we had now. "Unless the Greek Orthodox Church is a lot more efficient than I think it is," I told them, "you'd better start making new arrangements for the wedding. We've had a little difficulty."

"What difficulty?" Pan said.

"The priest died," I said.

"Died," Pan repeated.

The rest of them were very silent, very still. Pan took a deep breath and ventured, "Well, he was an old man. I don't suppose it's very odd—"

"He didn't die of old age," I said brutally. Pan was a dodger. If you didn't hit him over the head with the things he didn't want to hear, he didn't hear them. "He died of fourteen stab wounds to the chest. In your basement."

Silence again. This time, there was an electric quality to it, as if I had touched a nerve they all shared. I looked from one to the other of them, confused. So far, no one had reacted to this death the way I expected. It suddenly occurred to me that either Costa or Agapé should have said something to Pan, *told* him, and that neither of them had.

There was a strong mid-morning sun coming through the wall of windows. The living room was full of light. It didn't matter. The house was beginning to seem just as appropriate a stage set for *Wuthering Heights* as it had in the stormy dark of the night before. My head was beginning to ache. My imagination was running away with me. And the Peterises were behaving like visitors from another planet.

"What about tomorrow night?" Caliope said. "What are we going to do about tomorrow night?"

"Nothing is going to stop tomorrow night," Marina said. Her voice made it sound as if God had spoken. "We don't need a priest for tomorrow night."

"No," Caliope said. "Of course not. We just need our heads examined."

"A priest is preferable," Marina said, "but hardly essential."

"All right," Caliope said. "Just let me tell you right now, I'm not going down in that basement."

I pushed myself away from the doorjamb. It was possible someone could make sense of all this, but it wasn't me. Now that I had started thinking about the night before, I was bumping into too many unpleasant realities, too many undigested horror-story fantasies. The Peterises were only making it worse. I wanted to get away from their craziness before it infected me.

"I'm going to make myself some tea in the kitchen," I said, forcing myself to be polite. I did not go so far as to ask any of them to join me.

Apparently, none of them wanted to.

I was on my second cup of tea—and my fourth aspirin—when Marina came into the kitchen. I was surprised. I had half expected Pan. We had business to discuss, weight and rate schedules for the shipment, editorial policies for the magazine, even the Great Question of whether to give my assistant a raise. Besides, Pan liked to dump the dirty work on me. I thought he'd get me alone at the first opportunity, just to make sure I was going to shovel the you-know-what without being bludgeoned into it.

Marina was an unknown quantity. I had never turned her into a caricature the way I did with Caliope, but I had been careful to stay out of her way. She had a sharp tongue and an aura of being in

65

absolute control, as if she could get me hired or fired at whim. She probably could. Pan gave Caliope expensive presents, but he leaned on Marina. He never made a decision without her.

"Pan looks rested," I said nervously when she came in. "That must have been a pretty calm trip to California."

"California?" She looked momentarily confused. Then her brow cleared, and she said, "Oh yes. With everything happening, with this about my husband and the house and the wedding, I keep forgetting about California."

I got up to get the kettle, as much to hide my disbelief as to do the polite thing by offering Marina some tea. A California office for *The Banner* was Pan's latest pet project. He was so fond of it, he wouldn't even give it to me to work on. When Pan disappeared for weeks at a time—and he'd been doing that often for the last year—he was always in California.

I set a strainer of loose tea over a cup and poured water through it. Apparently, when I'd ordered the kitchen things from Athens, I'd forgotten to order a tea ball.

"You know what bothers me about all this?" I said. "Nobody seems to care that the old man is dead. I mean, they care, but not about him. They don't say, 'Too bad,' or, 'What a terrible way to die,' or any of the other things you'd expect."

"It was a terrible way to die," Marina said. "But I didn't know him, this new priest. I knew the old one, but not him."

I brought her cup of tea to the table. "He was an old man," I said. "Sad."

"Most of them are." She took a thick spoonful of

honey and stirred it into the tea. "The other one, now, the one before this one who died so terribly, he was here for many years. He baptized Caliope and Panyotis."

I had to remind myself that Panyotis was Pan.

"I cried when the last one died," Marina went on, "but there was some connection. This one was . . . a stranger."

"The last one didn't go any easier," I said. "The man from the American consulate told me about it last night. The last one went the same way. Stabbed so many times he looked . . . cut up."

"Cut up," Marina said vaguely. "Did you say there was a man from the American consulate here? For a local murder?"

"No," I said. "For me. He was a friend of my father's. In law school, I think."

"Your father was at law school with the American consul?"

"With somebody from the consulate, yes." I had never gotten Robert Hobart's exact title.

Marina tapped her glass with the edge of her spoon, reflective. "I didn't realize your family was so—important."

"I don't think important's the word for it. It's just that people who've been at Harvard together, even just the law school, like to gossip about each other. And do things for each other. It makes them feel less insecure."

"Harvard," Marina said.

"My father's been saying ever since that it should have been Yale," I said. "Not so many Democrats."

Marina licked her lips. "He has money, your father?"

"Some."

"And influence."

"Some," I said again.

Marina sighed. "It's so hard to tell with Americans. Everybody wears blue jeans. In Athens, you could tell just by looking." She set her spoon down in her saucer with an audible snap. "You should put some brandy in what you're drinking. Calm down. You can't afford to be so upset. Someone you didn't know is dead, that's all."

"Well, there's also the fact that I accidentally fell on him," I said. "After he was dead."

"How awful for you." She shook her head vigorously. "Even so. We have work to do here. I have to bring off a wedding"—she gave me a sly smile—"which in this case may be more difficult than I'd imagined. And you have Panyotis's business to see to. The *tiri*. Yes?"

"Yes. But not today. If I don't get some sleep, I'll die."

"Get your sleep. If you can get it with the two of them fighting. Which they're going to do no matter what I tell them. I suppose I'll be lucky if they don't kill each other, but I can't think of everything. And she was a good choice, Agapé. Maybe the only choice."

"Pan certainly likes her," I admitted.

Marina snorted. "Panyotis is a good boy, but he's a boy. He likes anything without an appendage between its legs. Not that men are any different." She started to get heavily and painfully to her feet. I got out of my chair and came around the table to help her. "Arthritis," she said. "I forgot how humid it was here, how wet, in the winter."

I hated to see anyone in that much physical pain. It almost hurt to watch her move. "You should have had the wedding in New York," I told her. "Then you wouldn't have to be wandering around in all this mud and damp, making yourself worse."

She looked up at me, startled. "New York?" she said. "Well, yes, I suppose I could have done that, but how could it possibly have helped?"

"Air conditioning?" I suggested. "Dehumidifiers?"

"Ah, I see. You don't understand. I didn't come to Greece for the wedding. That could have gone on without me."

"Then what are you doing here?"

She leaned very close to me, searching my eyes. "You don't know what happens tomorrow night, on the anniversary of my husband's burial?"

I thought I did, but the way she was looking at me made me unsure. "You say prayers over the grave," I said, my voice wobbling a little. "And there's some kind of religious service."

Marina hooted. "Well, if there's a religious service, it's probably pagan, though I wouldn't say that around here if I were you. The priests go along because they can't stop it. Maybe they think they'll Christianize it if they officiate. And I—well, I'm still enough of a village Greek to be superstitious. You see?"

"Not exactly."

"Of course you don't. In the farming areas of this country there is a custom that if a soul has gone to God, then the flesh will have fallen away from its bones and turned to dust. But if the soul is caught by the devil, the flesh will be thick on the bones and foul."

"You're right," I said, feeling sick. "It doesn't sound Christian."

"Well, if the soul has gone to the devil, we pay the priest and he makes special prayers for its deliverance.

Well, they're starving, most of these country priests. It doesn't do any harm."

"You mean they always say the soul is with the devil."

"Oh no, dear. On the anniversary of the burial we dig up the bones and check."

8

I HAVE A very morbid imagination. I fully intended to ignore Marina's talk of digging up bones, suppress any tendency to recall the events of the night before, lock myself in my room, and spend the afternoon figuring out how I was going to pay the cover artist my art director hired for the May issue—at exactly double the entire art-and-writing budget for the spring season. I even tried to convince myself that Marina had been talking nonsense. God only knew the woman could sound sincere and maternal and sympathetic, but I had seen other sides of her. I didn't trust her. She looked like a peasant Greek trussed up in Saks Fifth Avenue clothes, but she talked like a Park Avenue lady, in a voice so rich and round it could have been the result of Farmington and Wellesley. She was shrewd always, and ruthless when she wanted to be. I had seen her go after the poor, newly immigrant boys on the newspaper staff with all her talons bared and rip them to shreds before they knew what was happening to them. I had seen her deal with the bankers, too, when the loans came due and the money was tied up in the expansion of *The Banner* and Pan was hiding out in Danny Boy's behind a copy of the *Ethniko Kirix* and a quart of real ale. The man from Morgan always came out looking as if someone had

just drugged him, tied him up, and shipped him to
Shanghai for immediate sale. The man from Chase
Manhattan looked worse. If Marina had some reason
to scare me to death with graveyard stories, she would
do it.

Had there been a glint of malice in her eyes, at the
end?

I didn't know. I didn't know the answer to my
other, more important question, either: what did the
basement look like now that the local police had
"cleaned it up"? I sat cross-legged on my bed with the
budget sheets laid out on the bedspread and thought
that I didn't trust the ordinary Greek male to clean up
anything. He wasn't brought up to it. A Greek mother
makes her son's bed until the son finds a wife to take
over the duty, and most Greek sons reach middle age
thinking that dishes wash themselves. I knew there
had been damage down there—at least one chair
smashed up and reduced to splinters—and blood. If
anything, all those men tramping around down there
had probably left it in even worse condition. And Pan
hadn't said anything. Pan was always on my case
when anything needed to be done, no matter how
incompatible with my job description. I'd expected
him to accost me in the hall and bark out a few orders
detailing me to take care of the mess. Instead, he'd
gone down to the basement, spent half an hour
rummaging around, and come upstairs without a
word to anybody. Then he'd disappeared.

I gathered all the budget sheets into a pile and threw
them on the floor. The problem with locking myself in
to get some work done was that away from the
distraction of people, I couldn't stop myself thinking.
The problem with trying to sleep was that I dreamed
—either long, grotesque nightmares with disembod-

ied hands floating like prehistoric bugs in amber, or more disquieting ones that starred a man in a black leather jacket, with golden hair. That was something else I'd been putting off: getting to the root of why John Borden had *affected* me so much. I have never been a romantic. My Friday night drink-after-work comments on men would do credit to Ti-Grace Atkinson. And I didn't even know John Borden. He'd popped into my life exactly twice, and popped out of it again. If the world made any sense, he'd probably disappeared forever.

I got off the bed and started hunting around for warm socks and thick shoes and a waterproof parka. Outside, the sun was holding steady, and I wanted to catch it. Kilithia was a tiny village, but there were more people in it than Peterises or Papageorgious. I thought I'd walk down the hill and see a few of them. Worse came to worse, I could always get myself lost. *That* would provide me with something to think about for the remainder of the afternoon.

I stopped in the basement before I went out. I hadn't intended to—what I'd *intended* was to go down the stairs, out the front door, and into the sunshine by the shortest possible route—but when I reached the first floor, I caught wind of an argument.

"Roses," Caliope was saying, "make me sneeze. I've told her *four times* roses make me sneeze."

"Putana," Agapé said.

"Why, you little *cunt,"* Caliope said.

I rubbed away the headache that was threatening to start at the base of my skull and decided on the better part of valor. Instead of going out the front door, which would mean having to cross the foyer in full view of the archway into the living room, I made a

73

sharp left and headed down the "servants' hall" to the kitchen entrance. Even then I might have gone straight back and out, but the basement door was open. It stood in my path like a tree thrown across a road by a storm. It swayed a little in the breeze from the open kitchen windows.

What made up my mind was the electricity. Pan had sent Costa Papageorgiou into Agios Constantinos for gasoline, and the generator was working full-time now. I was still a little angry with him for not telling me anything about it, but the anger was tempered with embarrassment. I had, after all, made all the arrangements for the house. I must have made the arrangements for the generator, too, and forgotten about it.

"If that—that sexual convenience thinks she's going to take over *my* life," Caliope said, "she's—"

I slipped into the stairwell and closed the door behind me. There was one of those modern, push-button light switches set in a plate just inside the door. I pushed both buttons and got a harsh, bright bulb light in the stairwell and something softer below. I fiddled with the switches until the hall light went out. At this stage in Caliope's hysterics, it was unlikely anyone would budge from the living room—they wouldn't dare—but I wasn't taking any chances. I didn't want to run into any of the nuts while I was making my escape.

Or while I was snooping, either.

I ran down the steps as if someone were chasing me, only to stop on the final landing, paralyzed by fear and imagination. What worried me most was that they had left the blood on the floor. I seemed to remember there had been pools and pools of it, a great sticky river in the darkness. The memory of my hand

sliding into all that warm plastic goo made me sick.
The idea of turning the final corner and staring out
over a sea of it—cold now, of course, and hardened—
made me sicker. I nearly turned around and ran back
up.

In the living room, somebody threw something,
heavy and hard, that landed against the floor with a
crash.

I took a deep breath and headed down.

It was bad, but not bad the way I had expected.
Someone had been more considerate about the blood
than I'd have believed. There was no sign of it on the
great expanse of shiny red-and-white-checkered vinyl
flooring. There might have been traces on the furniture, but it was hard to tell. The furniture had been
obliterated. Every piece of it had been hacked and
torn apart. I stood above a red and white ocean,
looking out on the flotsam and jetsam of some unim-
aginable species of ship.

Even in the destruction, it was clear what Pan had
meant to do with this room. I'd dealt with the
architect in Athens once or twice, but I'd never seen
the finished product, and I was sorry about that. Cut
off from views of the whitewashed Greek countryside,
the pine paneling didn't look as ridiculous as I had
expected it to. The basement was a jazzed-up version
of what American builders call a recreation room, but
much warmer and more inviting, much more luxuriously comfortable than those places dream of being.
Even the brass fit, and I hate brass. The brass bar rail
and round brass table lamps looked like gold placed
near a fire, giving off reflections of the flame.

Unfortunately, whoever had been at the furniture
had been at the walls, too. The paneling was gouged

and pitted. Great surface strips of it had been peeled off and left in the rubble, wilted Christmas ribbons in a pile of discarded bows.

I descended the last two steps and began to plow aimlessly through the debris, wondering what it had all been about. Whoever had been down here had been bent on destroying everything. Only the brass and a huge, ugly faded copy of Delacroix's *The Massacre of Chios* had survived. The Delacroix hung forlornly on one otherwise naked wall, imprisoned in a heavy, age-stained, overly ornate frame. There had been another painting—all sharp-edged triangles and bright primary colors, much more Pan's style than the operatic melodrama of the Delacroix—but it had been taken down and torn into strips. Like the walls, the bar had been gutted and pockmarked. Like the furniture, it had been splintered, although only parts of it had actually been pounded into the anonymous wash of shards on the floor. Maybe Robert Hobart was right. Maybe whoever had come down here last night had been insane, full of pent-up hatred and undigested violence. I certainly couldn't think of another explanation for all this awfulness.

Slowly, I made my way to the middle of the room, stopping in a pile of rubble that reached my ankles. They said the insane could summon more strength than normal people of their size and weight could manage, but I didn't know if I believed it. At least, I didn't know how *far* I believed it. It seemed impossible to me that a small person, a woman or a child or a less than average-size man, could have caused this devastation. I wanted my villain big and rough and very well muscled.

Like Costa Papageorgiou.

I stepped back a little, feeling thrown off balance.

Costa Papageorgiou, who may have beaten his wife to death because she'd produced a girl. Costa Papageorgiou, who didn't like me or anyone else and always seemed one step away from an explosion. Costa could have taken apart that basement room without even breathing hard, even on a mellow day.

I reached into my pocket for cigarettes, thought better of it, put them back. Lighting a match in all that floating foam rubber would probably be fatal. I swung my head from side to side, wondering what I was supposed to do now. Surely I would have to do something. Pan must have had business in the village or in Agios Constantinos. It was the only explanation I could think of for his not having already asked me to take care of this problem. It was exactly the kind of problem he was so fond of asking me to take care of. Dirty work.

I was going through a list of the best possible options for restoration work—hiring some women from the village to help with the cleaning, getting in touch with the interior decorator in Athens, convincing Pan to open his checkbook one last time to replace the furniture—when it hit me that something was wrong. Something was *off*. I turned around and around in place, trying to pinpoint what had bothered me. Something was here that shouldn't be here. Or something was somewhere it didn't belong. Or something *wasn't* here that should be here. I turned around and around, making myself dizzy, feeling more frustrated and angry by the minute. I forced myself to stare long minutes at each and every object in the room, asking myself if this was it, or this, or that. It didn't help. I couldn't get hold of it.

I backed toward the stairwell, feeling not only helpless and frustrated, but frightened as well. My imagination was playing tricks on me again. I was getting claustrophobic, feeling trapped and suffocated in an underground cavern that only *seemed* to be well lit. There were shadows hidden in the lights and homicidal maniacs in the shadows.

I had made it onto the first step when the noise from upstairs broke my mood.

"Roses!" Caliope shrieked. "I'll tell you what she can do with her roses. She can shove her roses up her *ass,* is what she can do with her roses."

"Hasta diavolo," Agapé shrieked back.

I shook my head violently, clearing the cobwebs. I was in Pan's basement, alone, and my only danger came from those two maniacs in the living room. If I didn't get out of here soon, they would catch me.

I shoved my hands into my pockets and went pounding upstairs, intent on making it out the door before they came looking for me.

On the mountain, the sun was still holding. In the village, the people had decided to trust it. They had come out of their houses, bringing chairs with them, and set themselves down to rest in the street. Gathering in the street to gossip and snoop was the great Greek village pastime. You saw it even in Athens, in the older and poorer and more cohesive neighborhoods. In Kilithia, the widows brought their knitting and their sharp, restless eyes and shouted to each other over the pedestrian traffic in the muddy dirt streets. It would have been enchanting if the widows had all been old. Some of them, however, were no more than eighteen or nineteen years old. In a place like Kilithia, they would be expected to wear black, and to concentrate on mourning, for the rest of their lives.

I moved between them for a while, aimless and a little aggravated. The scene in the basement had done nothing to lighten the mood Marina had put me in, and the walk down the mountain from Pan's squatter's palace had been difficult and wearying. The widows looked hostile to me, resentful and envious and bitter. Their eyes followed my bright parka and jeans, wanting me gone.

I turned into the town's only *kafenion*, thinking I needed sustenance. The Kilithia villagers had never been friendly, of course—as I said before, Themnos is *not* a tourist island—but I had never walked through town feeling as if a lot of old women wanted to kill me. A lot of them worked for me, making tin replicas of *tiri* or doing badly varnished miniature reproductions of ancient icons for importation to the States. That had been Marina's idea. Park Avenue voice or no Park Avenue voice, in some ways she really was still a village Greek. She wanted the money brought home and spread around, where it might do some good.

I bought a bottle of *portokolatha*—nasty carbonated orange stuff, manufactured in Thessalonika—and had the owner open it for me. Then I stood for a while near the cash register, wondering what to do. The men did not stare at me with hostility, but they did stare. In a way, hostility would have been preferable. I didn't need extrasensory perception to know they had all heard stories about American women— fast, loose, easy American women—and were dying to test the truth of them.

I stepped back into the street, felt something fall on my head, and looked up into the mass of black, boiling clouds that was a new weather front moving in. All around me, the widows were gathering up their knitting and their chairs, getting ready to go inside. They didn't look at me, but they didn't look at each other, either. The malicious babble of gossip had ceased. They had closed in on themselves, shutting out the rest of the world. Secrets were bait. They hadn't wasted all of theirs on this small fishing expedition. I thought of the widow stoned to death in *Zorba the Greek,* and nearly gagged.

Overhead, there was a rumble of something that was not quite thunder, but somehow worse. Rain started to fall in thick, soundless drops, slowly and steadily, like Chinese water torture. I looked hesitantly back at the door to the *kafenion.* It would be safely out of the rain, and I needed a place out of the rain. I did not need that ragged collection of Greek farmers, dreaming pornographic dreams over outsized shot glasses of ouzo and ice.

I turned up the hill, thinking I'd go back to Pan's house and trust to a hot bath and a youthful constitution to ward off pneumonia. The rain came down steadily, irrevocably, as if God had decided to flood the world, drop by drop, through eternity. Women slammed their shutters closed, making Kilithia look abandoned and dead. Above me, the mountain lost itself in darkness and wind. It had become something wild, and alive.

I was coming abreast of the local Greek church—Agia Maria—when I heard the first hard slam of metal against stone. At first, I didn't know what it was. The edge of the weather front was burbling and coughing over my head, muffling all earthly sound. As for the mark it must have made, I wouldn't have noticed it. Greece has been through as many wars as any contentious banana republic—with a few civil wars thrown in, just to ward off boredom. There isn't a building in the country built before 1900 that hasn't been scarred by bullets and mortar. Agia Maria was pockmarked with shell holes and defaced by the results of three separate, unsuccessful attempts to burn it down.

I stopped because I was getting tired. If coming down had been a chore, going back up was damn near killing me. The mud kept sliding away under my feet, sucking me two steps back for every three I took forward. I leaned against the side of the church and stretched and shook the rain out of my hair, wishing I had something to cover my head. I was getting drenched.

I was still leaning against the church when the second one came, very close, not half an inch from my nose. The third one followed without pause, while I was still brushing stone dust off my face. That time, I got it.

Bullets. Not ancient bullet holes, mementos of distant wars, but real bullets, hard and fast and silent under the cover of thunder.

I whipped around, straining to see in the darkness, not even thinking how stupidly I must be behaving. I was giving my attacker a nice, broad target. Part of me even realized that. It was just that I couldn't let it go. I couldn't run without knowing who was following me. The thought of that was worse than the thought of dying.

The fourth bullet changed my mind. It ripped right through the flapping edge of my parka, leaving a ragged-round black hole that made the canvas look burned. I threw a last, desperate glance at the deserted emptiness of the Kilithia streets, turned on my heel, and plunged through Agia Maria's heavy iron-hinged front door.

The fifth bullet landed right behind me, hitting the wood with a thud and a whine. I ran through the vestibule and into the small, crowded main room of the church—and collapsed between two pews.

It had to be fifteen minutes before I was able to breathe again—really breathe, so I knew air was going in and coming out and the rest of my body was working normally. Even then, my muscles were still twitching and jumping under my skin, refusing to obey commands to calm down and allow me to think rationally. Maybe there was no rational response to what I'd just been through. Certainly there was no rational reason for anybody to shoot at me. Who in the name of God would want to shoot at a twenty-five-year-old yuppie in shoulder-to-footsoles L. L. Bean?

I had also trapped myself in the church. There was always that to think about.

I got first to my knees and then to my feet, then sank back into the pew behind me, exhausted by even those small efforts. The church was lovely, a miniature Byzantine jewel, but I didn't have the heart to investigate it. I could hardly see straight. I twisted my neck back and forth, back and forth, trying to unkink it. All I managed was to give myself an excruciating backache.

When I first heard the commotion, I very nearly screamed. I *did* jump out of my pew, whirl around, and crouch, just as if I'd had a weapon to use against my attacker.

Fortunately, the figure emerging from the dimness

of the vestibule was not a black-masked attacker armed with high-powered rifle and silencer.

It was Pan, weather-beaten and streaked with mud from exposure to the storm, knocking into candle stands and overturning pews in his clumsy advance on the altar.

9

THERE WAS A letter from my brother, Chas—hand-delivered, by special messenger, according to Marina—waiting at the house when I got there. It was a good thing. By the time Pan had pulled up to the door of his squatter's palace, I was ready to kill him. If something hadn't happened to break my mood, I probably would have.

He had not been screamingly sympathetic. "It had to be some kind of hallucination," he kept saying, first in the church, then in our run through the rain to the side street where his car was parked, then in the car, all the way home. "Nobody's going to shoot at *you*. And nobody on Themnos would know a silencer to save their lives."

"Okay," I said, after the fifth repetition of this. "Where did the hole in my parka come from?"

Pan stared at the hole in my parka. "Looks like a cigarette burn to me," he said. "And don't tell me it's not possible. You know how you smoke cigarettes. You don't smoke cigarettes. You light them and wave them around like incense."

"I haven't lit one, for incense or any other reason, all day."

He dispelled this with a wave of his hand. "You lit one and forgot. You probably do it all the time."

"I never do it at all."

"How would you know? That's the point of forgetting. You don't remember. And it's like I'd said. Nobody *knows* you here, for God's sake. Who'd want to kill you?"

I settled back on those absurd orange seats, wanting to kick him, even irritated that he drove so remarkably well. The Pan I knew never did anything well. He was a blusterer, a blunderer, and a fool, and there were times I thought that if he didn't have his mother behind him, he'd be living dead broke on the streets of New York. Of course, I'd never seen him drive before. People in New York don't drive much. People who've been born and brought up in Manhattan often never get their license at all. It was somehow insulting to find that Pan could drive that pink and orange pimpmobile with all the skill and panache of a Mario Andretti, even over dirt roads, through ruts and potholes and mudslides.

In fact, behind the wheel of his car, Pan became another person altogether—self-confident, self-sufficient, even masterly. I thought it must be the kind of transformation actors made when they changed themselves from everyday neurotics into legendary superheroes.

I turned away and looked out at the storm. The last thing I wanted was to start thinking of Pan as a superhero. It was ridiculous, and it would probably be fatal. I had a staggering amount of pride invested in my picture of Pan as consummate idiot.

"If you ever bothered to read your own newspaper," I told him, "you might be aware of the fact that Greece has had an epidemic of terrorism lately. This is exactly the kind of thing they do. And they don't have to know you or even think you're particularly important, either."

"A terrorist on Themnos," Pan said.

"Why not on Themnos? Anyway, at the moment, I can't think of any other explanation."

"You can't think of any other explanation because it never happened. Look, sweetheart, in the first place, I do read my own newspaper. I read it every day in the composing room. Terrorists don't have to think you're important, but they do have to think you'll give them access to the international media, and there's hardly any local media on Themnos. We barely get television. The local constable answers his own questions. And Interpol probably couldn't find us on a map."

"In Agios Constantinos—"

"—there are seven hundred and fifty people," Pan said. "Seven hundred and fifty people. They probably wouldn't let that be a town in New York State."

I rubbed my eyes, hard, as if it would accomplish something. "Pan," I said. "There's a bullet hole in my parka. You could stop the car right now, look down, and see it. You have seen it. Now, it has to have come from somewhere, and it has to have come from something silenced or I would have heard the report. A terrorist seems like a dandy explanation to me, but if you've got a better one—"

"I've been giving you a better one all the way up this goddamn f——king road," Pan said. He beeped loudly at a sheep that had come skittering, lost, across our path. "Has it occurred to you that terrorists don't look like you and me? Or maybe they could look like you and me, but they certainly don't look like village Greeks, which is all you've got on this island. The kind of person you're talking about would stick out like a sore thumb."

"This is not," I told him, "a Robert Ludlum novel.

This is real life. Most of the IRA terrorists look like those nice Catholic boys people's mothers want them to marry. He could be anyone. Even a she."

"He couldn't be anybody. He'd walk differently. He'd *move* differently. He'd have been *trained,* for Christ's sake."

"Look at what's-his-name, who tried to kill the pope."

"Never mind what's-his-name who tried to kill the pope. I know most of these people, Kerry, or I used to know them when they were children—"

"When you were a child. You haven't set foot on this island since you were twelve."

"Yeah. Right. Well, there's not a s——tload of reason to come. Anyway, I live in Astoria and I still know a village Greek when I see one and that's what these people are. Village Greeks. Rubes, Kerry. The only person I've seen in town who could possibly fit the employment picture as an international terrorist is this crazy American in a black leather jacket whose political activity probably consists of tithing to f——king Greenpeace."

"Don't swear so much," I said absently, caught on that bit about the black leather jacket. It was completely absurd, of course. If John Borden had had some kind of Interpol record, Robert Hobart would never have been as friendly to him, or as deferential, as he had been in Pan's house after the murder of the priest. The fact that Robert Hobart was a weak-chinned idiot, I told myself, was beside the point.

Besides, John Borden had such—arresting eyes.

I shook my head violently. I had to be losing my mind.

"Americans," Pan told me, "do not tend to be fertile recruiting ground for international terrorism."

"You ought to be locked up for that kind of syntax," I said.

"To hell with my syntax. I'm telling you a home truth. There was some hail, all right? It was dark. You were tired. You imagined it."

"And the hole in my jacket is from a cigarette I've forgotten all about."

"Right."

He pulled up to the door of the squatter's palace, applied the brake, and let the engine idle. I got out without waiting for him, running across the blessedly narrow mud plain and up the steps to the front door with all the force I'd have liked to apply to his face. For some reason, I was angrier with him for his slur against John Borden's character than I was for any of the rest of it. It felt so gratuitous somehow, as if an opponent, during a debate on the relative literary merits of Swinburne and Oscar Wilde, had changed the subject long enough to note that Oscar Wilde was a homosexual. As if it was supposed to matter.

I let myself into the foyer just as Marina was coming out the living-room door, holding a square white envelope in one hand.

"You're back," she said, looking very pleased with herself. "Very good. This came while you were out, brought right to the door, and I didn't know—"

I took the letter from her hand. "My brother," I said. "My brother brought this to the door?"

"You have a brother in Greece?"

If I'd had less on my mind, I might have paid attention to the fact that she'd gone very still, almost watchful. Under the circumstances, I was too busy thinking of ways to murder Pan.

"He's an anthropology student," I said. "Cultural anthropology. He's a doctoral candidate at Columbia.

He's doing his field work in Greece, on Themnos mostly, and—" I stopped, disoriented. "But you know him," I said. "At least I thought you did. Pan knows him, anyway. That was how I got this job. Chas introduced me to Pan. I'm sure he said he'd known you all forever."

"Ah," Marina said. "Chas. Yes, I know Chas. But this wasn't Chas, the man who came to the door."

"Chas is the only brother I have," I said. I tore open the letter, half expecting to find a lot of weird hieroglyphics that had nothing to do with Chas at all, but there it was, the old familiar scrawl. I smiled slightly. "Well, he may not have brought the letter, but he certainly wrote it," I said. "I think this chicken scratch is probably forgery-proof."

"Well? That's good, then. He must have asked a friend to bring it. It was an American, that I know. A very unusual-looking American."

I looked up sharply. "Blond?" I said. "In a black leather jacket?"

Marina smiled wryly. "Very blond. And in a very black leather jacket. And with a body like a—what? Like a statue? I don't know. I thought Caliope was going to disgrace herself. If I were her age, I might have disgraced myself."

"Right," I said. I looked down at the letter in my hands and licked my lips nervously. *I'm in Parakos,* it said. *Come spend the afternoon with me, day after tomorrow. I've got work to do, so I can't come get you myself, but I've got a friend—John—and he can take the morning off, so he'll come down and pick you up.* I took a deep breath. A friend named John. Of course. It worried me almost as much as the fact that Chas sounded so clipped and strained—anything but his ordinary expansive self.

89

"Are you all right, dear?" Marina said. "You look a little pale."

"Of course she's not all right," Pan said, pushing his way through the front door. "She's got some crazy idea somebody's been shooting at her."

"What?" Marina said.

"It's not a crazy idea," I said savagely, shoving the letter and all the worry it had brought with it into a pocket. I held the edge of my parka out for Marina to see. "Look at this thing."

"She's not satisfied just to be shot at, either," Pan said. "She thinks it was a terrorist with a high-powered rifle and a silencer."

"That," I said, "was just a suggestion I made as to how and why what happened could have happened."

"Why not?" Pan said. "The moon is a great big wheel of green cheese God puts out for the heavenly mice to eat, which is how we get the phases—"

"Shh," Marina said. "Shh." She was still fingering my parka, frowning at the not-so-neat black hole near the edge. "You shouldn't jump to conclusions, Panyotis. It's not good for you."

"For Christ's sake," Pan said. "Mother, you couldn't possibly believe that some nut is running around this island with a weapon out of a James Bond movie taking pot shots at an editorial assistant—"

"I'm not an editorial assistant," I said.

"Taking pot shots at an editorial assistant," Pan plowed on, "for no good reason anyone can figure out and in complete—note, I said complete—secrecy. Invisibility, even. She's making this up."

Marina dropped the hem of my parka. "Maybe. Maybe she's making it up, and maybe she imagined it. And maybe not. Do you see?"

"No," Pan said. "I don't see."

I looked curiously from one to the other of them. Marina had folded her hands over her stomach, but instead of looking at the ground like a good Greek widow, she was staring straight into Pan's face. Her eyes somehow managed to look wide open and hooded at the same time, and they were very, very sharp. Pan stared back, stupefied and stupid, struck dumb.

Marina broke the pose first, rubbing her hands together in a characteristic Greek gesture of impatience and turning away.

"I say simply that we should not make up our minds without knowing all the facts," she said. "You perhaps didn't realize that Kerry is from a very important American family?"

Pan blinked. "Don't be ridiculous," he said. "We know her family."

"We know her brother," Marina corrected. "Her brother who is now on Themnos." A current of understanding passed between them.

Pan resisted it. "They don't have any money," he said feebly.

Marina waved this away. "Americans are not like us, true? Sometimes they have money and don't seem to."

"Mother," Pan said carefully. "We've known Chas Hansen for six years. We met him through Themnos people. I know what you're trying to do—"

"Did you know the American consul came last night after the—the death of the priest—to look after Kerry?"

"The American consul?" Pan said. He sounded as if he were strangling.

"Or a man from the consulate office," Marina said. "Kerry was not sure when she told me. Robert

Hobart." The name acted on Pan like dry ice on water. "He came to look after Kerry's interests during the investigation. He had been at school with her father. At Harvard."

"How good of him," Pan said.

"Yes," Marina agreed. "I thought it good of him, too. I say now only that we must consider the possibility that Kerry's . . . explanation of the circumstances may not be so farfetched as it might appear, on the surface. Just because these are things we did not know doesn't mean they are things nobody knows."

"An international terrorist." Pan stared at his mother with frank admiration. *"An international terrorist."*

Marina patted my hand maternally. "There," she said. "We shouldn't panic. We shouldn't even worry." She smiled into my eyes. "Panyotis may be right after all, yes? Possibly it is something you imagined. But possibly not. So—we will be careful."

"Of course," I said. "I'll be very careful."

"I knew you would." She dropped my hand and turned to Pan. "Now, we'll let Kerry go upstairs to rest before dinner, and you will help me with a problem. No?"

"Oh God," Pan said. "What have they done this time?"

"There is a minor dispute about the bridesmaids' gowns. You will be able to clear it up without difficulty." She turned back to me. "Go upstairs now, *pithakim.* Go upstairs and rest. You look ill."

"Yes," I said. "Yes, well, all right. I'll do that."

Marina beamed at me like a mother at an obedient child. There was nothing sinister there, nothing malicious and vicious, none of the things I sometimes imagined I saw in her eyes. As for Pan, he was just Pan, bumbling and mother-dominated and vain. The only thing out of place in his makeup was his damnable genius at driving a car.

I turned away from them and headed up the stairs.

I forgot all about them once I'd locked myself safely in my room. It was a mistake, but I did it anyway. Nothing seemed as important as taking a good, hard look at Chas's note. I even momentarily forgot about being shot at. A strange conversation between Marina and Pan, even one as thick with oddnesses and double meanings as the one I'd just heard, didn't stand a chance.

Unfortunately, there was nothing to find in Chas's letter but what I'd already found. There was the odd phrasing, the clipped, constipated sentences giving the facts and nothing more. My brother has always been exuberantly verbose, filling his letters with charming but unnecessary details and irreverent side comments and nonsense analyses of current events. Even his academic papers are like that. He has to go over them, after he's finished them, and take out the lunatic parts.

I read it again. Not a word about the work he was doing—what, where, or how. Not a word about where he was living, either. And not a word about his "friend John."

It had to be the same John. I believe in coincidences, but not of such magnitude. John Borden had known I was going to Kilithia. He hadn't got it from me or from the cabdriver. He must have got it from Chas.

So why hadn't he said so?

I stashed the letter on the night table and stretched out on the bed. The more often I ran into John Borden, the stranger he seemed—and the more uneasy I got. Now he was a friend of Chas's, a friend I'd never met or even heard of. I'd have remembered if I had.

And Pan was right. John Borden did look like a movie-stereotype international spy. I'd been thinking the same thing myself just the night before.

I let my eyes drift shut and my mind float, far above the screeching argument Caliope and Agapé had started somewhere below me. Caliope. Agapé. Marina. Pan. Costa. John Borden.

Oh yes. John Borden. Sailing toward sleep, floating free of my defenses, I liked the idea of John Borden taking me away somewhere all too well.

10

THE CEREMONY THE next night was called a resurrection. It started at five, the hour when, in summer, the long afternoon sleep ended and businesses reopened for the evening promenade. There was never much of a promenade in Kilithia and only one business, but the villagers did their best for the Peterises and their own sense of religious fitness. By the time Marina emerged from the front door of Pan's house, dressed in the heavy black of the Greek widow, her hair and face covered by a winding scarf, the path down the mountain was clotted with people waiting bareheaded in the rain.

I probably should have stayed home. After the scare Marina's explanation had given me, I fully expected the procession to reduce me to stuttering idiocy. I'd had a bad day, too. Caliope and Agapé had appealed to me three times in matters of importance to the wedding (color of the ribbons for the reserved pews in church, color of the veiling for the bridesmaids' hair, choice of two wedding gowns from an Athens designer's catalog), and torn me to shreds before I'd ever had a chance to open my mouth. Pan had been fretful, demanding, and determinedly illogical, going over the *Greek Time* budget sheets as if he'd never seen them before and questioning expenditures—like the cost of the printing—he already knew were inflexible. I wasn't able to get anything done on the shipping of the offerings, either. I spent most of the late morning slogging through the mud, going from one village house to the other, finding no one home. After a while, I began to think people were home but refusing to answer my calls, a craziness that made me a little worried about myself. Why in the name of God would people hide from me, especially when I'd always been the one to pay them? It made me think Pan might be half right about the state of my nerves. I *was* getting a little paranoid. I *might* be imagining things.

I went back to the house and took the kind of long midday rest most Americans have no patience for, letting myself float unconcernedly above a sea of noise: Caliope and Agapé in yet another argument; Pan in the drive, haggling with the mourning women; Costa Papageorgiou pounding up and down the back hall, slamming things in and out of closets, heaven only knew to what purpose. I knew Pan would probably be furious with me for taking Greek hours, but I honestly didn't care. For the moment, I didn't care if he fired me. As for going to see Chas in the morning, if Pan objected to that, I had every intention of telling him, finally, exactly what I thought of him.

About four-thirty, the really interesting things started to happen. Subconsciously, I think I had expected a repetition of the funeral, which, aside from the wailing mourning women, was mostly stiff dignity and religious ritual, with a priest walking at the head of the crowd, carrying a great gold cross on a staff. The Greek Orthodox Church keeps an ancient rite, a service dating back to the year 1000, when all the churches in the world kept it with them. The Greek Orthodox Church never changes anything or allows the possibility of change. And it can tame anything. Some of the larger churches in Greece, like the one in Corfu town, keep the actual mummified bodies of their patron saints in open biers and carry them through the streets on the saints' feast days. The practice should be macabre, repellent, but it isn't. The priests walk at the head of the biers, dressed in long robes stiffly embroidered in red and green and gold and blue, carrying crosses and icons, and it all looks like the funeral of a particularly important man or a solemn benediction.

The Greek Orthodox Church had not managed to tame this. It wasn't just the fact that there was no priest. He would have been lost in the crowd under any circumstances. His voice would not have been heard above the keening. For funerals in Greece, you hire professional mourning women, widows who, for a price, scream and rant and tear their hair and lament the passing of the deceased. Pan had hired them for this, too, but here they were more like cheerleaders than a Greek chorus. They gathered at our door in the fading light, shawls pulled forward to hide their faces, and sent up a piercing, ululating moan that echoed across the mountain like the cries the spirits of the dead were supposed to make in the old mythology of All Hallow's Eve. The people on the path answered them, on a lower but no less urgent note. The thick, relentless wave of pain and grief and supplication crashed again and again into Themnos Mountain, battering mud and stone the way the ocean batters the coast in a hurricane.

I stood at my window and watched them, their cries getting wilder and wilder as the sky went to blackness. The mourning women underneath me brought out a torch and lit it, sending up a dangerous flame. Torches went up all along the path, down to the hollow near the church. They looked like bonfires inexplicably burning in midair.

I was just thinking I had to get dressed and go—had to see this close up—when there was a knock on my door. Marina didn't wait to be asked in. She pushed through, one hand pinning her shawl under her chin, and waited for me to say something. In her way, she was as strange and timeless as the mourners on the mountain. Her eyes seemed to give off a bright sharp light, like X rays, that saw all the way through to my bones.

I brushed awkwardly at my robe, wondering what this woman wanted of me. I'd wondered that before —Marina was the kind of woman who made you think of things like that—but the question had never seemed as important as it did in that moment.

"I was just going to get dressed and come down," I said. "I was looking—" I gestured helplessly toward the window.

She inclined her head to me, so slightly I half thought I was imagining it. "It is a very beautiful thing," she said. "One of the most beautiful I know."

I said, "Of course," though it came out so muffled by nerves and uneasiness, I wasn't sure she could hear it. Then she smiled, and I smiled back, pretending she was putting me at ease. The only thing that could have put me at ease at that point would have been a one-way ticket back to the States.

I watched her steadily until she was out of the room, with the door shut behind her. I didn't want to turn my back to her.

By the time I got downstairs, I was shaky but in control. I slipped out the door without anyone notic- ing me and took a place behind Caliope, at the very back of the small knot of family that would head the procession to the church, meaning to slip back further as we made our way downhill. Marina may have thought this a beautiful thing, but her family didn't agree with her. Pan was wound up tight, ready to go off the moment anyone touched or even spoke to him, and his eyes were haunted. Caliope, dressed for the first time in her life like the peasant Greek she expended so much effort not to be, was close to hysterics.

Agapé and Costa were calmer, but I put that down to familiarity. They must have seen hundreds of these ceremonies. They probably thought of them as entertainment. I thought Costa especially would be attracted to the underlying violence of it all, but it was Agapé who was glowing with excitement and anticipation, the way she glowed when Pan said she could order something new from Athens.

Marina put her hand out and touched the arm of the mourning woman closest to her. They went forward haltingly, to the head of the little group, Marina wincing with the pain of arthritis. They hesitated for a moment, looking downhill, and in the flare of the torch fire I got a sudden glimpse of Marina's companion—not one of the women I had hired when I'd come to arrange the funeral, but someone new, a very young girl with clear skin and wide eyes and restless hands, shivering with cold and fear under the thin covering of her shawl. She looked terrified.

I reached into my pocket for cigarettes, lit one, then dropped it in the mud as I caught Pan's stare of furious disapproval. It was no time to tell him I didn't actually want to smoke the thing. I wasn't even sure my explanation—that I wanted a light of my own, one I could control—would make any sense.

Suddenly, Marina sent up a wail of her own, sharper and more heartrending than anything the professional mourners could manage. It acted as a signal to the others. The mourning women increased their volume. The people on the mountain waved their torches and began to chant, slowly, something that sounded like a funeral poem. Somewhere in the distance someone started to sing. The high sweet voice drifted through the crowd like a ghost, calling up memories of loss and sadness and the long slow road through life to death.

Then we began to move, so slowly it felt like floating across still water on a raft, down the path and through the people and toward the church. Torches flared on every side of us. Women put out their arms to touch our clothes, pulling at the fabric as if to tear it. The chant rose and rose and rose, blotting out everything else, catching us in sound the way fruit is caught in gelatin.

It did more than affect me. It damn near swallowed me up, so that by the time I was halfway down the mountain, I was breathing in hitches and trying to pinch myself awake. I felt a short half second from collapsing from dizziness and fright, and I was beginning to panic. It was like being drowned, and I didn't like it. I wanted to run—to escape, because I was beginning to feel that if I didn't escape, I would cease to exist.

All around me, people I knew—even very familiar people, like Pan—*had* ceased to exist, had been digested into the body of the chant and become part of the sound and the movement. I looked into their faces and saw . . . nothing.

Then somebody put a hand on my arm, and I screamed.

* * *

100

I say I screamed. In fact I know I screamed, but you wouldn't have been able to tell from the behavior of most of the people around me. Nobody looked at me or jumped, the way people do when they hear an unexpected loud noise. They just stared ahead and went on chanting, louder and louder, as if working themselves up to something drastic.

The man holding me, however, reacted violently. He clamped a hand over my mouth and jumped a little at the noise I made, so for a moment the weight of his body was bearing down on mine. I slipped and thought I was going to fall. Then he righted himself and me and pushed us to firmer ground.

"For God's sake," he said in my ear. "What do you think you're doing?"

It was like a finger snap before the eyes of a hypnotist's subject. The scene dried up. Instead of a dream sequence, full of occult practices and magicians who could change shape at will, there was only a steep barren mountain dotted with people carrying torches, quite ordinary people, farmers and the wives and children of farmers, unlettered Greek peasants with a surprising talent for melodrama. The fear left me before the adrenaline did. My heart was still pounding wildly, but instead of being panicked and terrified, I was furious.

I tore John Borden's hand away from my mouth, whipped around, and shouted, "What the hell do *you* think you're doing? You scared me half to death."

This time, people did turn to look at us, sometimes with disapproval, but mostly with curiosity and a little amusement. The old women thought they knew exactly what was going on here: young love and the blushing beginnings of passion and the long, soppy road that leads to marriage.

Right.

I shook water out of my hair. "All you had to do was say something," I told him. "You didn't have to come up from behind and grab me like that."

"I didn't grab you," John said irritably. "I just touched your arm to get your attention."

"Which explains perfectly why I nearly jumped out of my skin."

John started to say something, stopped himself, then threw his hands violently in the air. We had been moving slowly and steadily downhill without realizing it, and now we were surrounded by people, men as well as women. A few of the men caught John's gesture and nearly laughed out loud. *They* thought they knew what was going on here, too. They had been through it all before.

"Look," John said. "I just came up to see if you wanted to get away from here. That's all. I wasn't trying to scare you. I wasn't trying to kill you—which was what it sounded like with that scream you made —and I certainly wasn't looking for an argument, which is what I got. All I wanted to know was if this was freaking you out a little and if maybe you'd like to go watch from the point."

"Right," I said.

"Oh Christ," he said.

"How far is this point?" I asked him. I sounded more reasonable than I had since he showed up, and he noticed, but I tried to ignore it. My problem was simple: I didn't want to give him ideas, or feed his ego, but I didn't want him to leave, either. I had a feeling that as soon as he disappeared, my dream sequence would come back.

He turned on his heel and pointed to the west, to a little knoll just above the cemetery. "It's dry up there," he said, "because there's a tree cover, practically the only one on the island. And you can see very well, probably better than you can from the ground."

"Better," I said dubiously. I wasn't sure I wanted to see better. They were, after all, exhuming a body. If I knew anything from my steady diet of detective stories, it was that bodies buried a year were unlikely to be nothing but bare skeletons.

"You don't have to look, you know," he said. "But it is a good vantage point if you want to, and it is away from all this."

I hesitated. I certainly wanted to be away from "all this," but I had a feeling that the knoll, although affording an excellent view of the cemetery, would not give anyone a view of *us*. Did I want to be secreted in a dark place with John Borden?

I looked into the crowd for some sign of Pan or Caliope or Marina.

"Don't worry about it," John said. "They're way up ahead. They can't see us."

"I'm not worried." I scanned the crowd again, this time for any familiar face. I saw no one. "The thing is," I said, "she asked me to come. Marina. She came to my room and asked me to come."

"To this?" John sounded surprised.

"Of course to this," I said. "What did you think I was talking about? Dartmouth winter carnival?"

"This is not exactly a wedding, Miss Hansen. It's not the kind of thing you invite people to."

I shot him one of my better angry looks. "I'm just trying to figure out what I'm supposed to do here," I said. "Which is getting to be damn near impossible, because everything is very confusing and *you're not helping.*"

He threw his arms in the air again, stopped them while they were still above his head, then brought them down, hard, on my shoulders. "Okay," he said. "We'll start from the beginning. Do you or do you not want to come up to the knoll with me?"

"Oh," I said. "Well. Of course I do."

Then I brushed his hands off my shoulders, turned around, and started walking toward the place he called the point.

I let him get ahead of me after a while. From where we had been standing on the mountain, the way to that minuscule promontory overlooking Pan's father's grave—and those of almost everyone else who had ever died in Kilithia—looked easy. In practice, it was something like cutting a road through the Burmese jungle. Here our problem was mud, not vegetation, but it was very lively mud. It seemed to expand and contract at will, catching at our feet and throwing us into wet piles of thorned scrub brush. By the time we got to the trees, I felt scratched and bitten and flailed alive.

John ducked into the tree cover, made his way to the edge of the promontory, and looked over.

"Come here," he whispered urgently. "They've made it over to the grave. They've even started to dig."

I hesitated again. What was I doing here, exactly? I didn't want to see them dig up that grave. And I didn't like the excitement in John Borden's face at the prospect.

"Kerry?" he said.

I made myself go forward. The unfortunate truth was, there was no way to go back. I wouldn't have been able to find my way.

"Look at that," he said as I pulled up beside him. "That's your friend Pan, saying the prayer over the grave. That would have been the priest's part if he hadn't died first. And Kyria Peteris—Marina?—you didn't see her, but she took the first shovel of dirt."

I started to crouch beside him, but he waved me away. He had a small square of nylon in his pocket. He took it out and began to unfold it and unfold it, until it was a single thin blue sheet the size of a mattress for a double bed. He laid it out on the ground and patted it affectionately.

"That'll take care of any lingering damp," he said. He lay flat on his stomach, close to the edge, with his head just jutting out into the air over the cemetery. "You can come and look now, you know," he said. "They won't be doing anything really awful for a while yet."

"You sound like you know all about it." I didn't move.

"My father was Greek," he said absently. "My mother was a Swede, that's why the blond. Anyway, maybe I should say my grandfather was Greek. My father was born in New York. My *papou* came from a village in the mountains around Salonika. He died when I was twelve. We took him back there, back home, to be buried, and we came a year later for one of these." He pointed over the promontory. "There was a priest at ours, but it doesn't make much difference. They're always the same."

"I was just thinking that before," I said. "I mean, that the priest wouldn't make much difference."

"It's like those people who dance on coals," John said. "They've got a Christian explanation for what they're doing, but it's not a Christian thing at all. It's pagan, as old as the country."

I walked slowly across the nylon and gave a cautious peek at the scene below. The men had reached the casket, a rough, spare oblong wooden box warped by the extremes of heat and damp that make up the year's weather on a Greek island. The lid had shrunk and curled until it was free of the sides and was now held to the rest of the box by the thin, rusted tin of the hinges and hasp. I winced and stepped back. Pan had requested that particular casket—told me where to go and who to see and what to pay—but although it had looked very impressive at the funeral, I could now see it was cheap and badly made. I was ready to kill Pan all over again. He was not just well off, but fabulously rich by the standards of an island like Themnos. He could have afforded to do better by his father.

Now Marina stepped out of the crowd, still holding on to the arm of the young girl she had approached at the house, and began to slide into the pit. The girl went with her, even at this distance looking a little sick and frightened. I reminded myself that she must have done this before, unless her husband had been lost at sea, which was unlikely. If she'd been married to a sailor, she'd have been living in Agios Constantinos or on another island.

Marina reached for the edge of the casket and began to hammer feebly at the hasp. I stepped quickly away from the edge before she had a chance to get it free.

"Whoosh," I said. My stomach felt distinctly unsettled, and I hadn't actually seen anything.

John Borden said, "What?" I didn't answer. He hadn't really been asking me anything. He probably hadn't heard what I said. He had pulled himself far forward, so it seemed half his body was hanging in the air, and was staring intently down at the scene in the tiny cemetery. I wrinkled my nose in disgust. He had been right about one thing: the view was excellent, especially lit the way it was by a dozen blazing torches. He would undoubtedly be able to see every scrap of flesh clinging to every splintered bone.

"Don't you find all this a little morbid?" I asked him. "I mean, for God's sake, it's a dead body."

This time he heard me. "Death," he quoted pompously, "is as natural as birth."

I snorted. "You shouldn't spout clichés," I said. "It doesn't suit your image. And we're not talking about death here, we're talking about—"

"Shhh!"

His voice was so low and urgent, it stopped me dead. I stared in surprise as he pushed himself farther and farther from the edge of the promontory, putting more and more of his body into the dangerous openness beyond the safety of the tiny cliff.

"There she goes," he said. "There she goes, I thought that was what—oh *shit.*"

He moved so fast, I hardly saw him do it. One moment he was pitched over the edge of the knoll, the next he was on his feet, his whole body tense and liquid. I had just long enough to recognize how graceful he was, like a tightrope walker, when he whirled, grabbed me by the shoulders, and shouted into my face.

"*Shit.* Who'd have believed they'd try anything *here?*"

11

I SHOULD HAVE been furious. In fact, I *was* furious, at least in the beginning, which was just as well. As soon as John stopped shouting at me, he dropped his arms, turned around, and went running into the mud and the brush without me. It happened so quickly, I didn't have time to realize I had anything to react to. One minute I was wincing against the deep baritone blasts of his anger, the next, I was alone on that knoll, lit from below by the torches in the cemetery and surrounded by chants and cries and sudden, piercing wails. And shouts. The shouts were what finally did it for me, made me realize that the sounds from the cemetery were not normal, even for an abnormality like this exhumation. People down there were shouting at each other, and they were in panic. And angry.

I made myself go to the edge of the promontory. I went slowly and carefully and reluctantly—and with half my mind calling John Borden the names I thought he deserved to be called—but I got myself to the lip and made myself look over. It was the first time I realized how very low that knoll was. I was barely a full head above the man standing closest to me and less than eight feet above the surface of old Kyriou Peteris's grave. I should have had as good a view as John had had, but I didn't. No one was standing around *now* with their torches held erect and steady like soldiers' rifles in a military parade. Some of the torches had been abandoned, dropped to the ground, where they were sputtering and dying in the mud. The men who held the others seemed to find it impossible to stand still. They ran around and around the edge of the grave, shouting to each other and the people in the pit, pushing at anyone who got in their way. The pit itself was chaos. Instead of a single man digging or Marina and her companion hacking away at the coffin hasp by themselves, there now seemed to be a hundred people in the hole, all of them tearing and shouting at each other. Even Pan and Agapé were in there, Agapé holding on to Marina for dear life, Pan with his seven-hundred-dollar Brooks Brothers suit in shreds. Pan's face came into the light for a moment, haggard and wild, and disappeared again. Then I saw the body—what I thought had to be Pan's father's body—a bare, perfectly intact leg and a small gnarled foot. The skin there looked as supple and vibrant as the skin of the living, the leg as washed and rosy as the leg of someone who had just come out of a hot bath.

I stepped away from the lip, back into the darkness of the pines, where I could neither see nor be seen. I was feeling distinctly sick, and underneath the sickness, my anger was growing. John Borden. God *damn* John Borden. Here I was, stranded alone in the pines, the solitary audience for a scene from a George Romero movie I hadn't chosen to see.

I wiped rain off my face—it had begun to drizzle again, that slow, celestial Chinese water-torture drip —and searched the edge of the pine clearing for something that looked like a path. It was important to find direction here, because beyond the pines, there would be nothing but open mountainside littered with scrub and no landmarks to find my way. If I went the wrong way, I would have nothing but sound to rely on to lead me home, and sound in a place like Themnos is treacherous. The juxtaposition of mountain and sea does something odd to the acoustics, so the voices of people calling out to help you only lead you away from comfort.

I went to the very edge of the clearing and walked every inch of it, looking for trampled grass and wet footsteps. There was either nothing like that or too much of it—three separate places where someone might have made her way through to start down the mountain.

I looked into the sky the way the old village women did when they wanted a special audience with God. I was not, however, asking for help finding my way down the mountain.

I was asking for a lightning bolt to strike John Borden dead.

It took me nearly half an hour to find my way to the cemetery again, half an hour of mostly false trails and mud and twigs and that murderous stinging weed the village women call witch grass. My anger lasted all the way through it. In fact for a while, it got worse. I could hardly believe he'd left me on the knoll to fend for myself—left me without a word of sensible explanation—and every time I did make myself believe it, something in my head exploded. I thought of him giving directions to my cabdriver, wandering around Pan's house as if he owned it (and finding and starting the generator, which I hadn't even known was there). I thought of him whispering to nervous, wimpy Robert Hobart, failed diplomat extraordinaire, as if the two of them were international spies and I was the kind of half-witted civilian likely to blow all chances for world peace with a single indiscreet word. In the wild, dark landscape of Themnos Mountain in a night storm, Pan's insinuations about the possible connection between John Borden and international terrorism were ludicrous. John Borden wasn't an international terrorist or an international spy or even a very good amateur detective. He was a spoiled brat with too high an opinion of himself, and when I got hold of him again, I was going to let him know I knew it.

I was saved partially by exhaustion—*you* try wandering around a steep mountain face in the dark, in a storm, in a pair of Saks Fifth Avenue heels—and partially by a phenomenon my mother had warned me about, but I'd never before experienced. Out-of-context, my mother called it, and for once was exactly right. I was beginning to think I'd be slogging through the mud forever when I saw lights. Then, as I made my way toward them, something—relief?—made me let down my guard. I wandered over the last ridge onto the narrow path near the cemetery wall in a state that was something like sleepwalking. And then I saw him.

What I did not see was the John Borden who had left me on the knoll or the John Borden who was standing in the middle of all those Greeks shouting directions and arguing about some situation I did not yet comprehend. Instead, I got the picture of a man as cleanly severed from the circumstances of the world as a necklace on black velvet in a Cartier window. Out-of-context wasn't the half of it. He looked more artistic ideal than man, taller and stronger and finer than the flesh-and-blood creatures around him, golden and shining where they were dark and dull. He was very good-looking, of course, but it wasn't just that. That, I had noticed the first time I saw him. What I thought I saw now was something that came from inside him, a kind of power, which was exciting and strange and dangerous and powerful.

I shook my head violently, hoping to clear it. Even in my half-sleepwalking state, I knew I had to be going crazy. John Borden. Half a minute ago, I'd been ready to kill John Borden.

The movement I made must have caught his attention. He looked up, blinked, seemed confused, then snapped to attention.

"Kerry," he shouted. "Oh, Kerry, for God's sake—"

I stepped back a little. He was coming at me very swiftly across the rutted hollows of that ancient cemetery. I was still far enough into my sleepwalking state to find the movement of his body, the closing of that gap, exciting and disturbing. I couldn't stop myself staring at his supple gracefulness, couldn't stop the thrumming beat it called up at the base of my throat, but at the same time I was pulling back. My inner resistance was tremendous. I felt as if I were shrinking into my skin, and I wanted to run.

He got to me before I realized he would. He jumped over the cemetery wall—it was about knee height for him—and grabbed me by the shoulders again. I was beginning to think grabbing me by the shoulders was John Borden's first reaction to finding me with him in any moment of stress.

"Oh, good *lord,*" he said. "I left you up there. I left you—"

"I know where you left me," I said peevishly, stepping back a little. The barriers of my inner resistance were as high as they were going to go, and they weren't high enough. I could feel his fingers through the elegant but inadequate coat I had worn to honor the importance of Marina's ceremony. Long, elegant fingers. What my mother would have called surgeon's hands.

What my father would have called jewel thief's hands.

I shook myself free of him and rubbed more rain from my face. He shoved his hands into his pockets and looked over his shoulder at the scene in the cemetery. I couldn't see past him to whatever was there, and I didn't try.

"Do you want to tell me what's going on?" I asked him.

He turned back to me. It was as if a light had been switched off behind his eyes when I wasn't looking. He was cold and watchful and still, like a stone statue with eyes that moved.

"No," he said.

"Oh," I said. *"Fine."*

He started to run a hand through his hair, pulling so hard I thought he was going to tear golden strands of it out by the roots. "I want you to get out of here," he said, almost whispering. "I want you to turn around and go back to the house and tell anybody who asks that you were here, on the ground, in the back, where you couldn't see anything. All right?"

"No," I said. "Of course it's not all right. And I *couldn't* see anything, so could you please tell me—"

I stopped because Pan had come up behind him—a very surreal Pan, clothes in tatters, hands and face covered in mud and grime, something like satisfaction in his eyes.

"Pan," I said. My knees felt, and my voice sounded, weak.

John whipped around, stuck his wandering hand into his pocket again, and looked Pan up and down.

Pan stared straight into John Borden's eyes. "The

113

constable's here," he said. "I was right. It was an accident."

"Like hell it was," John said.

"Marina fell into the pit. A lot of people jumped in to help her. The girl fell in the crush and—"

"And somebody stepped on her neck?"

"Possibly."

"Horse manure."

Pan turned away, shrugging. I could see the scene in the cemetery now, though there was so much confusion, it wasn't entirely clear what was going on. *Somebody stepped on her neck.* I shivered slightly. From where I stood, I could see an old woman, bent with dowager's hump and nearly prostrate with tears and wailing.

"Somebody died," I said.

The two men turned to look at me.

"Of course somebody died," Pan said. "Where the hell have you been?"

"In a state of terminal confusion," I bit back. I was in no mood to take any of his nonsense, or any of anybody else's, either. *"Who* died?"

"One of the mourning women." Pan shrugged again. I could tell he thought of the mourning women the way Regency aristocrats had thought of the lower classes—anonymous and expendable. It made me very angry.

"Just *one* of the wailing women?" I asked him. "Not some particular one with a jealous brother-in-law or some dower property her husband's family would like to have?"

"Oh, wonderful," Pan said. He jerked a thumb in John's direction. "Now you're starting to sound like him. I thought you didn't see anything."

"I didn't," I said.

"Good. Take my word for it. There was a little

confusion. The confusion turned into a lot of crazy chaos—which is what everything turns into in this idiotic country sooner or later—and there was a tragedy. One of the mourning women was *accidentally* killed. All right?"

"I don't know," I said.

"Fuck you," Pan said.

"At least she's keeping an open mind," John said.

Pan let out a snort that made him sound very much like a horse. "As for you," he told John Borden, "I don't know who you think you are or what you think you are, but this is a Greek farming village, not graduate school. If you want to make trouble, I suggest you return to the ivied halls of Columbia, where they'll indulge you."

"Fine speech," John said blandly.

"You," Pan said to me, "get ready to come back to the house." Then he turned his back on us and walked off.

I watched him go, and with him the air of incipient comedy that always seemed to surround him. Pan *could* make a fine speech—in fact, he was a well-educated and highly intelligent man—but there was something so essentially buffoonish about him that it was impossible to take him, or anything in which he had a part, entirely seriously. Pan on his dignity was just a little like a cat in clothes.

Once he was gone, however, there was no way *not* to take the scene seriously. The old, crying woman now looked sad and sinister at once, a witch-crone wailing over a caldron. I thought of the leg and foot I had seen from the knoll—not Pan's father's at all, but that of a woman who might have been alive when I saw her—and shivered.

I looked at John Borden. "Which of the mourning women?" I asked him.

"I don't know her name," he said. "She was very young, maybe eighteen—"

"Oh," I said. I remembered the girl Marina had chosen to lean on, how frightened she had been. I felt very near tears. "I saw her up at the house," I started to say. "She was—she didn't like all this."

"Did you see anything . . . in particular?"

"In particular? Of course not. What would there be in particular to see?"

"Nothing, probably." He sighed. "The trouble is—" He stopped himself. "Go back to the house," he said. "I'll pick you up tomorrow morning at nine, all right?"

I fixed my eyes on the figure of the man I knew from two nights before to be the local constable. He was standing in the center of a group of men, nodding sagely as half a dozen voices shouted at him at once.

"If I go back up to the house without finding out what's going on," I said, "I'm not going to be able to sleep at all."

"Peteris can give you the outline," John suggested.

"Pan can give me *his* outline," I corrected. "You think somebody killed that girl. Murdered her. Deliberately."

"It can't be murder if it wasn't deliberate."

"Don't *fence* with me."

"No." He backed up until he was against the cemetery wall and then sat down on it. The light, coming from behind him, left his face in shadow. His eyes looked blank. "If I could, I'd get you out of here right now," he said. "I'd just pack you into my car and take you to your brother."

"Why don't you?"

"I've got something I have to do tonight. And I'm not exactly sure where Chas is right at the moment, either."

"In bed," I suggested.

"Alone?"

I thought I was pretty good at recognizing a diversion when I saw one. "You think somebody murdered that girl," I said. "Why?"

"If I could do a halfway decent job of explaining why, I'd do it for the constable."

"It must have been something you saw from the knoll," I said. "Nothing else makes sense."

"All right. It was something I saw from the knoll."

There was something in his voice I didn't like, something tentative. *"Did* you see something from the knoll?"

"Oh yes."

"Then why don't you go to the constable and tell him?"

"It wouldn't change his mind."

"What?"

"It wouldn't change his mind," John repeated. "It wasn't that kind of thing—I didn't see someone throw her down or anything like that. And what I did see, I don't think he'd think it was important."

"But you do," I said.

"Oh yes."

I was getting a headache. I was also losing what patience I had, which is precious little under the best of circumstances. "I'm *tired* of listening to you talk like a script for 'Mission Impossible,'" I said, "and running around behaving like a character from something worse. And I'm tired of being treated like an idiot who doesn't know her own mind. What's going on here, anyway? What *are* you?"

He snapped to attention, coming off the wall and closing the gap between us. He stopped short of grabbing my shoulders again—thank *heaven*—but he stood very close nevertheless, close enough for me to feel his breath on my face. I could feel the beat at the base of my throat again, insistent and ticklish, as if my own body were laughing at me.

"I am," John Borden said, "a doctoral candidate in anthropology at Columbia University. That's all."

I turned quickly away from him. I believed a lot of things. I believed that John Borden was a friend of my brother Chas's, that he would take me to see him, even that his attentions were the twentieth-century version of honorable. He wanted to help, not hurt, and he meant me no harm. I believed all those things instinctively. What I did not believe was that John Borden was a doctoral candidate in anthropology at Columbia University.

"I'd better be getting back to Pan," I said.

"Get a good night's sleep. We've got a long drive in the morning."

"Do we really?"

"Kerry—"

"Oh, never *mind.*"

I started tramping toward the cemetery wall, feeling that beat in my throat and wishing I could make myself feel nothing more than that urge to kill him I'd had on the knoll. It struck me that I'd been very near this cemetery wall when that oddness had happened, the incident I still thought of as someone trying to shoot at me. I had been wavering in my belief in that explanation ever since it happened. Even when I believed it absolutely, I tended to think of it as something random, some nut or anti-American fanatic shooting at the first foreigner who crossed his path. Now I had the sickening feeling that not only had someone shot at me, but someone had shot at *me*, Kerry Hansen, a known quantity and a chosen target.

I turned back, meaning to tell him what had happened and ask him if he had an explanation for it, thinking *that* might get him talking if nothing else would. I never got a chance.

He was right behind me when I turned, so close I almost fell right into his arms.

And then he kissed me.

12

"IF THIS BITCH," Caliope said, "thinks I'm going to parade around in public, even what passes for public in this godforsaken hole, looking like an obese canary with the trots—"

"Look at this person," Agapé said. "This bloated board without a knothole that calls itself a woman—"

"You piss on the ground, you little whore," Caliope said. "I step over your puddles every time I leave the house—"

"*Skilo ye no meno.*"

"*Putana.*"

"*Stou golou sou.*"

"*Ya moto mitera—*"

I opened my eyes in the sun and stared at the ceiling above me, wondering if they were ever going to stop, and if they did, if I was ever going to be able to go to sleep again. I had the distinct impression that I hadn't had any sleep for a long time. There was the ceremony and the girl dying, and— I sat up abruptly and began to rub my eyes. There had been a hundred disturbing dreams, of course—one in particular, in which I found a disembodied hand and a disembodied leg in the mud, both belonging to someone still alive—but what was striking me most strongly hadn't been a

120

dream at all. I could still feel the soft leather of John Borden's jacket on my face, the roughened surface of his hands on my arm. I could even still feel the kiss, small as it was, fast as it was. He hadn't taken me roughly in his arms and played Rhett Butler to my Scarlett O'Hara. He hadn't even given me a good, hearty Rock Hudson–Doris Day smack. He'd hardly brushed his lips against mine. It had been totally insignificant. Totally. It was just that—

I swung my legs off the bed and began to rub my temples instead of my eyes, frantically and violently. I needed increased circulation to the brain and the common sense that was supposed to come with it. I kept thinking there was something I should have noticed or something I should have done—or been doing?—that was getting buried under all this sleep-sodden idiocy about John Borden. Whatever it was wouldn't come, not even when the argument on the floor below me passed beyond words and began to be fought in smashing plaster.

"I'll rip her *throat* out," Caliope said.

I thought it might be a very good idea. Then somebody could rip Caliope's throat out, and all the screaming would stop.

Chas.

I got slowly out of bed, wincing a little as my bare feet hit the cold, uncarpeted marble near the window. Had I really forgotten about Chas? It seemed I had. In all the confusion—I mentally classified John Borden as a confusion, which was what he was—I had gone to sleep and woken up without remembering even once that this was the day John Borden was going to take me to Chas. Almost better than that, he was going to take me *away*—away from Caliope and Agapé, away from Pan, away from people who might or might not have been shooting at me in the village, and away from a Kilithia girl who got her neck broken in the mud. I looked at the bedroom window and frowned. It all seemed preposterous in the light of day, but there hadn't been much light in the days this trip. And preposterous or not, it was all, unfortunately, true. I could still see the men standing in a circle around the pit that had been Pan's father's grave, arguing ways and means by torchlight.

I threw open the closet and started to pull out clothes, jeans and turtleneck, and a big fuzzy sweater for the trip, a "good dress" in case Chas wanted to go into Agios Constantinos for dinner, even a clean nightgown. There was always the chance Chas would want me to stay late, even too late to get back to Kilithia, and if he did, I wasn't going to argue. I had had enough of Kilithia, thank you, enough of mysteries and ancient rituals and people dying off like flies. I'd known a girl in college—one of those pale blondes from wealthy families whose trust funds exceed their craniums in capacity—who had been enamored of spending her summers in "unspoiled" places like Tierra del Fuego and Timbuktu. I knew a lot of people who were impressed with her, too. I never saw the point. What I like are Paris hotels—or even the Grande Bretagne in Athens—with rosewood and chandeliers in the bar and central heating advanced enough to let me wear silk in a snowstorm.

"When I get finished with her," Caliope said, "there's going to be nothing left of her for Pan to marry—"

I looked down at the turtleneck in my hand. Pale blue silk, custom made by whoever my mother was going to these days. A Christmas present. "Just your kind of thing, dear, but a little more feminine." Ah, yes. A little more feminine. A little more delicate. Something fragile enough to let a man know you're *female*.

John Borden.

I put the pale blue silk turtleneck back and got out one of my more customary L. L. Bean cottons. I was getting definitely screwy on the subject of John Borden. I didn't need to make it worse by dressing up for him. I laid out the clothes on the bed and grabbed my robe. I was headed for the shower when I heard the third volley of smashing plaster.

"I am not," Caliope said, "going to go to that wedding dressed in lemon-yellow satin looking like Miss Piggy in an evening gown—"

I locked myself into the bathroom, turned on the water, and stepped into the first form of soundproofing ever invented.

I was happy when I got out, in spite of everything. The shower is a good place to think, and for once, I had done my thinking on subjects of importance instead of fantasizing about John Borden or constructing plausible but unprovable scenarios that would explain someone having shot at me. I had been thinking about Pan. The longer I stood under the water, the cleaner and more fully awake I got, the clearer the situation became. It even touched on the problem of the sniper.

The fact was, I had no part in whatever was going on in Kilithia. That something was going on—something cohesive, which would tie in the murdered priest and the dead girl and the sniper—I was only half sure of, since I couldn't think of any way all the things that had happened could be brought together. What I was sure of, however, was that the only interest I held for anyone in Kilithia, or anywhere else on Themnos, was in my position as Pan's employee. If someone was shooting at me, it had to be because of Pan. As I've said, my father is not famous, and although he has more than enough money, he's not David Rockefeller, either. He's a top-of-the-line, upper-middle-class corporation lawyer, self-made, vile-tempered, and inflexible—hardly the classic victim of an assassination plot. *Especially* an assassination plot against his children. No, if someone had shot at me—and I was sure someone had—it was either because of Pan or because something I did for Pan was getting in the way of something else. I could not, at the moment, think what that might be, but I didn't have to. I'd had a revelation.

The *second* fact was: it was past time I got Pan Peteris out of my life. And his family. And his friends. And the remorseless craziness that was the attempt to produce a small English-language magazine in the midst of the chaos created by a man who did not know what he wanted to do, had never known what he wanted to do, and would never know what he wanted to do. The only thing Pan ever seemed able to focus on for more than ten minutes at a time was the import/export business, and even then he was far less worried about the product he was producing than the schedule of the shipments. He couldn't concentrate on his newspaper, his magazine, or his future wife. He noticed me the way housewives notice kitchen appliances—if I didn't seem to be working, he checked me out. Oh yes, it was time I cut myself loose from Pan Peteris. Not because of what was happening in Kilithia this trip—I didn't know, or want to know, enough about it to make a case in *that* direction—but because after two years' experience, I didn't have to put up with it anymore. I could write a respectable résumé. I could get another job.

I marched happily down the hall, humming to myself, wondering how I would find Chas, wondering what John Borden would think of all these career plans if I asked his advice. I'd just had time enough to be appalled by that last intrusion of John Borden into my brain when I opened my bedroom door and found Pan waiting for me.

He was sitting on my bed, playing absently with the clothes I'd laid out and listening dejectedly to the argument still going on downstairs.

"Skata, you little *insect,"* Caliope said right before the crash of more smashing plaster on marble.

Pan winced and looked up at me standing in the doorway. "That must have been the Nike," he said sadly. "They already got the Athena and the Winged Victory and four of Diana's nymphs."

"Diana's nymphs," I said.

"The statues in the niches in the living room." Pan sighed. "They've been breaking them all morning."

"I've been hearing."

"By the time they get done, there isn't going to be a thing left down there, and I can't find my mother anywhere. Not anywhere."

I crossed the room and started to throw clothes into my day pack. "Well, she's not here, either," I told him, "so why don't you get out of here and let me get dressed?" I grabbed an extra pair of socks and stuffed them into the front pocket. It would have been wonderful to quit there and then, but I wouldn't have put it past this idiot to cancel my return ticket to the States the moment I left his employ. "I don't know what time it is," I told him, "but I'm probably late,

125

and I want to get moving. Somebody's supposed to be picking me up at nine."

"Picking you up," Pan said. He straightened a little. "That's right, that's why I came up here. There's a man waiting for you downstairs."

"John Borden."

"He says he's supposed to take you somewhere."

"He's definitely supposed to take me somewhere. Pan, don't sit on that sweater. It's cashmere."

Pan stared at me. "But you can't just go running off in the middle of the day without telling me. You just can't."

"Why not?"

"But you have work to do!"

I stopped packing long enough to take a good, deep breath. "Pan," I said. "The only work I have to do is count the shipment, which will take two hours. I have to get it done sometime between now and next Tuesday, which is several days away. I promise I'll be back in time."

"You're going to be away overnight?"

"I'm going to see Chas. I don't have any idea how long I'll be away. Not long, probably. He's doing field work for his dissertation."

"But you can't do that without telling me!"

"Pan," I said. "To quote the man of a distant hour, let me make one thing perfectly clear. I will do what I want to do when I want to do it, with or without your permission. If you shut up, get out of here, and let me get going, I will be back shortly to take care of that shipment. If you don't—"

"It's completely improper," Pan said, working himself into a fury of dignity. "People just don't behave this way. I told that man downstairs. I couldn't possibly let you go the next few days—"

126

"You're going to have to."

"I told him you wouldn't be going out—"

"You did *what?*"

"He wouldn't *listen* to me."

"Good," I said, trying to stuff my anger somewhere safe.

"I've got to have you here to help me with the girls," Pan said plaintively.

"Don't even think of it."

Pan looked away, rubbing his lips with the back of his hand. I waited a few moments to see if he would leave—as far as I could tell, all conversation had been exhausted—but when he went on sitting on my bed ignoring me, I decided to waste no more time arguing. I gathered up the clothes I wanted to wear and shut myself in the walk-in closet. The light in there was weak but adequate. And I didn't want to waste any more time.

I was stripped down to my underwear when I realized I'd brought the blue silk turtleneck instead of the black cotton I'd chosen to replace it. After a moment of thought, I put it on. Getting back into my robe and going out to where Pan was undoubtedly still waiting for me was just too much of a chore. I wriggled into my jeans, put my best black cashmere crewneck over my head, and opened the closet door to face the music again.

He was no longer sitting on the bed. He was standing by the window, holding the curtains back, and looking at something in the drive. I was pretty sure I knew what he was looking at. I came up behind him and looked down at John Borden waiting behind the wheel of a Jeep.

"John Borden," Pan said. His voice sounded odd, strangled somehow, and his mood had completely changed. He slid his eyes toward me without turning his head, making himself look sly and secretive.

"John Borden," he said again. "You know, Kerry, maybe I'm just looking out for your interests. Maybe I'm just trying to keep you out of trouble."

"Which is supposed to mean what?"

He gestured toward the Jeep. "Who is he, anyway? Do you *know* him?"

"He's a friend of Chas's," I said. "Chas wrote me about him."

"And you've met him before," Pan said helpfully.

I drew away. Sly and secretive had become something else, something nasty, and suddenly I didn't want to be in the same room with this man. He was smiling slightly, but it wasn't the old Pan Peteris buffoon smile, incompetent and unthreatening. He looked oily, dirty, menacing, and *big*. That was one of the things about Pan in his usual bumbling state: you forgot what a large man he was. Not fat, but large.

I turned away and snatched up my day pack, intent on getting out of that room as quickly as possible. I hadn't packed my makeup or even the bright gold bangles I wore for jewelry for a going-out night, but I didn't want to take the time to get them. Pan had turned his back to the window and was leaning against it, arms folded across his chest. He was smiling at me.

"I don't know what you think you're trying to do," I told him, "but I wish you'd stop doing it."

"Just looking out for the help," he said lightly.

"I am not the help." I jerked the last of the day pack's zippers closed and looked up at him. "I'm leaving now," I told him. "You're perfectly welcome to stay in this room and contemplate the unmade bed if you want to."

"Don't be ridiculous," Pan said. "I'll see you to the door."

I bit my lip. I didn't want him to do any such thing, and he knew it, which was why he was doing it. Unfortunately, causing a stink about it would make me sound just as paranoid as he wanted me to think I was. When he wasn't busy trying to make me paranoid.

With as much dignity, and as much cool, as I could muster, I slipped one of the day pack's straps over my shoulder and marched to the door Pan was now holding open for me. It was extremely difficult to be cool when he was smiling at me like that.

"You're sure you haven't forgotten anything?" he said as I passed him.

"Quite."

"And you wouldn't like a little advance on your salary so you can buy—souvenirs?"

"I ought to take you up on it just for the novelty," I said. "That's definitely the first and probably the last time you ever ask."

"But you won't take me up on it?"

"I don't buy souvenirs."

"No, you don't. It's beginning to occur to me that I don't know what you do." He looked me up and down then, as if seeing me for the first time. Then he gave me another of those great big phony smiles and gestured toward the stairs.

"Shall we deliver you to your friend?"

I rushed by him, caught up in speed and the promise of escape. I made it to the stairs before he had a chance to get the bedroom door closed. I made it halfway to the first floor before I collided with Costa, and I was moving with such determined force, he didn't quite manage to stop me.

Big, knife-scarred, evil-eyed Costa, my eternal nemesis, my private bogeyman.

He was smiling, too.

13

By the time I got out to the Jeep, I was jumpy and nervous, my early morning buoyancy washed away in a wave of panic I was sure was senseless. Senseless or not, it was awful—as awful, or worse, as the way I'd been feeling since I first heard noises in Pan's basement. Terrible things were *supposed* to happen on dark and stormy nights. That's why children hide under blankets and tell ghost stories in thunderstorms. Bright sunny mornings, especially bright sunny mornings on a Greek island, are supposed to make you feel all gooey and melted with romantic sentiment. Besides, what in the name of heaven was I afraid of? Pan? Pan hadn't even been in Greece when all this insanity started. As for Costa—

I decided not to think about Costa. It was my private opinion that Costa Papageorgiou was personally responsible for anything that happened within traveling distance of him, and he'd certainly been perfectly placed to kill that priest, but personal prejudice was not proof, or even good reasoning. I'd seen Costa in the cemetery last night. By the time that mess was finished for the night, almost everyone there had been covered with mud and matted with dead vegetation. Costa had looked clean enough to have just stepped out of a bath.

I climbed into the Jeep—it was one of those converted army-surplus vehicles, with the footboard a very tall giant's step above the ground—belted myself into my seat, and tried to remind myself that whatever all this was about, it had nothing to do with me. I didn't know what was going on. I didn't want to know what was going on. I wasn't connected to what was going on.

I turned to John Borden and gave him a weak hello and what must have been a weaker smile. I expected to be affected by him the way I usually was—with a little drop at the pit of my stomach or a little dryness of the mouth. I expected him to notice how upset I was. I got none of it.

He revved the Jeep to life, popped the gears, and started us on a slow roll down the mountain toward Kilithia and what passed for a road.

We were on the other side of Kilithia, still going downhill, but west, away from Agios Constantinos, a way I'd never been, when he decided to start talking to me.

"Had a little trouble with your boss?" he suggested.

I was staring through the windshield at a vast landscape I'd never suspected Themnos of harboring, a long slope of gentle hills holding a dozen sheepherders' villages, a wash of vegetation that was almost green, even a few real trees, straight and alive and leafy instead of the stunted dwarfs I was used to on the rest of the island. The place almost looked habitable. It certainly looked tame. I was so used to thinking of Themnos as savage country, it was a kind of shock.

John prodded my knee gently. "Kerry? I said—"

"Yes," I said. "Sorry. I—this doesn't look like the rest of the island."

"Thank God."

132

I smiled a little. "I guess so. I just can't get myself used to it."

"Wait'll you see where we're going." He pointed ahead, where the road, the blacktopping getting better and better by the mile, curved into the distance. "Believe it or not, there are actually civilized places on this island. Or a civilized place, at any rate. That's where we're going."

"Not Agios Constantinos?"

"Good lord, no. A place called Dyphos. In Dyphos there is a decent *kafenion,* a good hotel, and a beach."

I wrinkled my nose. "It's forty-five degrees," I said. "The water's probably worse."

"So wear a wetsuit." He leaned forward and began rummaging in an airline bag. He came up with the Greek version of a cheese danish—one of those dry, brown flying saucers so dehydrated they can soak up spills better than Bounty. "I keep this for emergencies," he said. "I figure this is one. He let you get any breakfast?"

"I didn't let me get any breakfast." I waved the danish away. He was beginning to affect me the way I'd expected him to. He really had a very nice smile and very unusual eyes. It was his eyes that tipped the balance. They made him not only good-looking, but exciting.

I looked away, out my side of the Jeep. "I'm glad you didn't just leave when he said I wasn't coming. Honestly, how he could have the unmitigated gall to do something like that—"

"Well, that's his stock in trade, isn't it? Unmitigated gall, I mean. At least that's what Chas tells me."

"Oh well," I said. "Sometimes I think his stock in trade is bumbling, but I suppose that can't be entirely true. He certainly makes enough money."

"Does he?"

"Well, he lives out in Queens, and that's not expensive—not for New York, anyway—but he lives in Astoria, so maybe it's just nostalgia. I mean, there are a lot of Greeks there, and he grew up there, from adolescence anyway, so maybe he just likes the neighborhood. But he does own his house."

"Three mortgages," John said.

I shook my head. "I don't know about your Greek grandfather, but the Greeks I know in Astoria don't like to mortgage if they can help it. And if they can't help it, they'll pay off the mortgage before they start on something else—and the one thing you have to say about Pan is that he's *always* starting something else."

"How many Greek-language newspapers can the man run?"

"One. And one English-language magazine. Then he bought a new house to live with Agapé in, right across the street from his mother's. And he opened a California office—you ought to see what a mess *that* is. And expensive. I heard the comptroller screaming at him about it just before I came out this time. Plane tickets. Hotel reservations. And whatever it is he's spending to set up—finding an office, I guess, and getting paper printed and phones installed and that kind of thing."

"You guess?"

"It's Pan's pet project. For once, he doesn't want a little galley slave to do all his work for him."

John stared at the road, frowning. "California," he said. "California, California, California. He out there a lot?"

"Why are we talking about Pan?" I asked him. "I was just thinking this morning that it was about time I let the Greeks take care of the Greeks and returned to the real world. *And* how wonderful it was going to be not to have to think about Pan or the magazine or the offerings or any of the rest of it for the whole day."

"What do you want to talk about?"

"Chas," I said. "I haven't seen him in months. And he doesn't write the way he used to. Not lately, anyway. He used to send me these great long letters full of everything in the universe, and now I hardly even get postcards."

"Chas," he said lightly. He was still staring at the road—which was only natural, under the circumstances—but I began to get the uncomfortable feeling he was concentrating less on his driving than on not looking at me.

I turned away from that thought the way I'd turned away from so many others and said, "I get so worried about Chas lately. He was never any good under pressure, and all a doctoral dissertation is is pressure. Years of it. He just isn't behaving like himself. Even my mother says his letters are strange, and my mother is the original unobservant flake."

"Ah, yes," John said. "The space cadet. Chas talks about her a great deal."

"About my mother?"

"And about your father. I take it you both have a problem there."

"Nothing that won't get fixed eventually. *Are* you going to tell me about Chas?"

"There's nothing to tell. He's working a little too hard. He could use more rest. The usual."

I settled back into my seat, dissatisfied. We were getting near the sea. You could see it in the contours of the country. The hills were flattening, inch by imperceptible inch, so that the picturesque hilliness of a few miles back was changed now to a long, undulating slope whose earth was almost like sand. In the distance, I could see the outskirts of a small village, the whitewashed walls of small houses, the faded canvas awnings of shops, even a few of the tiny black lattice-work fences some tavernas use to close off their outdoor seating area from the rest of the sidewalk. It seemed impossible that there would actually be a village in Themnos with sidewalks, but there it was.

I looked at John Borden again. He was still staring at the road, but whatever had made me think his primary purpose was to avoid looking at me was gone. He was just a man behind the wheel of a car, taking sensible care on an erratic road.

He also had a very nice profile, all sharp edges and strongly drawn lines. True to recent form, I almost automatically noticed his profile.

I picked at the danish I had left lying in my lap. "Sometimes I think I should call my father and apologize and—oh, I don't know. It's hard to know. He wants me to go to law school, and I don't want to go. I'd make a terrible lawyer and it would bore me silly. But if I called him and said that and told him I was stranded, he'd at least get me out of here."

"You want to get out of here?"

"Wouldn't you, at this point? First someone gets killed in the basement, then someone shoots at me, then—"

"What?"

I blinked, astonished. "But I told you about that—"

"You did nothing of the kind. Who shot at you? When?"

"In Kilithia the other day. The day before yester-day, I think. Anyway, I was near the church, and when I realized what was happening, I went inside and then—what are you *doing?"*

What he was doing was stopping the Jeep. He pulled far over to the side, into the dirt of what must have been the edge of someone's farm, and cut the motor entirely.

"What happened?" he asked levelly. His voice was considerably calmer than his eyes. His eyes were murderous. "Start at the beginning," he said, "and tell me all of it."

I shrank against my door. "There isn't any all of it," I said, almost angrily. It can be a gift to be able to sound angry when you are frightened, and sometimes I have it. And I was getting very frightened of John Borden. This was the other side of that strong jaw and powerful profile and those nice, mysterious eyes. This was not a man you wanted to have mad at you, even a little bit. I folded my arms across my chest and glared at him as best I could.

"Who the *hell* do you think you are?" I shouted at him. "Why should I have told you anything? I hardly know you. I'm not even sure I like you much. You keep popping into my life like a cold I can't shake, and you're always demanding that I *do* things."

I got to him, just a little. I saw the anger spurt like flame into his eyes half a second before he managed to get control of himself.

His voice, when it came, was flat and emotionless. "All right," he said. "Let's start from the beginning. *Who* shot at you?"

"I don't know who shot at me. Don't be—"

He cut me off. "Who do you think shot at you?"

I turned away, angry and frightened. I had a terrible feeling he could go on and on like this for hours in that toneless voice.

"I don't know who shot at me. I don't know who I think shot at me. The whole thing was so strange, sometimes I'm not even sure someone did shoot at me. Nothing happened to me. I'm sitting right here and I'm fine, but I'm very upset and all I want to do at this moment is go home."

"Home?"

"Well, to Chas at this moment."

He leaned forward and started the Jeep up again, slipping into low gear for the fight through soft earth to the road. I turned my head away from him, not wanting him to see that my anger was dissolving into something much less dignified. I was on the verge of tears. The part of my mind that still had a little spirit left told me I had every right to be.

We were on the outskirts of Dyphos, making a glide into the maze of narrow streets that led to the sea, when he spoke again.

"I shouted at you," he said quietly.

I looked at him. "Very observant."

"Does it do any good to say I don't want to see you hurt?"

"Not much," I said. "But at least it's better than anything you've tried so far."

"That's big of you."

"You were behaving like a—I can't even find a twentieth-century word for it."

"I think the term normally employed is *brute.*"

"Don't patronize me."

"Right," he said. He rubbed his hands nervously across his mouth.

I got out my much-battered and mostly unused pack of cigarettes and lit one, thinking smoking would probably be all right if you could manage to do it only in emergencies. This was certainly an emergency. John was staring at me, ignoring the road completely, and I knew I was going to have to look at him eventually. The prospect made my stomach roll.

"Kerry," he said carefully. "I know what I'm about

to ask you isn't going to make much sense. But it *does* make sense. Can you just answer me and—and trust me?"

"Trust you with what?"

"Kerry—"

"I'm sick to death of people saying Kerry. I woke up this morning in a very good mood, and between you and Pan Peteris, it's been effectively destroyed. I don't want to talk anymore. I want to go see Chas."

"Don't worry about Chas. He's waiting at Papaspirou. With any luck, having a large breakfast."

"Papaspirou," I said.

"Listen," he said. "We'll have the day with Chas, maybe tomorrow, and then I'll deliver you to Bob Hobart. He'll arrange for the embassy in Athens to lend you the plane fare home."

"Oh, fine. Who's he expect to get it back from, my father?"

"It has nothing to do with your father. The embassy will advance plane fare to any American citizen stranded abroad."

I took a deep breath, steadying myself. "Back to New York," I said.

"Back to New York," he agreed. "And I think you were right. I think it's time you told Pan Peteris where he can put his job."

I flicked the ash of my cigarette into the Jeep's dilapidated ashtray. "If it doesn't have anything to do with my father, it doesn't have anything to do with you, either," I said. "I could go to Hobart on my own. I don't have to answer any of your questions."

"Of course not."

I bit my lip. Now that I was beginning to calm down, I was dying to know what he wanted to ask me. Being with John Borden was a little like riding the

Crazy Caterpillar at a state fair—up and down and back and forth without rhyme or reason, in the dark.

"All right," I said finally. "What do you want to know?"

John started staring at the road again, and this time I *knew* he was deliberately not looking at me. "February twelfth last year," he said. "I want to know if Pan Peteris was in California—or anywhere else but his office—on February twelfth of last year."

"February twelfth of last year," I repeated in shock.

John looked uneasily into my eyes. "Kerry," he started.

"Kerry *nothing*," I exploded. "I don't know what's going on here, but it's beginning to get me very nervous. *You're* beginning to get me very nervous. I don't know what it is you think you're trying to pull—"

"*Kerry.*"

"I wouldn't have any idea where Pan was on February twelfth last year. I came to Themnos to arrange his father's funeral, and that was the tenth. On the twelfth, I was on a plane to New York—which you probably know. What are you, anyway, CIA?"

"Oh, for God's sake."

"Don't swear at me," I said. "Among the many other things I'm sick of, I'm heartily sick of people swearing at me. You said Chas was at Papaspirou, right?"

"Kerry, you can't—"

"Oh yes I can." The car was still moving, but slowly, and I opened the door on my side without worry. A moment later, I had my seat belt off. "I'll find my own way, thank you."

"Kerry, Chas is—"

But I didn't wait to hear him tell me what he thought Chas was. I was chugging down a side street, hands in my pockets, eyes pointed straight ahead, telling myself Papaspirou was probably a *kafenion* and that I wouldn't have trouble finding it.

14

MY BROTHER CHAS is not a fighter. I don't mean simply that he never liked schoolyard brawls or contact sports or even loud arguments, although all of that is true. Chas always wanted not only to *be* the things my father wanted him to be, but to *want* to be those things. Considering the difference between what my father wanted Chas to be and what Chas is, there was bound to be trouble, but I don't think either of them expected that for a long time. My mother did and I did, but they didn't. Chas went off to the very expensive prep school my father picked out for him—where he picked up that nickname, shortened from Charles, so, like the rest of the boys, he sounded like a ghost from *Brideshead Revisited*—and when he couldn't force himself to go out for lacrosse or even debate, he made himself editor of the school paper instead. He went placidly off to Williams, too, because my father thought the "little three" had more social cachet than Yale and Princeton and more intellectual rigor than Harvard. Chas majored in history, a good foundation for law school. If my father worried sometimes—"Margaret, it makes me nervous, he's so *passive*"—it was always when Chas was out of the house and couldn't hear. If Chas was unhappy, he never told anyone. That was part of the problem, too. When Chas stepped off the dais after his college graduation and informed my father that not only was he not going to law school, he hadn't even bothered to apply, my father damn near gave up the ghost right there in the Williams Yard.

Chas would never have made much of a lawyer. His first instinct in any dispute is to pour oil on troubled waters or to make as many soothing noises as necessary to get whoever is yelling at him to stop. He would have failed miserably in a courtroom, and he knew it. He was not, however, a wimp. My father would have slaughtered him in a debate. In the emotional tug-of-war that was their "argument" between the virtues of law school and the glories of graduate study in anthropology, my father never had a chance. Chas agreed with everything my father said and never wasted energy in shouting matches. He just sat, his scholarship in one hand and his acceptance to Columbia in the other, and waited. *Passive,* my father realized, was not a word that applied to Chas. *Stubborn* was the word that applied to Chas. My father cut off the money and—convinced, as so many self-made men are, that his children had been brought up with so much privilege they were "soft"—waited for the cave-in. It never happened. Even now, after five years of what can only be called cold war, it hadn't happened. For once, if there were going to be any compromises, my father was going to have to make them.

I turned down the side street the last little old lady had pointed me to—I had been asking directions only of little old ladies, saying "Papaspirou" in a loud voice and waiting patiently, because I got a little nervous around young Greek males—and scanned the sidewalks for some sign of a *kafenion.* Nothing, just houses whose narrow balconies were crowded with old women sitting in the sun. I crammed my hands into my pockets and went ahead anyway, figuring there would be another old woman somewhere and another set of directions. If I'd started out in a calmer frame of mind, I probably would have been getting nervous about being lost. I had no idea how long I'd been walking. I had no idea how difficult Papaspirou was going to be to find, either, although John had tossed off the name as if everyone in two hundred miles would be able to recognize it. For some reason, it didn't matter. My native impatience—I'm more like my father than Chas will ever be—was not getting in the way. It was a beautiful day, cold but bright. Dyphos was a fairy-tale Greek village, with the smell of the sea in every street. Besides, I was carrying around a lot of fear and anger and upset-edness. It would probably be better for everybody if I managed to walk it off before I found Chas.

I stopped another old lady, got another set of directions, went down another side street. I always thought of Chas as my savior, in a way, even though what he did didn't save me from the consequences of what I decided to do later. He mellowed my father, just a little. I never got a note in the mail telling me I'd be unwelcome at home for Christmas, as Chas did his first year at Columbia graduate school, even when I'd run away to New York and (with Chas's help) taken what was referred to in my family as "that ridiculous job." I never came home for a weekend only to be treated to absolute silence, either. (By my father. My mother is incapable of silence, even in sleep.) I simply had my money cut off and got treated to endless lectures on how *every other girl* my age was taking advantage of the *wonderful* changes brought on by women's lib, so why wasn't I?

Another old lady, another set of directions, another side street. I'd been through it so many times I wasn't paying attention. My mind had slipped from Chas to Pan to, of course, John Borden. Somehow, every train of thought I had these days ended with reveries of one kind or another of John Borden. I suppose I was feeling a little contrite. Chas freezes under pressure. I explode. I was beginning to worry that the scene I had put him through in the Jeep had more to do with pressure I'd been under than with anything John had done. As I said before, I am not an introspective person. I might as well go further and say that I am not a person who likes to think about unpleasantness. Quite frankly, if I'm feeling bad in any way, even physically, I try to pretend I'm not. This time, I'd spent days and days shoving fear and revulsion as far into my subconscious as they would go, and I was beginning to pay for it. The bad feelings were roiling around down there, looking for a way into the light. When John Borden had refused to take the role I'd assigned to him—disinterested bystander, frivolous diversion, magician with the ability to make people disappear—I'd damn near clobbered him.

I had also smoked a cigarette, which was making me feel a little sick. I stopped at the edge of the almost nonexistent sidewalk I was walking on and took a deep breath of air, sea air, warm and salty and a little sweet. There was a strong, cool breeze blowing, pushing the hair away from my face. I remember thinking how odd that was. In narrow streets hemmed in by low buildings, what breeze there is tends to settle near the ground, so on hot days you can walk the alleyways of a place like Dyphos with perfectly air-conditioned ankles. I looked up, wondering if it was beginning to cloud over or build up to a hurricane or do something else that might explain cool air on my face, and then I saw it: the sea and the yacht harbor and Papaspirou.

John had been right to sound as if everyone in two hundred miles had heard of the place. Everyone certainly should have. The cove was tiny, the yacht harbor no more than a token of prosperity, but Papaspirou was not only huge, but outrageous. It was a hotel and a restaurant as well as a *kafenion,* and it stretched west along the coast as far as I could see. It looked like a Turkish pasha's hashish dream. There were turrets and onion domes, crazy tilting walls of plaster and crazy tilting walls of stone, terraces and esplanades and arches that held up nothing and went nowhere. It was also (mostly) pink. I put my hand over my mouth and tried very hard not to laugh out loud, so as not to give offense to the bright, patently proud young girls who marched up and down through the acres of *kafenion* tables in shortened versions of folk dress. If I'd been looking for a magic antidote to the war zone back in Kilithia, I had found more than I'd hoped for.

I started walking between the *kafenion* tables, humming a little to myself, thinking that everything was going to be all right after all. A couple of days in a place like this could defeat reality for anyone, even the kind of terrible reality I had left behind in Kilithia. The place was mostly empty, as it would be this deep into winter, and I wondered who came to stay in the summer months. Themnos, as I have said, is not a tourist island. There are no Olympic commuter flights to Agios Constantinos or anywhere else in the vicinity, and no public transportation of a sort schoolteachers from Iowa or lawyers from Minneapolis would find remotely acceptable. Nor was the harbor big enough to accommodate the boats of the only other possibility I could think of— the big-money people from Italy and France and Switzerland, the kind of people who'd had so much money for so long they wanted nothing but to enjoy themselves as far from the eyes of the watching world as they could get. Papaspirou was an impossibility, maybe even a mirage. I watched the young girls in their short dresses marching up and down between the empty tables, straightening chairs, righting listing umbrellas, and thought of them going on like that, with nothing to serve, all summer long.

There was a small knot of people at a collection of tables near the center of the esplanade closest to the sea, and I headed for them, thinking that if Chas was waiting, he would probably be waiting there. I started to move a little faster. It had been a long time since I'd seen Chas and even longer since I'd been able to have a decent conversation with him. First, he'd been involved in a particularly nasty rite of graduate school passage known as prelims, then in preparing the proposal for his dissertation, then in field work. I missed the conversations we'd had when I first came to New York, long discursive talks that always ended by making me feel that a brighter future was not only possible, but inevitable.

I got to the first of the occupied tables and began to slow down, thinking I would scan the faces carefully to be sure I didn't miss him. I didn't have to. I saw John Borden right away. My eyes went to him, with all the instinctual assurance of a homing pigeon returning to his coop. Beside him was a man I would have sworn I'd never met in my life, an *old* man, sallow and shaky and gray, maybe with some kind of degenerative muscle disease that made it impossible for him to sit still.

Chas.

I think I blamed John Borden for Chas's condition right away—blamed him and refused to be rational about it, because John Borden seemed to be responsible for so much, or maybe just involved in so much, that adding this to it didn't seem to make much difference. I was not being very rational, as I said. For one thing, I was in shock. What in the name of God could possibly have happened to Chas—what could he have been doing—to make him look like this? I knew my brother. He drank a glass of champagne every New Year's Eve. He wouldn't know an illegal substance from a banana. The only explanations I could think of for the condition he was in were illness or such a radical, prolonged lack of sleep and food that it was life-threatening. I didn't want to think about the first possibility. As for the second, if that was what was happening, then I knew, as surely as I knew I had gray eyes, that it had something to do with that mess back in Kilithia.

I marched up to their table, intending to take the man I was now thinking of as "that bastard" by surprise. I should have known better. He saw me coming before I got halfway to the table. He was on his feet when I got to him, holding out a chair for me.

"Kerry," he said, pleasantly but nervously. I couldn't blame him for the nervousness. I was probably breathing fire.

"What have you *done* to him?" I hissed in his ear. I hadn't meant Chas to overhear, but he did. My mother always said my whispers could be heard ocean to ocean. I glared at John Borden and sat down abruptly in the chair, not giving him a chance to ease it in for me. I could do without John Borden's help or the pained and increasingly agitated look on Chas's face.

"You look awful," I told Chas angrily. "You look *dead.*"

"Kerry," Chas started uneasily. He shot John Borden a helpless, haunted look that twisted my heart. I wanted to put my arms around my brother's shoulders and hold him until the hurt went away or sing lullabies until he could go to sleep, but those solutions seemed so pitifully childish and so unlikely of success. Instead, I turned on John Borden, positive, after the look Chas had given him, that he was responsible for this.

"What have you gotten him involved in?" I demanded. "And don't tell me you're doing your dissertation at Columbia, because I didn't believe it before and I don't believe it now. *Are* you CIA?"

"Kerry." Chas sounded shocked.

"Are you trying to get me killed?" John Borden said. "Of course I'm not CIA, but if you keep saying so in that *carrying* voice of yours—"

"They can hear you in Turkey," Chas said.

"I don't care." I stared from one to the other of them, revising my speculations to fit the fact that they were united against me. They were like a wall, bolstering each other up and shutting me out. I turned to Chas. "Listen," I said. "You don't know how to take care of yourself. I knew that when I was six and you were nine and I had to kick Emma Chadbourne in the shins for you. I don't know what you've been doing, but whatever it is, stop. Whatever he's been telling you, whatever this is isn't worth it. You're making yourself sick."

"He didn't get me into anything," Chas said desperately. "We'll explain the whole thing, but you've got to understand, he didn't—"

"Chas," I said gently. "I know you. You do not have the world's greatest talent for getting into trouble on your own."

"I may not be any good at thinking trouble *up,*" Chas said violently, "but at the moment, I've got a positive genius for letting it find *me.*" He gave John Borden another look, stronger this time. "You'd better explain it to her," he said. "At least give her the background. I can't keep all this crap straight in my mind even now."

It was the chance I'd been looking for—a solid reason to demand an explanation from John Borden —but I never got to take it. One of the waitresses came by with a drink for Chas and a cup of coffee for John—Chas, drinking liquor? before noon?—and asked me if I wanted anything. It isn't really necessary to order anything in a Greek *kafenion* when most of the tables are empty, but I sent her away with a request for tea, just to get her out of the way. As soon as she'd appeared, John and Chas had begun working overtime trying to look like carefree tourists.

Once she was out of sight, John sank a little lower in his chair, stared into his coffee, and said, "I'll tell you, but you've got to cooperate. I can't have you screaming the particulars all over Papaspirou."

"It could get me in a lot of trouble," Chas said hurriedly. "Serious trouble. Legal trouble."

I got my cigarettes out and laid them on the table. "All right," I said. "I'll be quiet and I'll be calm, *but.* And this is a big but. This had better be good, believe me, because if I think you're giving me nonsense—"

"No nonsense," John Borden said, suddenly all

crisp professionalism. "You remember something about a robbery last year, four men and a woman who robbed the National Bank of Greece of six million dollars in gold bullion?"

I frowned, suspicious. "Of course I remember. Except it was five men. It was the same day Pan's father died, and he bumped the story off *The Banner* —that's the paper—to put his father's obituary on the front page. We got furious phone calls about it for days. Mostly in Greek."

"It was four men and a woman," John said, "not five men. The woman spoke English and did the talking. She was Greek and she was young, but that's all anybody knows about her. That's all anybody knows about any of them, for sure. They were all wearing stocking masks. It was like something out of a television movie."

"That's what you've got to remember," Chas put in. "It *is* like a television movie. Like the whole thing was planned by people whose experience of these things was limited to—well, to the less intellectual productions of Culver City."

"That's the other thing we know about them," John continued. "They were amateurs and probably upstarts. Provincials. They were damn *bumblers.*" He hit the table with his fist. "That's what's so infuriating. They were tenth-rate, small-time thieves, and they managed to pull it off anyway."

"But how can you know that?" I asked him. "I mean, they did pull it off. Why doesn't that mean they knew what they were doing—"

"Because you don't learn what you're doing at that sort of thing without experience, and when you get experience, you acquire contacts. If these people had contacts, they'd be funneling that gold through Switzerland or Hong Kong or the Cayman Islands, places where there are people who know how to handle it. They're not. If they were, we'd never see that gold again. We would never even hear about it."

"And you're hearing about it?"

"You bet your sweet life we are. We're stumbling over it every time we turn around. Detroit. Los Angeles. New York. Places nobody in their right mind would bring it if they had a choice."

"Which makes you think they don't have a choice," I said.

"Exactly."

"But what does this have to do with Chas? For that matter, what does it have to do with you?"

Chas cleared his throat, loudly, painfully, nervously. "You remember when I came back from Greece last fall, in October, to clear up a few things at school?"

"You didn't even call me," I said.

"Yeah," Chas said. "Well, I didn't have time. I got stopped in Kennedy. I had five pounds of that stuff in one of my suitcases."

It was a bright, hard, glaring-sunshine day, with a breeze coming in from the sea—the real sea, not the harbor—that made the water in the cove rise into whitecaps in restless, uneven rhythm. There were birds, too, which was unusual for winter in Greece. I slid down in my chair and watched it all, thinking none of it looked real. The harbor, Papaspirou, even the two men sitting on the other side of the table—both six foot two but otherwise so different, my brother fine-boned and hollow-cheeked and ascetic, John Borden tense-muscled and high-cheekboned and disturbingly sensual—seemed like something I had

invented in a not particularly creative dream. My
mother always said Chas looked like a saint, a Roman
Catholic saint, and at the moment I believed her: he
looked like an early Church martyr. I don't know
what Mama would have made of John Borden. I
didn't know what to make of him myself.

The girl came back with my tea and put it down on
the table in front of me, with a small square napkin
under it to protect the painted iron surface that didn't
need protection.

"You know," I said, "this time last week, I had a
perfectly normal life. Dull, but perfectly normal."

John and Chas looked at each other with consider-
able alarm. I waved my tea in the air at them,
exasperated. "I'm perfectly fine," I said. "It's just—"
It was hard to say what it was "just." Or even where to
start asking questions. I turned to Chas. "I take it you
didn't do this on purpose," I said.

"I didn't even know it was there. Then I was
coming through customs and some guy got ambitious,
and I wasn't even worried about it. I just stood there
looking bored and getting pissed off because he was
holding me up." Chas smiled wanly. "I had one of
those embroidered net shirts you like. I was coming
right up to give it to you."

"Right," I said. Those shirts cost, at a minimum,
seventy-five to a hundred dollars apiece. Chas must
have gone without meals to get the money to buy one.
I turned to John Borden, not wanting to choke up and
start saying teary, sentimental things to my brother in
a situation where sentiment would only make things
worse. "What about you?" I asked John.

He reached into his back pocket, took out a black
wallet-folder, and opened it on the table. "United
States Treasury Department."

"Treasury Department," I said. I shook my head. "I thought the treasury department worried about the mint and the budget and a lot of boring—"

"We do," John said quickly. "But we also worry about the gold supply and about counterfeiting, and we do some stuff with ATF."

"ATF?"

"Alcohol, Tobacco, and Firearms."

"Oh." I took a long sip of my tea. "But you don't usually go running around foreign countries trying to find gold thieves, do you? I mean, you don't usually go running around foreign countries at all. I thought only the CIA did that, and then, half the time people don't even approve of that."

"Yes," John Borden said. "Well."

"You see," Chas said, "in this case—"

They looked at each other uneasily and shrugged, almost simultaneously.

John Borden sighed. "To tell you the truth," John said, "I've got a perfectly nice desk job back in Washington. Worrying about the gold supply."

"So what are you doing here?" I asked him.

"Well," he said, giving me a brilliant smile, "I'm on vacation."

"You're on vaca—for God's *sake*," I exploded. "You mean you're running around Themnos without any authorization and dragging him with you and chasing after a lot of people—good *lord*. I *read* about that robbery. They left two people dead in that bank. They're *dangerous*."

"I know they're dangerous," John said.

"He was just doing it for me," Chas put in quickly. "They'd have arrested me at Kennedy, except he stopped them. And now we're here trying to clear things up."

"I'm not just doing it for Chas," John said. "I'm also doing it for me. I've got a couple of problems of my own on this one."

"Yeah," Chas said. "The thing is, they nearly fired him."

"Fired him," I repeated dazedly.

"For letting me off," Chas said. "He was supposed to come to Kennedy and question me and either arrest me or turn me into a stool pigeon or something, and instead, he just said he believed me. And they said it was because we knew each other at college, and he was showing favoritism. And *he* said—"

"Never mind," I said. "I think I see the problem. Was what you said so hard to believe?"

"Not hard to believe," John said, "but completely unverifiable."

"Unverifiable or not, Pan Peteris asked me to bring in that package, and I took it out of his house, and the next time I see him—" Chas pounded his fist against the table angrily. "He said it was a present for Caliope. You know how good that made me feel? I've always felt so sorry for Caliope."

"Pan," I said. "But how could Pan be involved in this? He hasn't been to Greece for years."

"Exactly," John said. "That's one of my problems. Pan hasn't been out of the States for fifteen years. And Chas is in and out of Themnos, coming through Athens every time, like a Western Union messenger."

"When this is over," Chas said, "I'm going to get hold of that little bastard and wring his neck."

"You're going to behave yourself and let me turn him over to the Greek police." John got out a cigarette and lit it. "My boss thinks Chas is making it all up, and I suppose, rationally, I can't blame him. Chas was the one sitting in Kennedy Airport with five pounds of eighteen-carat gold in a plain brown wrapper. But once I started looking at this thing from the Pan angle, a lot of what started out looking weird began to make sense."

"Such as?"

"Such as the points of entry. We're looking for a reason why these people would bring this stuff into the States, the worst possible place. Pan Peteris does business in the States and in Greece and nowhere else. He doesn't have contacts in Zurich or Hong Kong or the Cayman Islands. And it's not just the United States of America in general, either. It's where the gold has shown up. Remember I said Detroit, Los Angeles, New York?"

"I remember."

"Well, we've also found a little in Tarpon Springs, Florida, in Dallas, in Chicago. Nothing in New Orleans, nothing in San Francisco, nothing in Atlanta."

"I don't see the point."

"The places the gold has turned up have large, very active Greek towns. The places where it hasn't, don't. And Pan Peteris does business in the Greek towns. With the newspaper and that magazine you run, and with those trinkets he brings in."

"You've checked the shipments?"

"We stopped two of them at the point of entry. Worry beads. Fake icons. Plaster statues of the Parthenon. We tore those boxes apart, and there was nothing."

"What about the people you found the gold *on?*" I asked him. "Couldn't they tell you where they got it?"

John nodded. "They could and they did. But we're picking up very small quantities, and always in raids on fences, and by the time it got to a fence, it had been through too many hands. Never mind the fact that people who deal with fences don't always give their correct name and address."

"But that's absurd," I said. "They can't—whoever they are—they can't move six million dollars in gold bullion through small-time fences."

"That's what my boss keeps saying." John smiled. "The thing is, once you start thinking about it, it's not as stupid as it sounds. Even if you grant me that we're dealing with Pan Peteris, and his resources only extend to small-time fences, the way this is being handled, it's very hard to trace. We've had almost a million dollars of this stuff turn up in the States already, and we don't have a single solid line on anyone."

"Chas said he picked up the package at the house," I said. "Did somebody search it? With all the construction that was going on—"

"We thought of that, too. Somebody from the Greek police went through it, and then we had one of our own people go through it, too. Not a thing."

"Did somebody question Pan?"

Chas came to life. "That *bastard*," he said again. "When they got to him, he was all injured innocence and polite shock. According to *him*, he never asked me to pick up any package. He hadn't even talked to me in years."

"He went further than that," John Borden said. "But I don't see any point in going into it. I still think he's a good candidate. There's a lot more to go on than just gold turning up in cities where Pan sells his trinkets."

"Like what?"

"One"—John held a finger in the air—"four men and a woman held up the National Bank of Greece. The guards there were pretty sure they managed to shoot one of them. Pan's father was away from

Kilithia at the time of the robbery. He got home the next day and died soon after that. Of a bullet wound."

"How can you possibly know that?"

"That's what I was doing on the knoll the other night. Watching Marina Peteris take a bullet out of that coffin."

"Marina," I said. "If I didn't know Marina hadn't been out of New York in years, I could see her holding up a bank."

"Not possible. The woman at the bank was young. Though I'll give you this: I like the idea of Marina as mastermind."

"At least she has a mind," I said. "Which is more than I can say for Pan."

"I think that bullet explains a lot of things," John said. "What happened to the two priests. What happened to the girl the other night. The first priest would have prepared Pan's father's body for burial, given it the Orthodox rites for the dead. I don't know what those are, exactly, but he might have seen the wound. Which would mean he would have to go. The same with the girl. Marina took her into the pit. She had to take somebody because of her arthritis, and by custom, it had to be a woman and not her daughter. The daughter wouldn't go into the father's grave."

"Caliope wouldn't go into anyone's grave," I said. "She wouldn't hear of it. But why not Agapé?"

"I don't know. Maybe because Marina knew she was going to have to kill off whoever went in there with her, and she wants Agapé to marry Pan."

"You think Marina killed the girl?"

"No. I think Marina started the fuss that started the confusion, on purpose. I think Pan killed the girl. Or Costa Papageorgiou. If it was Costa, by the way, it could explain why the girl was someone other than

Agapé. Costa might have balked at murdering his own daughter."

I was going to tell John that from what I'd heard, Costa hadn't balked at killing his own wife, but I didn't. The whole thing was so appalling, I was having a hard time taking it in. I looked into all that bright sunshine and thought how much more appropriate it would have been if the rain had lasted.

"Maybe Pan's father was involved in all this," I said, "but I can't see how Pan could be involved in anything but fencing the metal. I can see Costa Papageorgiou as a murderer with no problem at all, but not Pan. And Costa was in the house the other night when—when the second priest was killed."

"My boss's position exactly," John said, "when he's being rational and giving me the benefit of the doubt. But it won't work, Kerry. We're dealing with amateurs, and we're dealing with Greeks. With every person added to the conspiracy, the likelihood of exposure increases exponentially. And Pan's getting rich. He's getting rich for no good reason anyone can tell—certainly not from his legitimate businesses. Those books are so cooked they're hash—and by much more than his percentage as a middleman would account for. Or even his percentage as a middleman and his father's as a participant."

"So if he's involved, he must have been involved big."

"Exactly."

"But he couldn't have been here, John."

"I know."

"And the second priest? All that mess in the basement?"

"I don't know. Any more than I know who the woman was. Of the men, one, as I told you, I'm sure

159

was Pan's father. One I'm fairly sure was Costa Papageorgiou. One may have been a man called Yannis Tefillides. A sailor, if you will. He came from Kilithia, but he joined the navy during the junta. And got his ass kicked out in short order, too, and not for political reasons. He used to like to get his fellow sailors drunk to the gills and then pick their pockets when they passed out."

"He sounds like a charming man."

"Oh, he was. Unfortunately for your brother and myself, he went down in a small fishing boat about a month after the robbery. He was a great friend of Costa Papageorgiou. And of Pan's father."

I sighed. "One and one and one makes three," I said. "I suppose you're going to tell me the fourth is Pan."

"It has to be. He has to have been there somehow, Kerry. I just have to find out how."

"To save my brother's neck and your own."

"Exactly."

"And you can't stop, because if you do, your boss will arrest Chas and fire you."

"Also exactly. Old Iron Pants thinks I just can't believe any member of the hallowed Williams College class of 1983 could possibly be mixed up in bank robbery, gold smuggling, and international skulduggery."

"It would be next to treason even to suggest it," I said.

"Of course. On the other hand, it would help if I could figure out how the gold is getting into the United States."

"And how Pan is managing to get into Greece without getting his passport stamped," I finished for him.

160

"Exactly." He grinned at me.

I wanted to hit him over the head and tell him to stop saying *exactly* in that terribly self-satisfied tone of voice, but I didn't. Chas had fallen asleep in his chair on the other side of the table. He was snoring away happily, looking blissfully at peace. I wondered how long it had been since he'd had a decent night's sleep—or afternoon's, for that matter. I didn't think I wanted to ask.

"I think we ought to get him to the hotel, put him to bed, and give him an unlimited account with room service. Assuming they have room service."

"They have everything," John said cheerfully. "They're going broke, but they have everything."

"Well, help me with him." I got out of my seat, went around to the far side of the table, and prodded Chas gently on the shoulder. It did no good at all. He was out for the count, as they say in New York. John got hold of Chas's other arm and pulled, much less gently than I would have dared, but that didn't work, either.

"When we get him settled upstairs, why don't we go off and do what we'd intended to do in the first place. Put a picnic together. Go sit on the beach. Flop around in the water in wetsuits."

"No skulduggery, as you put it? No espionage? No hiding in basements or going through people's suitcases or—"

"I suppose I deserve all this."

"I suppose you do."

"I make a very pleasant companion when I'm not being obsessed. I really do."

"I never doubted it." I looked down at Chas's inert form and frowned. "Does Robert Hobart know what you're doing?" I asked John. "I mean, does he realize you're here investigating the gold robbery?"

"He thinks I'm a nice young treasury agent on vacation."

"Of course," I said. "I should have known."

15

IT TOOK ALMOST an hour to get Chas settled in one of the high-ceilinged rooms in the vast and empty hotel wing of Papaspirou—in fact, it took ten minutes just to wake him up—and by the time he was bedded down under a suitable number of blankets in his cool and airy room, I was more in the mood to collapse than go wandering around the beach with John Borden. My own room was right across the hall from Chas's, and its big double brass bed beckoned me, whispering promises of room service on the other end of an antique phone. If I'd had something to read and if I'd felt less guilty, I might have begged off the outing and spent the afternoon with Hercule Poirot and hot lemon tea. Instead, I changed my blue silk turtleneck and cashmere sweater for things more suited to the beach and headed for the lobby. I really was feeling guilty. I had misjudged John Borden terribly. I had every reason to feel grateful to him for the trouble he was taking on Chas's behalf. *And* for the trouble he had already taken. On the other hand . . . I shrugged off the temptation to introspection. My mother was always telling me that a woman with healthy self-respect didn't rearrange her life to suit a man's convenience and I believed her, but I had a sneaking suspicion that I might have gone on this expedition no matter how tired I was. John Borden intrigued me. In a few short hours, he had changed from suspicious character to knight in shining armor, no matter how foolhardy. It was a powerful image.

He was waiting for me near the desk when I came down, pacing back and forth under a great tiered chandelier that seemed to hang from the ceiling by a thread. The chandelier gleamed as if every one of its prisms had been washed that morning. The white marble walls were shined until they reflected images as well as any mirror. I was impressed in spite of myself. Marble is cheap in Greece—it's the native stone—and labor is even cheaper, especially on a small island like Themnos. On the other hand, money isn't everything. Whoever had built this place would have had to have had several million to spare in New York, probably no more than two hundred thousand on Themnos. Wherever he was, he'd have to be very good at hiring and managing employees to get them to put in the kind of work that would make a place look like this.

Of course, he couldn't be everywhere. Which accounted for the fact that there was now a girl in a chambermaid's uniform hanging around the reception desk, making eyes at John Borden. He wasn't exactly making eyes back—he was pacing up and down as if the effort to stand still was painful—but he wasn't telling her to leave, either.

He saw me on the stairs and stopped, doing his best to smile jauntily. He'd promised me a day of complete rest, and apparently, he had every intention of working to give it to me.

"How's Chas?" he asked as I reached him.

"Mostly asleep." I waved vaguely in the direction of our rooms. "Last thing he said was something about

164

picking him up some Jane Austen. He was probably delirious."

"Maybe not." He held the door open for me and waited until I passed through, oblivious to the fact that the chambermaid, so charming and eager to please a moment before, was now pouting mightily. "The guy who owns this place is a little crazy. He put in everything he could think of he thought people of 'quality' couldn't live without. Last time I was here, there was a little hole-in-the-wall place that called itself an international bookstore. Lots of Penguin paperbacks. Lots of Agatha Christie and Dorothy L. Sayers."

"He must be losing his shirt," I said. I stopped on the broad terrace that led from the front door to the beach, such as it was, and looked at the spreading, fantasy-craziness of that Turkish hash dream. "Who comes here, anyway? How can he afford to keep it running?"

"He can't, at the moment. You know what transportation to Themnos is like—nonexistent. He hasn't been able to convince Olympic to schedule flights, though he did, believe it or not, build a small field just adequate for a 727. And the harbor's too small for the big cruise boats. He gets some of the charters and some of the people with their own pleasure boats to sail, but that's about it. On the other hand, if he does ever get Olympic to go along, I think he'll make a go of it. All this may look a little bizarre to Western eyes, but it's *exactly* the kind of thing the Athenian rich like."

"*I* like it," I said. I did, too. It was strange. It was, shall we say, overenthusiastic. It was also rather splendid. "I hope he can talk some sense into Olympic. I'd hate to see this disappear."

There was a long, curving flight of shallow steps leading to the beach, and I started down it, drifting slowly from one platformlike step to the other. After all the excitement of these last few days, I felt a little let down in the lull that was a winter afternoon at Papaspirou. Even John Borden wasn't getting his usual reaction from me. I looked out at the water of the tiny cove and wished it away. I wanted something else, or something more. I wasn't sure what.

"You want to tell me what you're thinking about? Or worrying about? Or whatever?"

I looked back at John Borden and smiled. I would have found it hard *not* to be attracted to him. He was a compelling man, as much because of something inside him as because of the way he looked. He had an intensity, a singleness of purpose and concentration, I was unused to seeing in people. Even my father only got really intense when he was angry. As for the boys I'd known in college—well, there was no comparison. There was one, Daniel, I'd thought of as the love of my life for a whole six months. After that, he'd started to bore me.

John Borden would never bore me.

I sat down on the last step and began to take off my shoes and socks so I could walk along the beach without getting sand in them. John sat down beside me, throwing the large canvas duffel he'd been carrying at my feet.

"What's that?" I asked him.

"Wetsuits. You can rent them upstairs. I guessed you at a size seven."

"Very good. I didn't realize you were taking inventory."

"Subtle, I may be. Dead, I am not."

I laughed. "Take these, then," I said, handing him

my shoes with the socks stuffed inside. "I'd just as soon not have to carry them when I walk. There's got to be room in that thing."

"Oh, there is." He took the shoes and looked away, fiddling with the metal snap-hook at the top of the duffel. "Kerry? You don't have to worry all this much, you know. I'm not a *complete* amateur. I have a vague idea of what I'm doing."

I winced, looking out to sea, looking anywhere but at John Borden's black-leather-clad back. Here was reality again, raining on my fantasy, and I wasn't sure I liked it. It did odd things to my perception of John Borden.

"Kerry?"

"I'm sorry," I said. "I was just thinking. I'm afraid I don't know exactly what you meant by all that."

"I meant I've had some experience with these things. Not much, but some."

"You mean you *are* CIA?"

"No." I had said it lightly, and he'd taken it that way, laughing a little, but he got serious again very quickly. "I didn't go to Williams right after high school. I couldn't have, no matter what I'd done, because my grades stank, my deportment record left something to be desired, and there wasn't any money."

"Your father?"

"Died when I was a junior."

"I'm sorry."

"I am, too. He was a good man. An unusually good man. And I made his life hell."

"Don't tell me," I said, trying to keep it light. "You were a greaser, with a motorcycle and a girlfriend with green hair and spike heels."

"We didn't have green hair in my day. And what I

was was a pain in the ass. I went wild as soon as I could and I stayed wild as long as I could and I made everybody miserable. If I hadn't had some renegade talent for academics, I'd have sat in the ninth grade until I was old enough to quit and then gone. Instead, I kept just getting by. And I suppose some people were pulling for me, some people at school, because I never got expelled. Even when I showed up for a history test one afternoon dead drunk."

"Was there some reason for this?"

"I had a brother. An older brother. Let's just say Tom always did everything right."

"Ah," I said.

"People always say 'ah' like that. Anyway, Tom always did everything right until one day he did everything wrong off the high dive at the Olympic pool at the civic center in Calder, Massachusetts. And drowned."

"I'm sorry," I said again. "You haven't had an easy life, have you?"

"That wasn't an easy period, no. First Tom and then my father, six months later. My mother always says Tom's going killed him, but then she always says he liked me best. It's hard to know what to believe. Anyway, this was really all leading up to something. Between high school and Williams, I did a little growing up. In the army."

"You enlisted?" This was more interesting than disturbing. In the kind of schools my father sent Chas and me to, people not only did not enlist, they looked on the reestablishment of a civilian draft as tantamount to the rise of fascism. It wasn't that they were unpatriotic. In the event of a war, they would undoubtedly have followed the example of their English counterparts in 1914 and gone off to fight for freedom and glory in the most idealistic manner possible. It was just that in the safety of peace, they considered the army at best useless and at worst scuzzy.

"I not only enlisted," John said now, "I got some sense talked into my head. And I found something to do where I didn't have to compete with Tom. And I found a few things I was good at."

"How long did you stay?"

"Five years."

"Five years as an enlisted man?"

"No. Six months as an enlisted man. Then six months in OCS. Then four years in army intelligence."

I was not, I thought, ever going to get the bottom of my stomach back. It had dropped away from me at John's last words, and now it was disappearing somewhere in the bowels of the earth. Army intelligence. I thought of the books and movies my father liked so much, by Robert Ludlum and John le Carré and Ian Fleming, where guns and bombs and blood and death were almost incidentals. It suddenly occurred to me that there were people in the world who would find the things that had been happening to me in the past week perfectly *normal*. It was a shocking thought. Even when I'd accused John of being CIA, I'd been throwing the accusation around the way some college students call their professors Nazis. There'd been no *reality* behind it, no gut-level understanding that there really were CIA agents and spies and God only knew what else. I don't think I'd even fully believed the existence of criminals until then—and I'd just been shot at. Army intelligence. What did they do in army intelligence?

"Kerry," John said gently. "That was years ago."

I stood up and started walking across the coarse sand, hardly noticing that the grains were the size of pebbles, with sharp edges that dug into the skin of my feet. He caught up to me before I'd gone very far, falling into step beside me, reining in his long legs so that he didn't outpace me or hurry my walk.

"I feel like an absolute idiot," he said. "I just wanted to let you know that I'd had *some* training. I'm not rushing into this, or rushing your brother into this, on the strength of a few bad novels and an inflated idea of my own competence."

I wrapped my arms around my body, trying to stay warm, but it didn't help. "This is going to sound crazy," I said, "and probably stupid and naive, but I don't think I believed in all this stuff before this week. I mean, I believed in it intellectually. I read the papers. I know people mug people and people rob banks and people do worse than that, I guess. All you have to do is look at the Police Blotter section of the *New York Times*. But—and this is where it begins to sound stupid—I think I believed all that stuff the way I believed in the ghosts and goblins of a Stephen King novel. Meaning, not really. Am I making any sense?"

"Quite a bit of it. It's what happens to people who are mugged for the first time. It just hits them all of a sudden that all that violence is really real. And they can never look at the world in quite the same way again."

"Well, it didn't hit me when that priest was found in Pan's basement. And it didn't hit me with the girl last night, either. And as for getting shot at"—I shrugged—"I don't think that penetrated, either. Maybe that was why I could never fight hard enough when Pan told me I was making it up."

"*Pan* told you you were making it all up?" His tone was light, sardonic, and I shot him a grateful glance. It was comic relief, no matter how short-lived, and I needed it.

We had come to the edge of this side of the cove, an

outcropping of rock that divided Papaspirou's minuscule bathing area from its tiny harbor, and I climbed onto the jutting, ragged gray rocks until I found a seat.

"I suppose you liked it," I said. "Running around playing spy, being very macho."

"I hated it."

I stared at him in surprise. "But I thought it was what half the men in America wanted," I said. "Either to be James Bond or to make the NFL. My father is always reading these books—"

"I've read a lot of the same books."

"Not the same?"

"Beside the point," he said firmly. "You were calling yourself strange before because you'd never really believed these things could happen. Well, there's nothing strange about it. Normal people *don't* believe these things can happen. Which, by the way, is my personal explanation for why there's so much resistance to letting women participate in combat. Not that men want some area of power to themselves exclusively, but that they want to be able to come home to people who don't know the things they do. Who are too nice and too normal to think anybody could take death and destruction and violence seriously."

"Well, if that's what men want in women, I've just lost it."

"It's a good thing. Walking around with that attitude is not the best way to stay healthy when somebody's trying to kill you."

"*Is* somebody trying to kill me? Me in particular, I mean. Not just some stray American who happens to be handy for the purpose."

"There's a lot of gold wandering around someplace, Kerry, and Pan Peteris knows where it is. I may not be able to prove it yet, but I'm sure of it."

171

"And I know too much and Pan wants to kill me for it?"

"You may know something you don't know you know."

"Odd," I said as his words struck home. "I was thinking that just this morning. That something strange had happened and I hadn't caught it. And then later." I frowned. "I can't remember," I said finally. "I don't think I even want to remember."

"You could try."

"No, I couldn't." I jumped off my rock and started walking toward the water. I'd had enough of Pan Peteris's present and John Borden's past, enough of all this talk about violence and all this thinking about how different the world was from what I'd always thought it to be. I let my feet sink into the wet sand at the tide line and the water wash shards of shells over my toes. Greece could be so beautiful in the sunshine, beautiful and clean and cold. That was all I wanted to think about.

"I like Papaspirou," I said, not turning around to face him. "It doesn't connect to anything, not architecturally or aesthetically or culturally or politically, not in any way at all. It's like Oz."

He didn't say anything, but I sensed the change. The air around me was suddenly electric with tension.

I spun around, anxious and suspicious and angry. "Now what?" I demanded. "What's Papaspirou got to do with anything?"

He had the good manners to look embarrassed. "Like I said, it's not doing too well financially. So the guy who owns it rents rooms in it, by the month, where some of the local heavy hitters keep girls they'd rather their wives didn't know about. The rooms are registered to the girls, for discretion's sake. I've been checking them out."

"And?"

"And two don't check out at all. I can't find out who they belong to or what they're doing here."

"Why would you think that had anything to do with Pan?"

He licked his lips. "Caves," he said finally. "Like a lot of Greek islands, Themnos is lousy with caves. Papaspirou is built over a whole network of them."

"I see." I did, too. There was all that gold that no one had been able to find, and there were all those caves under Papaspirou. I wiped salt spray out of my face. The worst thing about this nightmare was the way it took in everything, every part of my life, so that there was nothing I could do and nowhere I could go to get away from thinking about it.

I thought of the little hole-in-the-wall "international bookstore" John had told me about and all that Agatha Christie and Dorothy L. Sayers. I wanted to be locked in my room with my phone off the hook, lost in a world where murder was a game. I wanted to be there now, before it had a chance to hit me that I'd never be able to look at murder as a game again.

I was turning to start up the beach when I realized John had come close, moved in beside me when I wasn't thinking or looking. One minute I was staring at the water, hating all of this with as passionate a hatred as I'd ever been able to summon for anything. The next, I felt his arms sliding around my shoulders, bringing me close to him.

He *was* a compelling man. He almost broke through the wall of revulsion and fear I had thrown up around me, to protect me from the things I didn't want to know and didn't want to understand. There was sea salt on his lips. His tongue carried it into my mouth, and for a few seconds I lost myself in it and in him. I shut out the world and my life and everything that had gone wrong in both since the week started, and let myself drown in the waves of love and desire his body was sending out to me. He was not only making love to me, he was trying to heal me. He almost succeeded.

Almost, but not quite. The kiss had to break sometime. When it did, the illusion dissolved, and I was left standing on the beach in the arms of a man who was even more thickly involved in all this horror than I was. Worse, he had been involved in things like this before, and probably would be again.

I stepped away from him, jerky, nervous, torn. I wanted his arms around me again, and I didn't want him to touch me. I wanted to tell him it was all right and to tell him it wasn't. I wanted most of all to be back in my apartment in New York, my horrible one-room apartment with the cockroaches and the astronomical rent, where things were dull and ordinary and none of this had ever happened.

We stood staring at each other for a long time. Then I turned around and started walking away from him, slowly and alone, up the long flight of shallow steps to the hotel.

16

I FOUND THE hole-in-the-wall international bookstore on my way back to my room. It was even smaller than John had implied, but I found a dust-encrusted copy of *Northanger Abbey* for Chas and a British edition of *The Mysterious Affair at Styles* for myself. I bought them both—the prices were astronomical—and took them upstairs with me. God only knows why. I couldn't have thought I was going to read, any more than I could have thought I was going to sleep. My mind was on one of its racing jags, all revved up and already on its way who knew where. I would have been lucky if I'd been able to make myself sit still.

Oddly enough, once I'd coerced room service into bringing up a pot of tea and locked the door of my room behind the retreating waiter, the one thing I didn't think about was John's now-defunct membership in army intelligence or the way I felt about it. Other things he'd said began to catch at me, things all the talk about murder and mayhem had momentarily overwhelmed. I kept thinking of John making his way through Williams on his own—*Williams,* not the local state university. It was staggering. At last count, tuition, room, and board at Williams—and at places like that, almost everybody lives on campus—ran to something over ten thousand a year. Even with some form of the GI Bill still in operation, that was a heavy load. I couldn't help admiring him for going through with it—and for going out on his own, at eighteen, to live his life the way he wanted to live it. He might have made a few mistakes, but at least he'd made his own decisions. I knew too many people whose entire life-plans could crumble into dust at one wrong look from their parents—including, until about two years ago, me.

I pulled the great fan-backed wicker chair and the little tea table with the pot and cup and sugar bowl and spoon laid out on the room-service tray up to the window and curled up under a blanket to watch the sea. I hadn't even considered seeing a man seriously since I'd left college, partly because my experiences in college had been mostly disappointing and partly because I'd had too much on my mind just trying to survive in New York. Now that I looked back on what I did know of men, I realized that the most accurate description of it was: nothing. Even the boy I'd considered the love of my life for six months had failed to stir anything impressive in me physically, and my one foray in that direction—I was not a virgin; it would have been a social black mark of the first order to graduate from my college as a virgin— had left me wondering what all the fuss was about. I hadn't bothered to try again. In fact, I hadn't even been tempted to try again—until I met John Borden.

I squirmed a little in my chair. There was the fact, the very important little fact, that all my lack of introspection was working overtime to keep from me. If the impulse had been entirely physical—as it had been when I first met him—it wouldn't have been so worrisome. I *read* those working-girl magazines my mother sent me. I *knew* about lust at first sight. This wasn't it. What I felt for John Borden grew with almost everything I learned about him, even with the things I didn't like. I might retreat in the face of unpleasant revelations about army intelligence, but I didn't hate him for it or even want him to go away. I was so far from wanting him to go away, it was embarrassing. Yet I had been the one to walk away from him, and I'd done my best to make him feel responsible.

I poured myself another cup of tea. My window faced the wrong side of the hotel, looking into Themnos Mountain, not onto the sea. I couldn't tell if he'd stayed by the water or come up to the terrace. I did know that no one had passed in the hall and that he would have had to pass to get to his room. What was he doing down there? What was he thinking of me?

Somehow, finding the answers to those questions seemed far more important than figuring out where someone had hidden six million dollars in gold belonging to the government of Greece.

I must have fallen asleep. At least, I seemed to be dreaming—and dreaming about something pleasant. When I heard the knock on the door, I was disinclined to answer it. I was somewhere very nice, warm and soft and uncomplicated, and I wanted to stay there.

Unfortunately, whoever wanted to come in wasn't going to take no for an answer. The knocking went on and on, getting louder and louder, until I could no longer pull away from it into fantasy. On the other hand, I was still disinclined to move. I dug myself further into my blanket and yelled, "Come *in.*"

There was the sound of someone turning the doorknob, then rattling the door. "It's locked," Chas shouted at me. "Get over here and let me in, will you?"

I said, "Damn," loud enough for him to hear and got out of my chair to answer the door. The floor was cold and slick, as if the heat had gone off while I'd been asleep and the room had sunk to the temperature outside. I'd left my shoes and socks with John on the beach, so I had to navigate what felt like an ice-skating rink in my bare feet. I twisted the bolt and then pulled the door open as I was heading back to my chair. The president of the United States could have been at the door and it wouldn't have mattered. I wanted to be back in the warm.

By the time I was safely under my blanket again, Chas was not only in, but taking a seat on the wide hotel bed. I suppressed a few comments on the virtues of having long legs—and of being overtall in general—and smiled him a hello. The rest had done him good. He had dark circles under his eyes and he still looked hollow and underfed, but at least he didn't look like he was dying. His shakes were gone. There was even some of the old humor back in his face.

"What *did* you do to John Borden?" he asked me. "I was delegated to haul you out of here and down to dinner, and I got the distinct impression he was afraid you were going to beat him up."

I wouldn't have answered that one for money. "What time is it?" I asked. "It's dark out, but you can never tell at this time of year."

"It's after seven-thirty. And don't tell me you couldn't have been asleep that long, because you were. We tried to wake you about an hour ago."

"How do you know I was here an hour ago?"

"You were here an hour ago."

"Yes, I was." I stretched luxuriously under the

blanket. "I think it's being away from Kilithia and Pan and all that craziness. Even if your John Borden does think the caves under this place are riddled with loot, it still feels to me like somewhere out of time."

"Maybe it is. And we don't really know anything's there. We—he—was going to check—"

"Check when?"

"I'm supposed to be keeping you out of this."

I sighed. "I'd love to be kept out of it," I said. "I'd love never to have heard of it, frankly. At the moment, it seems a little late for that."

"Yeah. I guess it is." He ran a hand fretfully through his hair—too-long hair, I realized now. He'd been neglecting himself in more ways than I'd noticed at first. "You've no idea how guilty I feel about all this," he said. "Getting you that job with Pan—"

"That was two years ago," I said quickly.

"I know. But I've known Pan Peteris a long time, Kerry. And I've always known there was something fishy about him." Chas smiled bitterly. "I thought it had to do with sex. All those cheap women. Walking around with his pants stuffed, or whatever he does to make himself look like that. I wasn't worried on that score. That kind of vulnerability has never been your problem."

"I don't know if I can take that as a compliment."

"Take it as a compliment. *Vulnerability* was a high-level euphemism for what I was talking about. I just wish we'd been able to wake you up at six-thirty. We could have put you on the mail boat for Rhodes at seven. Then I'd have you out of this for good."

"Mmm," I said tentatively. I said "mmm" because I had to say something, and I'm not very good at making up lies on the spot. I *had* said something to John about being willing to go back to New York and I'd meant it at the time, but things were different now.

Chas was involved. I didn't know if Chas was on Themnos because he was doing field work for his dissertation or because keeping him on the island was the only way John Borden could protect him from arrest or because he was trying to help, but whatever it was, I knew I didn't want to leave him alone with all these crazy people. Chas just wasn't equipped to handle it. In the Middle Ages, he'd have been a great Christian ascetic, one of those men who dreamed their lives away over ancient manuscripts in monastery libraries. It was a quality that drove my father crazy and that I valued, but at the moment, neither of our evaluations addressed the salient point. The fact was, in a situation like this, Chas's ethereal nature was highly dangerous—to Chas.

"Kerry," Chas said warningly. "You *are* going home. You're going home on the first boat we can put you on."

"Of course I am," I said soothingly. "But that won't be for another three days, and I couldn't just leave from here, anyway. I have to go back to Kilithia and get my things."

"I'm not letting you within a hundred feet of that house," Chas said. "Or that slimy little—well, never mind what I want to call him. I'll get your things myself."

"You wouldn't know where to look or what to look for," I said. "And if I tried to tell you, I'd probably forget something."

"I know when you're up to something, Kerry, and I'm telling you right now—"

There was another knock on the door. Chas stopped mid-sentence. It was just as well. I had stopped listening to him.

"Who is it?" I called out.

"John. And there's a guy from room service out here. Says you've got a teapot."

"Door's open."

John opened the door himself, but stepped back to let the little man from room service pass. The little man from room service didn't speak English and didn't expect anyone but John to speak Greek. He gathered the tea things from the table, accepted the overlarge tip I gave him with vigorous smiling nods of his head, and raced out my door into the hall.

John stood until the door closed, then took a seat on the bed next to Chas, facing me. "How are you?" he asked.

"Rested," I told him.

"Still mad at me?"

"I was never mad at you."

"Oh, don't waste time on trivialities," Chas said irritably. "She's making noises like she won't go home."

"I'm doing nothing of the sort," I said. John Borden was shooting me looks that weren't in the least friendly. I didn't intend to go home until I could find a way to take Chas with me, but I knew it would be the worst kind of mistake to let either of them know that ahead of time. "I was just saying there wasn't another mail boat for three days, and I've got a lot of stuff at Pan's. I just want to go pick it up, for heaven's sake."

John was clearly suspicious. "I'm with him," he said, jerking his head toward Chas. "You're trying to find some way to stay in this mess."

"The thing I want most in the world is to get out of it," I said, which was the truth, "but cashmere sweaters cost a hundred fifty apiece and I've got three of them in Kilithia."

"Cashmere sweaters?"

"And other things."

"You're crazy."

"I'm insolvent."

"You're—"

I think he was about to say, "You're lying," but he didn't. My argument was just crazy enough to be the truth. Also, just "feminine" enough. Even in these days of liberation, men harbor a sneaking suspicion that women just don't think the way men do. I was confirming John's. He looked nonplussed, if still suspicious.

He was also no fool. I knew if I gave him time enough to think about this, he'd see through it, and I didn't want that. I started to make impatient, distracted movements under my blanket.

"I'm starving," I said. "If we're going back to Kilithia tonight, I want something to eat first. I don't think I've had anything all day."

"We're not going back to Kilithia tonight," John said. He looked at Chas and shrugged. "I suppose we've got to eat. There's a restaurant downstairs. I don't know how good it is."

"Well then." I smiled happily at both of them. "Why don't you two get out of here and let me get dressed. I'll meet you in the lobby as soon as I'm ready."

They didn't want to leave. Oh, how they didn't want to leave. The look in Chas's eyes told me clearly that what he wanted to do was bind me, gag me, wrap me up in a sheet, and transport me off Themnos—on a dolphin's back, if necessary—with all possible speed. John just looked as if he wanted to shake me.

I waited them out. A request for dinner after a day without food is hardly evidence of mental instability. They couldn't impugn my motives without making themselves sound paranoid and uncharitable.

It was a no-win situation, and they knew it. They left.

My mother always says no good can come from bad intention, but she's wrong. I know, because the first good thing to happen to us, the first "break in the case," as Agatha Christie would have said, came about because I had the very bad intention of listening to no one but myself and plunging right back into that mess in Kilithia. The fact that I had no idea where I would end up when I started talking is beside the point—as I said, my intentions were entirely bad. I wanted to elude the protective clutches of my two self-appointed knights in shining armor and station myself where I could keep an eye on Chas. I thought I knew a way to do this, but in order to carry it out, I had to keep their minds off me. The only thing I could think of that they were more interested in than getting me off Themnos was that robbery and that gold. John had given me a synopsis of his reading of the case, a synopsis with holes in it big enough to ride an elephant through. I'd known that from the beginning, but I'd been so concerned about Chas, so edgy at the thought of my own danger, and so blinded by the multiple attractions of John Borden that I hadn't given it much thought. Now I gave it more thought than I believed it deserved. I wanted to get down to dinner with enough questions to ask, enough niggling points to consider, to take up several hours of conversation. Since I didn't care what they talked about as long as they didn't talk about me, I made up a dizzying list of questions on no particular theme and in no particular order that made the Pan Peteris gold robbery business sound like Agatha Christie at her labyrinthine best.

I also took care to dress carefully, unbuttoning an

extra button on my shirtwaist-style "good dress," tying back my hair. I was not only attracted to John Borden, he was attracted to me. If he was a normal male—and I knew from experience he was at least that—I thought I could gain a few minutes on the basis of simple distraction. Not many, since John was a very self-controlled man, but a few.

I unearthed my quilted blue evening bag with its thin silver strap—another present from my mother— from where I had buried it at the bottom of my day pack and hurried downstairs, stuffing money and passport and cigarettes into it all the way. Physically, I was not quite together when I hit the lobby. Mentally, I was raring to go. Even the sight of John Borden in a suit didn't slow me up, and that man looked *good* in a suit. Seeing him in black leather, I'd thought that was his natural attire. Seeing him in a suit, I thought *that* was. He looked like he could have entered the Grand Casino at Monte Carlo with more authority than Prince Rainier.

I could just imagine him in black tie and evening jacket.

It was an affecting picture, but I was too wound up, and too intent on my object, to give in to it. I gave him an extra-wide, extra-meaningful smile I told myself was entirely artifice—and that made his eyebrows shoot to the middle of his forehead—but I also started talking almost immediately. I must have sounded like a movie unaccountably kicked into high speed. Both John and Chas gave me long, odd looks, which I ignored. Fortunately, they didn't take it into their heads to shut me up.

"It's the second priest," I said as they escorted me—I was holding on to both their arms—into the tiny, almost painfully picturesque restaurant. "That's what I was thinking about this morning. You've got an explanation for the first one and an explanation for the girl, but why would anyone want to kill the new priest and tear up Pan's basement?"

We were seated at a small table under an archway near the windows to the garden. Papaspirou's Garden, as the restaurant was called, was one of those whitewash-walled, archway-encumbered evocations of a tourist's conception of a remote Greek village taverna, complete with woven cotton bags hanging from the walls as decorations and plaster statues—just like the ones in Pan's living room—of the Parthenon and the ancient gods on every available surface. Normally, I would have hated it, no matter how good the food turned out to be. I had not only been to Greece, but to the nontouristy parts of Greece, enough times to know what the real thing looked like, and this wasn't it. At the moment, I didn't have time or thought to waste on decor. I didn't even have time or thought to waste on food. I let Chas order for me. I couldn't stay calm enough to read the menu.

I had expected a few initial difficulties, some attempts to get me back on the subject of my departure, but they didn't materialize. Instead of trying to deflect me, John took my question with complete seriousness. He even looked a little uncomfortable.

"I've been thinking about that myself," he said when the waiter brought our bottle of *retsina*. He poured me a glass, then offered the bottle to Chas, who refused. It was a very good sign. I gave my brother an affectionate pat on the hand.

"I never did like liquor," Chas said. "I can't figure out how I managed to drink so much of it over the past few months."

John waved away the explanation. "The second priest," he returned to the point, "is a problem in two respects. First, I don't understand why kill the man before the resurrection ceremony. After, yes, for the same reason the girl died. But why before? And why at all? The girl went down in the pit with Marina. She, Marina, and I were the only ones who could have seen Marina take that bullet out of the coffin. I could see because I knew what I was looking for and because of the strange way that knoll is placed. That's why I wanted to go up there. But the priest wouldn't have been in the pit. He'd have been at the rim of the grave, and he wouldn't have been looking for anything except bones. So kill him after if he happens to see something, but not before. Not before you know if you even have to."

"You were the one who figured out they were amateurs," Chas said. "Amateurs sometimes kill people they don't have to."

"Nobody kills the local Greek Orthodox priest— the most important and most visible man in the village—on a whim," John said stubbornly. "Kerry's right. There's got to be another explanation. Something in particular. Something we missed." He pounded the table angrily, a gesture I was beginning to recognize. "We keep missing things and missing things and missing things. I'm beginning to feel like an amateur myself."

The wine was beginning to relax me. (Actually, enough *retsina* could relax a homicidal rhinoceros.) I slid down a little in my chair and stared dreamily across the mostly empty dining room, marveling at just how easy this had been.

"Maybe he found out something," I said lazily. "Maybe he knows where the gold is hidden or something about that woman no one can find."

"If he knew something about that woman, I'd expect him to be dead," John Borden said. "Two guards got offed in that robbery, and as far as anyone can tell, she got every one of them. She's a vicious woman, whoever she is. But I don't see how he could have known anything about her. She's the one person I'm sure isn't from Kilithia."

"Why?" I asked.

"Because I've been through everybody in that village four times, and there isn't a woman of that age and build who speaks English."

Something started nagging at me again, but I couldn't catch it. I *had* heard a Greek woman speaking English recently. I just couldn't remember where. To be honest, I wasn't sure if what I was remembering was reality or dream. It was very hazy in my mind.

I picked up the bottle of *retsina* and refilled my glass. "The situation as I see it," I said a little pompously, "is that in order to get both Chas and you off the hook, we have to connect Pan Peteris with that robbery. Which means we either have to find the gold that's still missing—how much is still missing?"

"Almost all of it. Four-fifths, I'd guess."

"All right. Almost all of it, which means a lot of metal. Anyway, we either have to find the gold that's still missing and find it in a place that will connect him to it, or we have to find a way to prove he was in Greece at the time of the robbery."

"It would help if he was here at the time of the murders," Chas said. "At least, it would help me."

"It could have been Costa Papageorgiou," John said.

"I'm for Costa Papageorgiou," I said. "At heart, I think Pan is a wimp."

"Either way." Chas shrugged. "They had to be in it together. Costa is all over Pan's interests in Greece— the house, the businesses, everything. Pan couldn't hide all that metal without Costa knowing something about it. And Marina—Marina had to at least know what was going on. If she didn't, she wouldn't have retrieved that bullet."

"I suppose Marina is too old to be the woman at the bank," I said.

"Too old and too arthritic," John said.

"Caliope?"

"Too American. Whoever this was was young, curvy, and definitely Greek-Greek, not Greek-American. According to the English and American witnesses, she had an accent thick as a pea-soup fog."

I frowned into my wine. There seemed to be little pieces of cork floating in it. "I keep thinking about that basement being torn up, and the only explanation I come up with is somebody knew the gold was there and went looking for it—"

"But as I said, we've been over the house a dozen times, Greek police, Interpol people, even the U.S. Treasury Department at the request of the Greek government. There isn't a scrap of metal in the place."

"All right," I said. "But even if you'll grant you missed something, just for the sake of argument, the time frame doesn't work out. I know they don't absolutely have to have a priest at those resurrection ceremonies, but don't they prefer them?"

"Of course they prefer them," Chas said, "but what were they going to do, let him call the police on them?"

"How?" I said.

They stared at me. I stared right back at them.

"Look," I said. "Try to remember, this is Kilithia we're talking about. There's one phone in the entire village, and it belongs to Pan. That's it. Somehow, I can't see Costa Papageorgiou letting the priest phone the police from there. Which means he'd have had to go to Agios Constantinos to get them. Which means he'd have had to get to Agios Constantinos. There is exactly one car in the village of Kilithia, and that also belongs to Pan. Which means the priest would have had to get to Agios Constantinos by foot or by donkey. Or go to the local constable and have him go to Agios Constantinos the same way. That was a rainy, muddy day. It would have taken hours to get to Agios Constantinos without a car. By the time anyone made it back to Kilithia to investigate, they could have had the whole pile moved somewhere else, where nobody would think to look. So why bother to kill the priest?"

"Dear God in heaven," John said.

"She's got a point," Chas said.

"I know she's got a point," John said, "but—"

"Wait," I said. "Give me two things. First, it's a stupid thing to do to kill the village priest unless you have to, because it's going to bring down a lot of heat. Even someone like Costa Papageorgiou understands heat. Second, the basement, the wreckage down there, was a red herring."

"Why?" John said.

"Because it got rid of the heat. There'd been a priest killed before, in the same way. The police were inclined to look on it as the work of a crazy person. That mess in the basement convinced the police they were looking for a crazy person. No heat."

"All right," Chas said. "Then what?"

"Then we're left with this: they killed that priest because they had to. Which means they couldn't afford to just move the stuff around. Since there are plenty of places on Themnos Mountain to hide things if you want to, and places you could get to without too much trouble, too, we're back to the time element. There has to be something about the time element. Some deadline."

John perked up immediately. "I see what you're saying. Something's about to come off. Soon. Something they've gone to a lot of trouble to set up and don't want to abort."

"Exactly," I said. "But the trouble with that is, they've got to have a cover for it. Gold is heavy. You can't just haul however many pounds of it they have lying around out of a place like Kilithia without causing a lot of comment."

"Unless John's hunch is right," Chas said, frowning. "Maybe it's not in Kilithia. Maybe it's here, in the caves, and the priest was killed because he knew that and he was going to the police and they didn't have time to get here to move it. That would explain everything, wouldn't it?"

"Everything but how they got it here," I said. "They'd have had to hire boats—"

"Yannis Tefillides had a boat," John said.

"Yes," I said. "I know, but—" And then I saw it, right there in front of me, where it had been all the time. Gold turning up in all those cities where Pan sold his souvenirs. Gold coming in drop by drop, so slowly it would drive a patient man mad. Gold coming in only when it was absolutely necessary, to shore up the business or provide operating money or feed Pan's ego—something Pan would have considered absolutely necessary, even if no one else did. Pan was not a patient man. But he'd been patient this time, because he'd had to be.

I dropped my wineglass on the floor. It was half full. It made an ugly stain on the flagstone floor.

"Dear God," I said. "Dear sweet Lord in heaven."

They stared at me as if I'd lost it completely.

"Chas," I said. "The *tiri*."

"The *tiri?*" Chas looked blank. "Oh, the—holy *shit*."

"Exactly," I said.

"What are you two talking about?" John demanded.

I turned to him in a fury of determination and concentration, knowing I had to make sense. It was going to be difficult. "Start with the girl," I said. "The girl who was killed at the resurrection. I remember seeing her at the house. She looked terrified. I thought it was odd. Mourning women are widows, they've been through all that before. And I was wondering if she'd been forced into it or if she was so poor there wasn't anything else she could do, but that didn't make sense, either. Pan's the biggest employer in Kilithia. I know. I do his hiring for him. If she needed a job, she could have had a job."

"This is a *tiri?*" John said. "A *tiri* is one of those offerings things, isn't it? That they put in the church."

"Right," I said. "Gold and silver offerings."

John stared at me a minute. Then he shook his head slowly. "Pan couldn't import gold anything into the United States at this point. We'd have him."

"He isn't going to import gold," I said. "He's going to import tin. Tin replicas of gold offerings for the souvenir shops of America. Three hundred boxes of five hundred *tiri* each going out on Tuesday. Who's going to look through that many *tiri?*"

"Most of them would really be tin," John said.

"Exactly."

"And that priest was probably the only person in Kilithia who didn't know about that gold."

"Again, exactly."

"Oh boy," John said. "We checked his shipments and there wasn't anything, but of course there wasn't. We'd just picked Chas up. He couldn't take the chance."

"I don't think he would have taken the chance with

191

small shipments, anyway," I said. "I don't think Marina would have let him."

The waiter had come to clean up the glass, but John didn't notice him. He was beaming at me.

"Look at her," he said to Chas. "Beautiful, courageous, and a genius besides." He grabbed my face in his hands and gave me a kiss on the nose.

It was a sweet gesture, but I just wasn't in the mood for it. "I'm not courageous," I said, wrenching myself away. "And if you think I'm happy to be going back into that mess now that I *know,* you're out of your mind."

"But why would you have to go back?" John said. "Now that we've figured it out, all we have to do is call the police in Agios Constantinos and—" He faltered.

"Exactly," I said. "You don't have a shred of proof. I could always go in and lie my head off, but I'm not very good at it."

"Chas and I will go get one of those boxes," John said. "We'll just—"

"Just what? Force yourself into some little old lady's hut and start rummaging through her belongings? There is a constable in Kilithia. And he's probably in on this. Worse, the men have to be in on it, and if they are, you'll get your necks broken. You're stuck with me, gentlemen. I'm the only one of us who can get into one of those houses without arousing suspicion, and I'm the only one with a chance in hell of bringing a solid gold *tiri* out without getting killed."

17

WE DID NOT leave early the next morning. We wanted to, we even argued about it heavily at that interminable dinner, but in the end we decided it couldn't be done. It was too out of character. I am not, by choice, an early riser. I would rather reach my office late and stay at work late than get there on time and go home with everybody else. Pan was used to seeing me wander in, bleary-eyed and clutching a cup of coffee, somewhat after ten. If he saw me bounce through the doors of his squatter's palace at some ungodly hour, all wide-awake and ready to go, he'd know something was wrong.

Given the late hour of our departure, I should have been rested. I should at least have had enough sleep to be coherent. Instead, when the first faint light of dawn came through my windows, I was wide-awake and restless and running on so little REM time I was walking into walls. I was caught up not only in fear and anticipation, but in memory. There was so much to think about, I couldn't decide what to concentrate on. Sometimes I went over and over the arguments about whether or not to call in the police, and over and over what had happened when John walked me to my door after we'd put Chas to bed. In fact, I blamed it all on John, in every way I could think of, even

193

though I knew I was being ridiculous. And dishonest. I had known exactly what was going on in his mind long before he did anything about it. I even encouraged him, in my fashion. It was just that, later, blaming him was easier than indulging in the introspection I dislike so much.

"I still say there's somebody we ought to notify," he said when we were still in Chas's room. "Granted, the local constable wouldn't be the right person, just in case, and that idiot in Agios Constantinos might not come. But somebody—"

"All you're saying is that you're not so happy about playing cops and robbers when I'm playing one of the cops," I said. "It was just fine when you were the one rushing in half cocked."

"No, it wasn't. And I wasn't happy about Chas being here, believe me."

Chas gave us both a sick smile. "I'm not happy about Chas being here, either," he said. "Couldn't we just call your people in the States, have them go through those boxes more carefully than they usually would?"

"Sure. And what happens if we're wrong?"

"How could we be wrong?" Chas said.

John sighed. "Look, it's a great theory, the best we've had, and we're probably right. And I'll go down tonight and check out the caves, just the way I intended, to close that avenue off. But we don't really know yet, and three hundred boxes is an awful lot of boxes. Would he really be able to sell a hundred fifty thousand *tiri* under normal circumstances?"

I gave it a little thought. "Yes," I said finally. "We've got a lot of orders for them. The non-Greek population doesn't want them. But the immigrant Greeks use them, of course. They bring them to the church with a check to make up for the fact that they're not gold. And Pan's been holding back on the orders over the past year. I think it must have taken a long time to get enough tin ones backlogged and enough gold ones made to put together the kind of camouflage Pan wanted."

"Whatever," John said. "We still don't know enough to cover our rear ends. If we knew for sure there were some gold ones in every box or if we knew how to identify a box we knew had gold ones in it, that would be one thing. But a hundred fifty thousand of the things, probably less than a tenth of them gold—well, there's just too much chance they'd be missed."

"Nobody's going to go through that many offerings," I said, repeating my sentiment from dinner. "And we can't count on them to get lucky."

"Exactly."

Chas brightened. "The weight," he said. "Gold weighs a lot more than tin. I can't remember how much, but I remember it was a lot. Wouldn't those boxes be heavier than they should be?"

John and I were both shaking our heads. "Packing materials," John pointed out. "Even discrepancies between boxes could be explained by differing packing materials. Unless they got really stupid and decided to put all the gold ones in one box, and I don't think they will. I said Pan was an amateur, not a mental defective."

"Oh well." Chas flopped down on his bed. He had been working overtime for the last few hours trying to look cheerful, and the strain was beginning to tell. He hated the idea of putting me in danger. He still wanted to pack me onto a mail boat and off to Rhodes. Only his knowledge that I was absolutely correct in my assessment of the way the people of Kilithia would react to any strangers' attempts to get at that shipment, and his consciousness of his position as the U.S. Treasury Department's chief suspect in this particular case of gold smuggling, held him back.

I sat down next to him on the bed and patted his hand. "It'll be all right," I said. "Pan's been at me for days to go see to that shipment. I'm supposed to open the boxes and count the offerings. No one will suspect anything out of the ordinary."

"Of course not," Chas said. "You'll just wander in there, cool and collected, do your work, steal a gold offering, and walk out again. Looking like you'd done nothing more nerve-racking than have lunch."

"Chas," I said.

"You wear your life on your face, Kerry. They're going to take one look at you and know more than they'd get out of you by torture."

"Either that or we're all going to collapse in the middle of the project from lack of sleep," John said, getting up. He held out his hand to me. "Come, my love. We will go to the Casbah."

Chas laughed. "Oh God, Borden," he said. "I'd wish you luck, but the last person who made a pass at her got kicked in the shins."

"He wasn't the last person who made a pass at me," I said. "And he was a creep."

"He was a perfectly nice kid from Hotchkiss, and he adored you."

I waved away this discussion of my adolescent social life. "Get some sleep," I said. "John's right. We should be rested for tomorrow."

"And I look like a wreck," Chas said. "I know I look like a wreck."

I bent over and kissed him on the cheek. "Sweet dreams," I said.

"Gold-plated," he promised.

John waited just outside Chas's door, to "walk me to my room." It wasn't much of a walk, just across the hall. I fumbled in my bag for a minute, pretending to look for the keys that were practically all I had in there, to stretch the time a little. I needn't have bothered with the subterfuge. John took the keys from my hand as soon as I produced them, unlocked my door, and went into the room ahead of me.

"I know you're probably going to think this is foolish," he said, "but I have an irrepressible urge to look in your closets."

"And under my bed," I said, sitting down on the bed in question. "No, I don't think you're being foolish. I don't think you'll find anything, but I don't think you're being foolish."

He closed the door of the single closet and stared at the shining lamp on the bedside table. "Did you leave that on when you left the room?"

"Definitely. I always do that. It comes from living alone in Manhattan."

"Smart move." He came around the edge of the bed and sat down beside me, staring at his hands. "About this afternoon—"

"I'm sorry about this afternoon," I said quickly. "I just wasn't expecting all that. I overreacted."

"And I dumped it on your head in one big lump. *I'm* sorry about that. I could see you weren't handling it well. I should have shut up."

"And never told me at all?"

"No. With any luck, I'd have had to tell you sometime." He looked up at me and smiled. "Let's just say it would have been better if we'd had that conversation, say, six months from now, in a cozy little restaurant somewhere, when we were beginning to think of all this as an adventure we could tell our grandchildren about."

"Oh well," I said, beginning to feel very nervous. "They'll indulge us, of course, and not believe a word of it."

"Sometimes I hardly believe it now."

"Lucky you."

"Come here," he said.

I thought he was going to take my face in his hands as he had on the beach, but instead, he slid his arms around my neck, drawing me to him. I opened my lips to his with the kind of calm acceptance I had wanted, but not been able, to manage the first time. All *that* seemed very far away, de-energized by all our discussions of plans and possibilities, ways and means. *He* was very close, pressed against me, the weight of his body pulling us down until we were lying awkwardly across my bed. I felt the contours of his shoulders under his shirt. He was a much more muscular man than I had imagined him to be, seeing him in clothes.

He broke a little away from me and looked down into my eyes. His eyes had green flecks in them. Very fascinating green flecks. In fact, hypnotic green flecks. I thought I could watch those green flecks forever.

"I keep telling myself I'm not going to do this," he said, "until everything's over and I can do it right, but I seem to have a very weak will where you're concerned."

"You've never had a weak will in your life," I said.

"You'd be amazed." He kissed me again, lightly this time, as if he were teasing. "You ever been in love?"

"No," I said seriously. "I don't think I have."

"Well, it's got a few things going for it." He nibbled lightly at my ear. That was teasing, too, but it set up a pounding in my chest that almost frightened me. I wanted to draw him closer, hold him hard, so that he couldn't get away. No wonder kissing the boys I'd known at college had seemed so boring and senseless. Whatever attraction they'd held for me, it had never evoked this kind of physical response. For the first time, I was able to credit the stories some of my friends told me, about being carried away and just not able to help themselves. I'd always thought it was nonsense or self-rationalization. I'd been wrong.

I had not, however, been wrong about myself. Ambivalent was the way I'd always characterized my feelings about sex, and ambivalent was how I felt now. It wasn't that I didn't want . . . things to happen. I wanted things to happen so badly, every inch of my body ached, inside and out. It was just that I felt as if I were falling from a high window, falling through empty space at too high a speed for comfort.

"You know," I said the next time he paused long enough to let me breathe. "According to my friend in psychology school—"

"Psychology school?"

"She's getting a doctorate in clinical psychology."

"Oh."

"Anyway, according to her, there isn't any such thing as falling in love. There's bonding, but that takes longer. Do you think we're bonding?"

"I think psychology ought to be declared illegal."

"Nice point."

He propped his head up on one hand and began tracing connect-the-dots patterns across the front of my dress. The expression on his face was so playfully serious, I laughed. He looked like a small boy, working very hard to understand a particularly difficult concept in his arithmetic homework.

"Psychology," he said finally, "is a discipline created by people who do not know how to think, feel, or live, in order to provide themselves with an explanation for what everybody else seems to be doing."

"Very profound," I said. "Was it supposed to make sense?"

"Not really."

"I'm glad you know that."

"As I said, falling in love has its points. Chief among them is the permission to talk utter nonsense with complete impunity."

"Are you falling in love with me?" We were both suddenly very still and very quiet, quiet enough to hear the skittering sound of sand being blown across the terrace in the wind. The teasing look left his face, even his eyes, so that he was looking at me with almost terrifying seriousness.

"You know," he said, "I think I am."

"And what does it mean?" I'd intended to put the conversation back in a teasing mode, but my voice came out choked, wavery, harsh. I could have kicked myself.

He said, "More than you think it does."

It was more than I could handle, certainly. I sat up abruptly, needing to break the mood. Thinking about falling in lust, the way my mother's working-girl magazines assured me every young career women did, was one thing. Thinking about this was quite another. It was like an unexpected plunge off a high dive into unknown waters, and I didn't know if I was ready to make it. More honestly, I knew perfectly well I wanted to make it. I just also wanted a parachute to slow my fall.

John put his hand on my arm, lightly, undemandingly. "Kerry? Are you all right?"

"I'm fine," I said.

"You don't sound fine." He sat up and turned me around until I was facing him. "Did I do something stupid? Was I pushing you again?"

"Not exactly. I'm, um, well. I don't have a lot of experience with that sort of thing."

"I can tell."

"Is that a plus or a minus?"

"Neither. It's a fact of existence." His eyes widened in surprise and, I thought, consternation. "You're not a—I mean—"

"Would *that* have been a minus?" I asked him wryly.

"Of course not," he said. "It's just—"

"It was the emotional stuff I was talking about," I said.

"Ahhh." He sank back contentedly. "No one's stolen my true love's heart but me. I should stop going at it like a race-car driver?"

"I think it's a little late for that at this point. You just shouldn't think I'm, I don't know, rejecting you or something when I pull back a little."

"It hadn't even occurred to me."

"And somehow, I get the feeling I should have known that."

He laughed, sat up, stretched. "I'm thirty-two years old, Kerry Hansen. I have a whole different frame of reference. I'm afraid what I don't have is any more time."

I'll give love this much—it certainly takes your mind off everything else. I'd entirely forgotten about Pan and stolen gold and even Chas being in trouble with the police. I had a hard time making myself think about it now.

"You're going to go looking in the caves," I said, picking at my dress.

"I have to. Just in case."

"I know you have to."

He kissed me lightly, with closed lips. "It'll be all right," he said. "I don't think there's anything down there. I won't be in any danger. And once I've had a look around, we'll know. Right?"

"Right," I said.

He kissed me again. "Why don't we make an appointment to continue this discussion in the morning. And the afternoon. And a week from Tuesday—don't giggle. It's very bad for my ego."

"Well, it's very good for mine."

"Figures. Well, I'll let you get some sleep. And don't tell me you're not going to be able to sleep. I'm counting on you."

I got up and went to the door and let him out.

Later, when I heard his step in the hall, I waited until I knew he'd be too far ahead to notice and followed him. I went as far as the terrace, afraid to go any farther. I didn't want him to hear me or see me. I just wanted to watch him.

He looked very good in a wetsuit, as good as Christopher Reeve in tights. More importantly, he looked very natural. His golden hair spilled over against the dull black of the suit, catching light from the moon. Here was something I hadn't thought of: that no matter how much he'd "hated" army intelligence, action was integral to him. He might have a nice, comfortable desk job back in Washington, but he'd always be itching to get out and *do* something, even if it meant just taking up some kind of dangerous sport. I wondered how he'd feel, watching me sitting on the side lines, probably cringing. I supposed it wouldn't matter.

I watched until he went into the water. Then I went back to my room, telling myself I ought to get some sleep.

I've never been very good at doing what I ought to do.

18

MAYBE IT WAS just as well I didn't get any sleep. I wasn't as alert as I should have been, but I wasn't jumpy either, and jumpiness would have caused us all trouble. Jumpy or not, the adrenaline must have been flowing. Going down to breakfast, I told myself I would sleep in the car. Normally, I can sleep anywhere but on a plane—I have a tendency to feel that a plane stays in the air by the force of my will alone—and something like our trip from Dyphos to Kilithia would have been ideal. We were all talked out. Even at breakfast, we didn't do much more than grunt at each other. When we got into the Jeep, John gave Chas and me a lecture about taking precautions and not doing anything stupid, and then ran out of conversation. I was so tired, I didn't even resent the fact that the lecture was aimed at me. Chas, after all, had nothing to do and therefore couldn't (I thought) do anything stupid. I gave only passing thought to the niceness of John's being worried about me. That, and the feelings it arose from, I would have to deal with later. In the meantime, I could hardly deal with the weather. We rode up the steep grade of Themnos Mountain and into the wild barrenness of that landscape just as a storm was coming in from the other side. There was thunder in the distance, so far away it sounded like a giant grumbling awake under the earth. There were fitful patches of rain that never came down long enough or hard enough to make us feel it was worthwhile to stop and put on the canvas. There was darkness, but darkness with an odd quality to it, like day-for-night in a cheap movie. My imagination was running away with me and I knew it, but I couldn't stop myself. The great banks of clouds streaming in from the east made Themnos Mountain look like the setting for a gothic horror story—a horror story, mind you, not a gothic romance—and I could feel the monsters moving in from the netherworld, getting restless, getting ready to strike. I took out one of my beleaguered cigarettes, lit it, and smoked it for real, thinking all the time that it was a good thing I didn't get myself involved in crime on any regular basis. If I did, smoking could become a habit.

Just past Kilithia, at the bottom of the rise that led to Pan's house, John stopped the Jeep.

"I'm going to drop you at the door," he said. "It would look odd if I didn't."

"It'll look odd if you don't come inside," I said. "Chas and Pan have known each other forever."

"I don't think Pan expects Chas to stop in for coffee," John said. "I don't think we ought to let Chas anywhere near the man, anyway. There's likely to be a whole new category of murder done."

"I might commit it myself."

"Keep your shirt on."

"Really?" I tried quirking an eyebrow at him. Since I'd never tried quirking an eyebrow before and didn't have access to a mirror now, I don't know how well I did. "That wasn't what you were saying last night."

He gave me a reproachful look, but it was

indulgent-reproachful, and I knew I'd done the right thing. "You won't reconsider and just stop at one of those houses in Kilithia without going up?"

"No. You're the one who said we shouldn't do anything odd to tip them off. What if Pan has changed the rules while I've been with you two? If I were him, I wouldn't let me near one of those boxes. What if I show up at one of the houses and find out he's told everyone not to let me in?"

"What if you do?"

"Then, if we're right, he'll know we're on to him. And we'll have the same problem we had before."

John sighed. "I used to tell myself I preferred smart women," he said. "You're making me wonder."

"If something's gone wrong, I'll find out about it at the house. Then we can replan."

"And do what?"

"Break in, of course."

He was about to give me another lecture, but at that moment the rain really started coming down, and instead, he got out of the driver's seat and began struggling with the canvas. By the time he had it up, Chas had woken up and neither one of us wanted to discuss this any more than we had to around Chas. Chas was rested and sleepy and calm today. He'd been all right the night before. He was not, however, good under pressure, and both John and I knew it.

"Oh God," Chas said, squinting through the windshield. "We're practically there."

"And mud season's back," I said cheerfully, climbing into the back. "You've been out like a light since we left Dyphos."

"Avoidance." Chas waved it away. "You'll be careful, right? That bastard has probably killed two people—"

"I'll be careful," I promised.

I lit another cigarette and wedged myself in so I wouldn't rock too much as the Jeep went uphill. I knew John and Chas both thought Pan was responsible for at least some of the deaths in this case. I even knew they had good reasons for their interpretation. I just couldn't make myself believe it. Chas had known Pan much longer than I had, but he hadn't as much time with him as I had. The man was a sleaze, and probably a dangerous sleaze, but he was also a coward. He hated confrontations, and he didn't have a strong stomach for blood. I could see Pan shooting at me from a safe distance, hidden in the bushes, imagining himself to be a dangerous international criminal. I could not see him stabbing the Greek Orthodox priest with a short-bladed knife many times. I couldn't see him stepping on that poor girl's neck, either. It would have required more contact than he liked and more finesse than he possessed. I wanted to believe Pan Peteris a villain as much as John and Chas did. After what Pan had done to Chas, I'd have liked to see Pan hung. I just couldn't make the deaths in Kilithia fit any pattern he might have a part in.

What I hadn't told John and Chas was that I couldn't make those deaths fit a pattern Costa Papageorgiou might have a part in, either. There was something wrong about the way that priest had been stabbed. It was too emotional, too spiteful, too *feminine*. What had happened to the girl was feminine, too, in a way—so neat and quick and small. Costa's violence came in great explosions of brutality, thundering, anarchic upheavals of destruction. He would beat you to a pulp in a fit of anger. He would not plot and plan and maneuver. He could do nothing quietly. I could see him tearing the basement apart. I could not see him stabbing a man over and over again with a little knife when he had use of his fists.

But what did I have? There was John's mysterious woman, of course, but I didn't have her. I had only Caliope who, I knew perfectly well, had never left New York. She came to the office every day, if only to chase after poor little Thanassis Papanicolau, who was just over from Greece and probably homosexual. I had only Marina, who was too old and too arthritic to fit the description of the woman in the bank. I had only Agapé, who was ignorant and illiterate and barely seventeen and who did not speak English. The available suspects were so hopeless, I hadn't bothered to mention my suspicions to John and Chas. And yet the suspicions persisted. There *was* something feminine about the planning and execution of everything that had happened since I'd come to Kilithia this time—old-fashioned feminine, Eastern feminine, built on the quicksand of the sly deceitfulness that had been the single most important tool of survival in the harem.

I lit another cigarette, took three drags, then opened a corner of the canvas and threw the cigarette into the mud. Normally, I am very careful about cigarettes. I don't leave them littering the ground in country or city, even if I have to put them out under my heel, wrap them in a Kleenex, and carry them around in my pocket for lack of a trash can to throw them in. This time, I wanted to do something, anything, to pay Pan back for what he'd done to Chas. Throwing a cigarette into the mud of his unpaved drive was a stupid and ineffectual thing to do, but it was all I had.

I closed the flap just as John was slowing to a stop in front of Pan's door.

"You're going to be careful," he said as he was vaulting himself out of his seat so that I could get by and out.

"I'm going to be careful," I promised.

"You have till five o'clock." He tapped his watch. "If you're not at the *kafenion* in Kilithia at five o'clock, we're coming in to get you."

"With guns blazing," I said lightly.

"Don't laugh. You might need it."

I looked away. The heating oil must have come in at Agios Constantinos. The electric lights were blazing, far brighter than they would have been if Pan had been relying on the government service. It relaxed me immeasurably to think the house would be well lit.

"Five o'clock," I repeated.

John turned me to him and searched my face. I could feel the beat of my blood getting stronger with every moment he looked at me, but I swallowed it. This was no time for that sort of thing.

"I'd kiss you"—he sighed—"except that I have the feeling it would be dangerous to let you-know-who see me do it."

They were at it when I walked into the house, screeching at each other in a steady, monotonous whine as if they'd never rested since the last time I'd heard them.

"Nasturtiums," Caliope was shouting, "make me sneeze. They make me sneeze! And what's more, they make my eyes red. And she knows it. That little high-box bitch knows perfectly well—"

I slammed the door behind me, pushing at it as hard as I could, so that it made a satisfying crash when it snapped into its lock. There was nobody in the foyer and I didn't want to see anybody, but I didn't want to be accused of sneaking, either. The Peterises were the kind of people who would accuse you of sneaking if you happened to turn up somewhere before they heard you coming. The fact that an elephant could have walked through the foyer without being heard over Caliope's needle-edged shrieks was beside the point.

At most, I'd expected Marina to detach herself from the insanity and come to see who had come in. I certainly had not expected to interrupt Caliope's tirade. Nothing ever interrupted Caliope's tirades back in New York, and there, she'd only been concerned with making sure everyone in the office paid her the "proper respect." That she should come to a complete halt in the middle of telling her brother's future wife just what she thought of her was mind-boggling. Still, come to a complete halt she did. Before I slammed the door, the house was all cries and wails and threats. After, it was silent.

I hesitated in the foyer, wondering what I ought to do. It should have been easy. I was supposed to do whatever I would have done if I hadn't been up to anything. Unfortunately, I couldn't remember what it was I would have done. Escape to my room? Wait patiently for Marina and Caliope and Agapé to emerge or to call me inside? Go looking for Pan?

I was still racking my brains for an answer when Pan came into the foyer, looking exhausted and strained and sweaty. I couldn't help feeling a little bubble of pleasure at the way those two harpies were wearing him out.

"Kerry," he said. "You're home."

"I'm home," I agreed, smiling a little. The smile was sheer nervousness. Pan was looking me up and down, over and over again, his eyes sharp with excitement. I didn't like it. I didn't like it at all.

I started edging toward the stairs. "I'm going up to change," I said. "Then I'll go out and do the count. It shouldn't take me long."

"The count," Pan said, nodding sagely. "Yes. Well, Kerry—"

"Yes?"

He coughed. He was weaving back and forth, putting his weight first on one foot and then on the other, like a small boy who needed permission to go to the bathroom. That was the way he always seemed to me—a great hulking brute of a person who'd never managed to become fully adult.

"Well," he said again. "I suppose you've had a long talk with Chas?" His voice rose to make the question, but he wasn't really questioning. He knew I must have had a long talk with Chas. He just wanted to know what I was going to do about it.

It was a relief to be as honest as I wanted and needed to be. "I've had a long talk with Chas," I agreed. "And as far as I'm concerned, you're an unalloyed, dyed-in-the-wool son of a bitch."

"Kerry, Kerry," Pan chided me.

"What do you expect me to say? I don't know what you're up to or what you're not up to and I don't want to know, but if Chas said he picked that package up from you, he did. And you let him go down. And he got arrested. And it's a damn miracle he's out and around now. As far as I'm concerned, you can shove your job, your magazine, and your entire existence up your ass and let it keep company with your head."

"Now, Kerry," Pan said.

There was a musical "ahem" from the far end of the foyer, and I looked up to see Marina coming into the hall. I blushed a little. I don't normally swear. I never got into the habit in college, and since then I'd been working with Greeks, who generally don't. I still carried a taboo in my head against swearing at all in front of older people, especially older women. I had no idea how much Marina had overheard. It was disconcerting to think she might have overheard everything.

211

"Excuse me," I said.

Marina waved it away. "You are upset," she said. "You have every reason to be upset."

"And I didn't tell Chas to pick up any package," Pan said righteously. "I know you're not going to believe me—"

"You're right, I'm not."

"—but I'm telling the truth anyway."

"Pan," I said. "You wouldn't know the truth from a banana."

We stood staring at each other in silence. Pan looked guilty, but he always looks a little guilty. Marina looked . . . remote. She seemed to have retreated far inside herself. It was a pose that should have reminded me of a saint or a mystic or at least the brooding heroines of Brontë novels. Instead, it reminded me of a computer. Her face was impassive, but I could hear the calculations going on behind it.

Caliope and Agapé slid into the foyer from the living room, with Costa Papageorgiou behind them. Caliope looked sullen and stolid, resentful of the existence of everyone and everything on earth except herself. Agapé was smirking—about what, I had no way of knowing.

Costa Papageorgiou looked like Costa Papageorgiou. It was enough. He always made me want to run.

I was standing in the foyer of Pan's squatter's palace, faced by three people I was sure had been involved not only in the robbery of the National Bank of Greece, but in at least four murders. The sweat that was running down my back made me feel like I'd backed into a hot tub. Coming back to Pan's house suddenly seemed like a very bad idea. Caliope and Agapé, uninvolved though they might be, were no friends of mine. What friends I did have on this island were I didn't know where. John had said only that he and Chas would stay out of sight. I began to back slowly toward the stairs, half convinced that Pan or Costa or even Marina would put out a hand to stop me.

Instead, Marina said, "She wants to take a shower and rest. Isn't that only natural?"

Pan seemed to snap to attention. "Of course," he said. He looked sideways at his mother. "I wasn't thinking."

"You seldom do," Marina said dryly. She hobbled to me, holding out her hands. "You go and rest, dear. You'll feel better in a few hours."

It was the perfect escape clause, and I almost took it. I needed to get to my room, into rain clothes, and out the door again if I was going to get hold of one of those offerings by five o'clock. Then I thought how odd it would look, sneaking out of the house when I'd said I was going to rest. It would be better to be as straight as possible. And there was a chance that going upstairs to rest would sound out of character, as turning up early would have been. It might be insufficiently loyal to my brother.

"I'm not going to rest," I said virtuously. "I don't have time. I'm not going to leave you in the lurch—I'll bring the specs for the magazine down and do the count for the shipment this afternoon—but after that, I'm going to go. I don't think I can stay here anymore."

Costa Papageorgiou started to say something, angrily and excitedly, in Greek. Marina waved him silent with a short, sharp gesture that belied the serenity of her smile. Costa was not easily reined. He stared at Marina resentfully, dangerously, as if he lacked only an excuse to strike.

"Now, now," Marina said. "I know how you must

feel, but you're being very impractical. You can't just walk out the door and call a taxi."

"I could phone for one," I said, "but I don't have to. Chas is picking me up at five o'clock."

Pan's eyes widened in alarm. "But you can't do that!" he shouted. "You can't—" Marina silenced him with another gesture. He settled himself uncomfortably, staring at the floor. "There's too much to do here," he mumbled. "The wedding—"

"Marina can handle the wedding," I said. "I never promised to run your personal life for you, Pan. I've been doing far too much of that in the past two years. I'm going to get the business things out of the way, and then I'm going to go."

"But—" Pan started again.

I was already on the first step. The atmosphere in the foyer had become intolerable to me. It was like a particularly dangerous pool, full of currents and crosscurrents, eddies and countereddies. I was in danger of being sucked under. Then Marina began to move again, the clumsiness of her arthritic gait making hollow sounds against the marble floor.

"Go," she said, patting me on the hand. "Do what you have to do. It will be all right."

I didn't hesitate. Before anyone could say anything else, before I could lose my nerve, I turned on my heel and started running to the second floor.

Underneath me, in the stairwell, Costa and Agapé stood together, watching. Costa's eyes were murderous. Agapé's were bright and dry and avid in a fever of anticipation.

I locked the door as soon as I got into my room, locked it and put a chair in front of it. I was shaking so badly I could hardly stand, and I was ready to kick myself. I'd been so damn cool at my dinner with John and Chas, so damn sure of my ability to prance in and out of Pan's house, and his affairs, with all the aplomb of Laura Holt from "Remington Steele." I should have known better. Outside my window, thunder crashed and roared, lightning electrified the sky in broad, thin sheets. It was the worst kind of weather. The rain was tapering off. The wind was rising. I knew Themnos in that mood. I hated it.

I got out a cigarette and lit it, dragging deeply, over and over again, until it made me cough. There's something so rational, so ordinary, so down-to-earth about a cough. I stared at the lit tip of the cigarette and wondered what I thought I was doing. Normally, a pack of cigarettes lasts me a month. I was going through this one in a matter of days.

If I was going to be any use at all, I would have to get myself in gear. I got up—I had been sitting on the floor, next to the wall, huddled over like one of the street vendors who sold their trinkets on the sidewalks of the poorer sections of Athens—and wandered to the bureau. I wouldn't have time to pack, only to change. I opened the second drawer and reached blindly for a clean pair of jeans. I came up with a button-down shirt instead.

It took me a minute to realize what had happened. I am not a neat person, but I am organized. If I put things away at all, I am very careful about where. Once I'd decided to pick everything off the floor, I had put my jeans in the second drawer, my underwear in the first, and my shirts and sweaters in the third and fourth respectively. I did not mix types of clothes. It created too much confusion in the morning, when I was barely awake and in no shape to go hunting for things.

I opened the top drawer. There was underwear in there, but there were also sweaters and the little zip-up bag where I kept the few pieces of jewelry I wore. The zip-up bag belonged on the night table.

Someone had gone through my drawers, every one of them. And moved things around, quite deliberately.

Someone had been there, and wanted me to know it.

19

I SHOULD HAVE stopped right there. John and Chas and I had discussed possible courses of action in case I was discovered, and I had agreed, with what I'd thought at the time was heartfelt conviction, that at the first sign that there might be any faint possibility that I might under any circumstances get in trouble, I would give up the entire project, sit docilely in my room, and wait for the cavalry to arrive at five o'clock. Somebody had been in my room. Somebody had moved my things around. Somebody wanted me to know it. I should have taken out my copy of *The Mysterious Affair at Styles,* settled down in bed, and read it. It was what I'd promised to do.

What I did instead was to go into overdrive, trying to get myself weatherproofed as quickly as I could manage it. There was one thing I hadn't thought of when I'd made my promises to John and Chas. If the Peterises thought I knew something, they must also think the project was in danger. If they thought the project was in danger, there was every chance they'd do something to protect it, like remove incriminating evidence. If the most of the village was in on this—and they'd have to be—they could get those boxes moved or sanitized in no time at all. Of course, if we

217

were right, they wouldn't want to do it. They had too much riding on that shipment going out as planned. On the other hand, they had even more riding on not getting caught. I had no way of knowing if whoever had moved the things in my room suspected me of knowing about the gold or the shipment. I was sure that if they suspected me of knowing about either, they'd do something about it.

My problem, I told myself, was Chas. I had never been clear on Chas's legal status, but I had some vague idea that if this project of John Borden's didn't work out, the United States government might charge Chas with something. Smuggling, I supposed. Whatever it was, I couldn't let it happen. Especially when I could prevent it just by taking a short walk across town.

I bundled myself into my rain poncho and let myself into the hall. There was a lock to my door—I even had a key—but I didn't see the point in using it. Marina probably also had a key. She would have had to. Marina was old and often sick. It wouldn't be hard for someone to get at her keys, even if they didn't want her to know about it. Besides, I didn't trust her. She could have planned this little farce in my room herself and sent Caliope and Agapé to do her work for her. Like John, I favored her as the mastermind of the whole gold-smuggling mess. Certainly, Pan could never have thought it up on his own. He didn't have the mental wherewithal for even this amateurish an effort. From what I'd heard about Marina's husband, he hadn't been much better. A big, bluff Greek with full honors in the fight against the Nazis and the Greek civil war, but with little intelligence. As far as I could tell (from village gossip and comments from Caliope, who had known her father better than Pan had), Marina, like most village girls, had married for sex rather than companionship. There are many intelligent Greek men. There are also many beautiful Greek men. As in most places, the two categories almost never overlap.

In John Borden, of course, the categories overlapped. But John Borden was different.

I kicked all thought of John Borden out of my mind with a feeling of exasperation that bordered on anger. I didn't have time to get mushy and sentimental and starry-eyed. I was making my way down the hall to the stairs. I could hear low, agitated voices on the floor below me. Two people were having an argument but doing their best to keep it down. I wanted to get out the door without anyone seeing me, something it would be impossible to do if the arguers were parked at the bottom of the stairs. Pan's house was all bright and shiny and modern and new. There weren't even any drainpipes to shimmy down.

I reached the head of the stairs and stopped, listening. Whoever was talking was not directly below me. I could see no one at the bottom of the stairwell. I could, however, hear. Were they in the foyer? Were they further away, with the acoustics against them?

I sat on the top step and waited.

"You were supposed to follow them," Marina was saying. "To follow them means to keep them in sight. You didn't understand that?"

"Of course I understood it." Costa Papageorgiou sounded ready to break that old woman's body in half. "I followed them. I've done everything you asked me, Kiria, everything, it's not my fault—"

"It's entirely your fault."

"I can't keep her in a cage. And I can't follow two men in an army-surplus Jeep when I'm on foot."

There was an angry, clicking sound—Marina snapping her olivewood worry beads. "Do you at least understand the situation is critical? They will be here at five o'clock. They will expect to take her with them."

"You should have let me—"

"Don't be ridiculous. It couldn't be done in the open like that. The vice-consul has been here. There is great influence."

"There's great influence with the other one, too. And I don't like speaking in English. She could hear."

"She's in her room. There are three girls here to clean. They could hear."

"They wouldn't care."

"They wouldn't keep their mouths shut, either. We can't have any of this near us, Costa. We can't have any of this touch us. That is important. We must make them disappear."

"I will make them disappear."

"How?"

"When they come at five o'clock, we'll invite them in—"

"They won't come."

"We won't let her out unless they come in."

"They still won't come. They will go to Agios Constantinos and call the vice-consul."

"We'll tell them we'll kill her if they go."

"Yes? And if that works? What will we do about the Jeep? What will we do about that new priest—" There was a stream of Greek that I didn't understand. Then there was a crashing sound, as if someone had tipped over a pail. The Greek stopped. "An American priest. To send an American priest."

"It's just for the funeral. He'll be gone in a day or two—"

"We don't have a day or two. That girl, that girl. I

220

can't stand the thought of that girl. That pious, hypocritical, sanctimonious little whore."

"Well." Costa's voice was bland, but I could hear the smug maliciousness underneath. I realized with a shock that Costa hated Marina Peteris, hated her with a lively and personal viciousness that was rendered impotent only by his need of her. She was bringing him gold. If she hadn't been, he would have found an excuse to do her harm. "Yes," Costa said. "She was a very pious girl. She should have gone away to a convent. You should have paid for that, Kiria. It would have saved us many problems."

Marina dismissed this. "I would have had to start paying when she was a child. How were we to know what she was when she was a child? Why should she have been any different than any other child?"

"Why should she have grown up to spill all her sins to a priest?"

There was a little silence. When Marina's voice came again, it was sly, needling, oddly triumphant.

"She can't get away with it this time, you know. He wasn't here. I have proof of that. Not the old proof. New proof. Real proof. Solid. Everything else you could have put on him, but not this."

"I'm not trying to put anything on him. Or on you, Kiria."

"Oh yes you are. I know what you're doing. I've known it from the beginning. Put it out of your mind, Costa. You have work to do."

"I have to make them disappear."

"Help me upstairs. I'm going to rest."

"And if she goes out to check the shipment?"

"Stop her."

I heard steps on the stairs and began to retreat, too fast and with too little thought. I should have gone back to my room. That was where they expected me to be, and I couldn't get into trouble by being there. As I said, I wasn't thinking. *If she goes out to check the shipment, stop her.* That was clear enough, and it scared me to death. I knew exactly how Costa would like to stop me. He had certainly been talking about killing me—and John and Chas—when I first began to overhear the conversation. I should have been immobilized, but I wasn't. There was no surprise in any of this. Five people were already dead. What else should I have suspected but that, faced with unwanted interference, they should decide to kill a few more. My putative relationship with the vice-consul was the only thing saving me from being summarily dispatched. Even that wouldn't save my life. Marina would be perfectly happy to see me dead. She just thought the murder of a woman with "influence" required more care, more planning, than the removal of a pious peasant girl. That gave me time, but no other advantage.

Marina and Costa were advancing more quickly than I'd expected, taking into account Marina's arthritis. I looked frantically around for somewhere to hide. I wasn't worried they'd realize I'd overheard their conversation. I had backed up far enough along the hall to make that seem unlikely. I was worried they'd try to do something to keep me in my room—like tie me up and lock me in.

I pulled open the nearest door I could find, discovered a linen closet, and stuffed myself inside, on the bottom, under the lowest shelf. I just about fit. If I'd had the height I'd always wanted, I'd never have been able to get myself in there.

I pulled the door shut and waited. No, all that talk about killing me hadn't been a surprise, but the rest of the conversation had. I now had the real motives behind the killing of the second priest and the girl, and they made beautiful sense. Costa was right. It would have been much better for the Peterises to have paid that girl's dowry at a convent. Involving a pious Greek Orthodox in a scheme like this one, where murder had been done and would continue to be done, was asking for disaster. If the girl had made a regular ritual of personal confession—which is practiced in the Orthodox Church, but not popular—she had probably been close to a fanatic. Even if she had made only that one confession, pouring out her part in the smuggling and her knowledge of the circumstances of the death of the old priest (or her suppositions), it would have been enough. The new priest would have been alerted. Expecting, as all Greek priests do, to be the center of anything happening in the village in whose church they preside, he would not have let it rest.

As for the rest of it, I couldn't work my way through the confusion of pronouns. All those *he's* and *she's* seemed to switch at random. Costa and Marina knew what they were talking about because they knew the context. I couldn't even guess. *He* could not be held responsible for something, because Marina could prove—what? I didn't know. *She* was going to get stuck with it this time, but I didn't know who *she* was or what it was she could be stuck with. I had a vague feeling that the *she* in question was Agapé, but that only made everything even more confusing. I knew all there was to know about Agapé. She was a peasant Greek without the brains to tie her shoelaces without help and with the self-involved myopia of a Manhattan apartment cat. I had dealt with Agapé for months. I had suffered through her marriage negotiations. The only kind of trouble I could imagine her getting into would be with a man, and although she was stupid, she was also shrewd. She wouldn't have pulled something like that in a village the size of Kilithia on the eve of her wedding to a rich man.

And yet, there was *something*.

I huddled in the closet and tried to think. That *something* had been coming up, on and off, ever since John and Chas had told me what was going on. No, from before that—was that possible? I closed my eyes tight and made myself think. Something, something, something. Something wrong. Something off. Something I knew. I chased the phantom around in my head, never catching it.

I could hear them now, outside in the hall. They had reached the top of the stairs and were moving slowly toward me. Marina's room was at the far end of the hall. They would have to pass the linen closet to get to it. I held my breath. Marina was going on and on about something, her voice a monotonous murmur under the rumble of thunder. I heard Greek words and English ones, as if she were mixing her languages like a bilingual child.

Costa was speaking only English, mostly profanity. He used profanity the way most people used nouns.

They stopped talking. They stopped moving, too. Marina's step was heavy and arrhythmic. One minute it was moving closer to me, the next it was still. I bit my lip and wondered what they were doing out there.

"Wait," Marina said. "Maybe we should see how she's coming along."

"What for?"

There was another short silence. I wanted to scream. What would they do when they found I wasn't in my room? And just where in the hall were they? They couldn't be outside my bedroom door, because they were talking in normal voices, not expecting to be overheard. On the other hand, I could now hear them clearly, with none of the muffle effect I'd been getting a few moments before. They had to have come past my bedroom, closer to the linen closet. For all I knew, they were standing right on the other side of the door.

"It is possible," Marina said, "we are going to a lot of trouble for nothing."

"Nothing? The last thing she wants to do before she leaves is get a look at that shipment. You call that nothing?"

Marina clicked. "Americans are not like Greeks. They're very conscientious about their work. Kerry is especially so."

"So conscientious she'd do a job for a man she thinks betrayed her own brother?"

"Americans are not like Greeks that way, either." Marina started swinging her worry beads again. "It is hard to tell. They will go without sleep to get a job finished. They will go without food. They will cancel plans—put off visits to their families, go away late on vacations. And they do not believe in letting emotions . . . interfere."

"Women are nothing but emotions."

"And men are nothing but what they have in their pants. We will go and see. It cannot hurt us."

I heard them moving away from me again. By then, I was ready to do more than scream. I wanted to break something. The tension was unbearable. They were so close. They were about to have good reason for suspicion. I felt like a complete jerk. If I'd only had sense enough to go to my room instead of cornering myself in this ludicrous position in a linen closet, I might have been able to convince Marina I was innocuous. And thereby give myself more time.

They stopped moving again. I heard the sharp cracks that had to be Marina knocking on my bedroom door.

"Kerry?"

Of course there was no answer. There couldn't have been. I was disporting myself among the sheets and pillowcases.

"Kerry?" Marina spoke more loudly this time, as if she thought I might be asleep.

"Maybe she's gone to the can," Costa said.

"Look for yourself. The door to the facility is open." Her worry beads rapped together impatiently. "We will go in, Costa. Open the door."

This time I bit my lip hard enough to draw blood.

Outside in the hall, I heard the rattle of the doorknob, the creak of the hinges. No amount of daily oiling, no matter how meticulous, would ever make those hinges silent. The extremes of temperature, the wild jumps in barometric pressure, would make the wood swell and shrink around the metal until the warp was as wild and ungovernable as Themnos Mountain.

I counted very slowly to ten. It helped keep me from moving.

"For Christ's sake," Costa said. "Where could she have gone? We were standing right next to the front door."

"Out," Marina said harshly. "She has gone out. Through a window, through the servants' entrance, it doesn't matter."

"To look at the boxes," Costa said.

"Or to get something from them. Yes." Marina's

worry beads were clicking away, clicking and clicking and clicking, driving me mad.

"Get Pan," she said finally. "Both of you go. Find her. And when you find her—"

The rest was in Greek, but I didn't have to be a linguist to get the gist of it. If Marina had her way, I was as good as dead.

I MIGHT HAVE gotten out of that closet five minutes earlier than I did and saved myself and everyone else a lot of trouble later if it hadn't been for Caliope and Agapé. Costa and Marina were in the hall, making their way to Marina's bedroom. I had to allow enough time for Marina to get settled and Costa to leave. After that, the hall would be clear and I would be able to leave the closet. I had no idea where I was going to go. Marina had said something about a servants' entrance, but I didn't know where that was. As for windows, the suggestion made me think the old woman was going senile. I'd thought about jumping out a second-floor window once before on this trip and had come to the conclusion that all it was likely to get me was a broken leg or a broken neck. There are very few trees on an island like Themnos. There are very few trees, as Americans and western Europeans understand the word, anywhere in Greece. The few sickly plants that managed to grow near the walls of Pan's house would never hold my weight. They looked as if they would break in two on my first attempt to climb down them.

Agapé and Caliope started just as Costa and Marina reached Marina's bedroom door. The timing was so perfect, I would have thought they'd planned it if I hadn't known that the decision to "find" me had been made a few inches from my ear only minutes before the commotion started downstairs.

"You'll have to open the door for me," Marina said. "My hands—"

I never did find out what was wrong with her hands, although I could guess. There was a clatter and crash underneath me, the sound of another of those plaster statues meeting its doom, and Caliope screamed, "You're trying to *murder* me. You're trying to *murder* me. You little *bitch.*"

I wanted to weep. I'm not exaggerating when I say Caliope screamed. She'd passed some kind of point of no return in hysterics. Her voice was as high and shrill and *loud* as that whine you're supposed to hear before a bomb falls. It filled the second-floor hall. I couldn't hear voices. I couldn't hear footsteps. I couldn't hear myself think.

Agapé's voice, when it came, was no less obstructive. She didn't have Caliope's range—her voice was low and hoarse, a whiskey-and-cigarette voice—but she made up for it in volume. She bellowed. The stream of incomprehensible Greek came on like the pounding of horses' hooves in an ancient western movie. She even managed to drown out the thunder.

"Don't call *me* a whore, you cheap-jack *cunt,*" Caliope screamed. Again. It seemed like Caliope was going to go on screaming all day. "Nobody has to tell me what a Christless little—"

"Skata," Costa roared.

They must have heard him downstairs. He had the advantage of height, weight, and experience. He sounded like a large wild animal. The war paused mid-sentence.

In the lull, I heard Costa say, "I'll have to take care of them first. I'm always having to take care of them."

"Take care of your own," Marina said. "Nobody's worried about Caliope."

"I'm not worried about Agapé," Costa said. He let out a snort, an aborted laugh. "Maybe I'm the only one who isn't."

Downstairs, they'd apparently decided Costa was a mirage. Agapé's voice rose in a shriek—no words, just shriek, in curious imitation of the wailing women— that went on and on until I thought it was going to crack my head open.

Caliope screamed, "You're trying to *murder* me. You're trying to *murder* me. You're trying to break my *eardrums.*"

It might have been all right if Costa had come past the linen closet on his way downstairs, but he didn't. Costa was a big man. I would have felt the vibrations of the floor shaking as he went by, if nothing else. Instead, he just disappeared. There was probably something—the servants' stairs?—on the far end of the hall that I didn't know about. Unfortunately, there was something else I didn't know: whether Marina's door was open or closed. I hadn't heard it close, but I couldn't hear much of anything in all that craziness.

"I'm going to break this over your head, you little bitch," Caliope screamed. "I'm going to open your skull, you little cunt."

I hugged my knees closer to my chest. I'd never had the least inclination to explore Pan's house. I hadn't even paid attention when the architect lectured me about it. I'd considered it an exercise in unbridled vulgarity and beneath my notice. I was ready to kill myself for my snobbishness. If I'd allowed free rein to

my normal curiosity, I'd know what was on the other
end of the hall. I might even know a few ways out of
the house that Marina and Costa and Pan wouldn't
think of.

Costa's voice rose from the floor beneath my feet,
pounding out an angry wave of Greek that drowned
out the higher-pitched contributions of the other two.
I relaxed a little. Costa was downstairs. Marina was
upstairs, but she was an old woman. She was sick and
she didn't move well. Even if she saw me, I might be
able to get past her fast enough to escape before she
had the presence of mind to call out.

"Don't stick up for her," Caliope yelled. "I don't
care if you *are* her father, you know what she is—"

I reached very slowly for the doorknob, nearly
dislocating my shoulder in the process. I had no idea
how long I'd been in that closet. It felt like forever. I
had thought that kind of feeling was illusion. Now,
considering the way my joints creaked and my muscles were frozen in place, I wondered.

I turned the knob, meaning to pop the door open
just a crack, but my wrists were too stiff. I couldn't
keep the knob in my hold. It popped out of its groove,
propelled by the tension created by the warp in the
wood and the weight of my body against the door, and
swung open into the hall.

It swung too far. I couldn't just reach out and pull it
closed again. My safety was gone. Anyone coming
along the hall would see me, crouched like the puppet
in a jack-in-the-box under the bottom shelf of that
linen closet.

And what would *anyone* be doing crouched under
the bottom shelf of a linen closet?

I told myself it was probably time to move. I
couldn't stay in the linen closet. Eventually, when

they'd searched Kilithia and found no one who'd seen me, they'd start to search the house. It might take them a while to think of looking in closets, but it wouldn't take them forever. I had to get out of Pan's house and go—where?

It suddenly occurred to me that I had no idea where I was supposed to go. John and Chas should be warned off. It wasn't safe for them to come here. But I didn't know where they were, and I couldn't think of a single hiding place along any route they were likely to take to reach the house. The road workers and pavers and builders had laid waste the hill between Pan's house and Kilithia proper. The driveway might never have been surfaced, but the brush had been all but exterminated. There was hardly as much as a weed out there for me to hide behind. I couldn't hide in Kilithia, either. I didn't know who was in on this and who was not. Even if I had known, I couldn't predict which of the winding, tortuous side streets John and Chas would use on their way in.

I thought about my father, who always said my life was a series of disastrous choices that I forced on myself by procrastination. I thought about how nice it would be to prove him wrong, just once. I did not think about how frightened I was. If I let myself think about my rolling stomach or my pounding head or the way my heart felt ready to explode, I would be paralyzed.

Downstairs, the war had slid into truce mode, at least momentarily. There was no more shouting and no more screaming and no more crashing plaster. The house was almost too quiet.

I crawled out of the linen closet and tried to stand. It was very hard at first. All my muscles were cramped, and my joints ached in a way that gave me new sympathy for Marina's fight with arthritis. It was also hard to see. The weather front that had been rolling in when John and Chas and I drove up from Dyphos had arrived. Through the window at the far end of the hall, I could see the sky, black and angry in the middle of the afternoon. There was no rain, but there *was* wind, wild and hard and angry. I could feel it pushing against the walls of the house, trying to bring the building down.

I squinted into the darkness in the general direction of Marina's door: nothing. Marina's room might as well have been on another planet. I hesitated. It would be dangerous to pass Marina's door if it was still open, but it would probably be more dangerous to try to leave through the foyer. Caliope and Agapé were quiet, but that didn't mean they had gone. They could easily be sitting in the living room, staring at each other and sharpening their claws for another round.

I started, as slowly and carefully and quietly as I could, toward the far end of the hall. There *had* to be a way out there. Costa hadn't come past me to get downstairs. The problem was, I didn't know where that way out might lead—kitchen? laundry? pantry? —or who might be there waiting.

I passed Marina's door without breathing. It was shut. On the other side of it, the hall did a zigzag and a one-step dip that ended in a small platform. The platform was the top of a narrow flight of stairs.

I was so relieved, I damn near cheered. I think part of me had believed, in all that long slide down the hall, that I would reach the end and find nothing but a blank wall. I wanted to run down the stairs with no concern for the noise I made and no thought for my possible pursuers—just to run and run and run until I was out in the air and free. I think I must have been delirious. Even if I'd made it outside, the danger wouldn't have been over. It would have just been beginning.

It was footsteps in the hall that brought me to my senses—running footsteps. They came right toward me, pounding against the carpet, as free and unfettered as I'd wanted to be. They came so close, they knocked all the exhilaration out of me. I thought whoever it was, was going to come straight to my end of the hall and start down the very stairs where I was hiding. Then the footsteps stopped and I heard fists pounding against a wooden door.

"Kiria Peteris," Costa shouted. "Kiria Peteris."

"Endaxi," Marina said, her voice thin and querulous. *"Endaxi."*

Costa started ranting away in Greek, tripping over his words, pounding on the door. I heard John's name twice and Chas's once. That stopped me. Was it five o'clock already? Had they come, and been caught?

There was no way for me to find out. Marina and Costa were speaking only Greek now, and all I could catch were names. John. Chas. Agapé. Marina had quite a bit to say about Agapé. It made Costa sullen and defensive, if I could judge by intonation. He sounded like a little boy who expected to be praised for winning the sandlot baseball game, only to have his mother scold him for the state of his clothes instead.

"Deal with her," Marina said in English. "Get her under control. Now."

Costa swore.

Usually, Marina did not put up with bad language. To swear at her was to invite a lecture. This time she didn't bother. I heard her door shut, a little harder than necessary.

Costa swore again.

I stayed very still, wondering if he would come toward me and what I could do about it if he did. Every other part of the house was full of statues I could have used for weapons. This section, being for the use of domestics, was bare. Fortunately, Costa turned away and went toward the stairs to the foyer. If he hadn't, he would have fallen right over me.

It was not the kind of thing I wanted to think about when I was a hairsbreadth away from panic.

It took me a long time to find my way downstairs. It shouldn't have. The house was not all that badly laid out. The floor plan was rational enough. The back stairs led to a small open area that opened on three narrow halls, one to the pantry, one to the laundry, and one to the kitchen. So far, my predictions had been accurate. The trouble was, I didn't know which hall led where, although I did know there was no access to the outside from either the laundry or the pantry. To get free, I'd have to find my way to the kitchen.

I took my first wrong turn because it was the hallway farthest from the shouting. Two people—it sounded like Costa and Agapé—were having a knock-down-drag-out fight at the end of the first hallway to the left. I took the first hallway to the right to get as far away from it as possible. I ended up with sixty-six cans of Green Giant baby peas, thirty cans of niblets corn, and two dozen boxes of Sugar Smacks, all imported from the States. In California, it would have been enough to give Pan a shot at the Junk Food Defense.

Somehow, the sight of all that processed food restored my sanity. It was just so funny, so ordinarily, mundanely funny, the detail of a world where people did not steal six million dollars in gold and kill off anybody who got in the way of their keeping it. I picked up cans and put them down, even opened a box of Sugar Smacks and ate some. It did wonders for my nerves.

When I thought I'd calmed down enough to think straight again—I was appalled at the way I'd been behaving, with so little calculation in my movements that I might have been asking to be caught—I went back to the open space. The argument was over. Agapé was humming to herself. Her voice was cool and clear, even at that distance. I hesitated again. It was unlikely that Agapé would be in the laundry. A girl came in from the village to do the clothes, and as a rich man's fiancée, that work would have been considered beneath Agapé. She had to be in the kitchen, and the kitchen was where I wanted to go.

I considered going back to the pantry or into the laundry to wait until the coast was clear. I didn't like it. There was nowhere to hide in the pantry. There might be nowhere to hide in the laundry, either. And how would I know the coast was clear? I couldn't keep coming out to the open space to listen. I was too likely to be discovered.

I slipped into the hall to the kitchen, closer to Agapé and I didn't know who else. I had John and Chas to think about. Costa had been saying *something* about them upstairs, and he'd been excited. I didn't put it past that man to kill them first and make his apologies to Marina later. I didn't think he'd done it—if he had, Marina would probably have gone through the roof—but I didn't think it would be long before he did, either. John and Chas had to be either in or near the house. Costa had found them, or found out about them, before he'd gone out. Now I had to find them before he ran into them again.

I stopped just inside the arch that opened onto the kitchen. I would have preferred to meet up with nobody at all. If I had to run into somebody, though, Agapé would be the best choice. She was the only one besides Marina who was smaller than I was, and she had none of Marina's strength of mind. With surprise and height on my side, I would have a good shot at overpowering her if I had to.

She was standing near the sink, playing with her crystal. There were rows and rows of it on the counter, every glass washed and polished until it gleamed in the faint light of Pan's ultra-modern fluorescents. There was something else, too. There was a phone.

I drew in my breath sharply. I'd forgotten entirely about the phone. I'd been coming to Kilithia for two years. I'd learned early to banish futile longings for the convenience of a phone the moment I stepped into the village. Nobody in Kilithia had a phone.

Except, of course, for Pan. Pan had paid to have the cable laid, had imported instruments from Athens, had bribed a dozen Greek officials to get the house put on line in Agios Constantinos. The system hadn't been working when I first arrived, but it might be by now. If it was, I could call that policeman in Agios Constantinos and tell him what was happening.

What, exactly, was happening? I dismissed it. I would lie if I had to. It wouldn't matter as long as I could get that man up here.

The arch jutted out a little from the wall, and I plastered myself behind it, praying I hadn't gained any weight since coming to Greece this time. There wasn't much cover, and I wasn't an anorectic in any case.

As it turned out, it didn't matter. Agapé never looked in my direction. She polished crystal and hummed and took more crystal out of boxes, but if she got distracted, it was by something out the window. She spent some time looking at the weather, even talking to it, and once or twice she tapped her finger against the pane.

Somebody must have been out there. I was beginning to look frantically for a weapon, something I could hit her over the head with, when she suddenly went erect and leaned forward to press her face against the window glass. She had to pull herself up on the sink to do it. She dangled there for a moment, her feet in the air, then jumped down and headed for the outside door. I heard it open against the wind, then slam closed.

It was such a surprise to get exactly what I wanted, I had a hard time taking advantage of it. If I'd been faster, things might have turned out differently. As it was, I wasted precious minutes staring in stupefaction at the empty kitchen, wondering how I'd ever earned such luck.

When I got myself moving again, I went almost too fast. I stumbled twice getting to the phone, and there was nothing in my way. Then, with my hand on the receiver, I hesitated again. There was every chance in the world the line would be dead. I didn't want to face it.

I picked up the receiver and held it to my ear. The line buzzed, hummed, cleared. An impatient, contemptuous female voice said, *"Embross."*

Embross is the way people answer the phone in Greece. It means: start! get going! talk! Greeks are the only people I've ever heard of who can talk in a situation like that. I stared at the phone, wondering what I was supposed to say. The female voice came back on line.

"Embross," she said again, and let out a jumble of

Greek I couldn't have understood if I'd been damn near fluent.

I got myself together. "Agios Constantinos," I said, scrambling after what little phrase-book Greek I had. *"Politsia. Kiriou Louganis. Politsia."*

There was a snap on the line I would have sworn was bubble gum being cracked. Then there was a hum and another crackle and another long minute of dead air.

A male voice said, *"Embross."*

I had hold of my pitiful few words of Greek, and I wasn't about to let them go. *"Politsia?"* I said.

"Nai," he said. *Nai* is the Greek word for *yes.*

"Kiriou Louganis," I said. I didn't have the word for *emergency.* I had to rely on my voice. If it sounded half as frightened as I felt, I'd be put through without any trouble.

There was another hum on the line and another buzz and another long, clear silence. I thought I was going crazy.

"Kiriou Louganis," I said desperately. "Kiriou—"

"Nai," a voice said, sounding impatient and exasperated and oh, so beautifully familiar. I nearly passed out right there, in the middle of whatever speech the man was making.

"Listen," I said, interrupting him. "Listen, Kiriou Louganis, this is Kerry Hansen and I—"

I never got farther. I felt the prick in my ribs and someone's breath on my cheek, and whirled so quickly I dropped the phone. I'd expected anyone and anything but Agapé. She'd gone out the kitchen door. I was sure I'd have heard her come in again. Well, I hadn't. She was there and she had a knife and she was smiling. Her eyes were as bright and feverish as they'd been the night of the procession to the cemetery.

Costa was there, too. I'd been less than four feet

from him, and I'd never noticed. He was messily, bloodily dead, his chest pockmarked with stab wounds, the shreds that were all that was left of his shirt stained a bright, wet red. I wanted to be sick.

"Agapé," I said.

She picked up the phone and put it back in its cradle, cutting my lifeline to Agios Constantinos.

"We don't have phones in Kilithia," she said in perfect, if heavily accented, English. "They're not good for us."

It came together then, that *something* I had never been able to get out of my mind. Of course Agapé spoke English. I'd heard her before, when I was half asleep, and because I was half asleep and it was something I'd thought couldn't be true, I'd put it out of my mind. "This bloated board without a knothole," Agapé had called Caliope, and I'd heard her. They'd been screaming, as usual. I'd been in my room, with the door closed. Their argument had woken me up.

The morning of the day I left for Dyphos.

"Marina is going to be very angry with me," Agapé said. "She likes everything done with finesse. And I have no finesse. I like to go . . . right to the heart of things."

She was prodding me with the tip of her short-bladed knife, a country knife like the ones the shepherds use to cut burrs from the feet of their sheep during the long summer grazing. I backed away from it instinctively, unable to think of anything but what an idiot I'd been. I should have suspected Agapé might speak English even if I'd never heard her and everyone told me she couldn't. Costa had been able to speak English. Costa, her father, whom she had killed.

She had backed me to a far wall, near a door. I

didn't know where it opened or what was behind it, but I was plotting a way to go through it anyway. This woman wanted to kill me. In fact, she would enjoy killing me. The only chance I had now was to run.

She pushed the knife against my ribs again. This time, the blade went through the cloth and cut me.

I grabbed the doorknob, twisted, and pulled.

Looking back on it, I don't think I would have gotten away with it. She was crazy, and shameless. She wouldn't have cared how much noise I made or what kind of spectacle we produced, chasing each other through the streets of Kilithia. She would have had the advantage, as well, of knowing that the door did not lead outside. The only reason I'm alive is that I never got a chance to make my stupid move and she never got a chance to catch me at it.

I had the door wide open when we heard steps coming down the hall from the living room. It was Marina, leaning heavily on her cane, swearing and mumbling as she made her way toward me. I was ready to faint from fright. Marina was no friend of mine. Fortunately, she wasn't a friend of Agapé's, either. The girl's face drained of all color. She looked terrified.

"Agapé," Marina called. "Agapé, *pithakim.*"

Pithakim is a term of endearment in Greek, but it didn't sound like one the way Marina said it. Agapé panicked. The open door yawned at my back and she pushed me toward it, shoved me with more force than I'd have thought she could muster, and once I was past it, she slammed the door in my face.

It wasn't in my face for long. What was behind that door was a flight of stairs going down, and I fell. I fell and fell and fell, tumbling over and over, hitting my head repeatedly on the wooden steps. I hit the bottom in a clatter of wood and metal, disturbing unknown inhabitants of an alien place.

I had just enough time, before I passed out, to get my eyes adjusted to the lack of light and note that I was in an unfinished basement and realize that John Borden was in there with me.

21

HE HAD MANAGED to work his gag off by the time I came to. He hadn't been able to do much else. When I opened my eyes, I was staring at the ceiling. I stared at it for quite some time before I started to remember things. The first thing I remembered was that I had fallen and hit my head and passed out. Head wounds, especially those severe enough to make you lose consciousness, are tricky. They can be nothing at all or very, very dangerous. They can cause hematomas and embolisms and heaven knows what else. Anyone who has one should be taken to a hospital immediately.

The next thing I remembered was why a trip to the hospital was unlikely to take place immediately—and never mind the fact the Themnos doesn't have a hospital. I tried to think it through. I remembered Costa on the floor and Agapé with the knife in her hands. There was blood all over Agapé's skirt. I hadn't noticed that until she'd come close. She was wearing a peasant skirt, one of those brightly embroidered things. At a distance, the red of the blood blended with the red of the flowered vine along the hem, looking like part of the pattern.

I turned my head, very slowly. With all the rest of

the remembering I'd been doing, I'd also remembered that I was going to have to do a lot of things a person with a recent blow to the head shouldn't do, but it seemed sensible to postpone self-endangerment as long as possible.

"John?" I said.

He was sitting in a corner, his hands tied behind him, his legs tied together in front of him, a black kerchief hanging around his neck. When I'd come falling down the stairs, the kerchief had been partly stuffed into his mouth and partly wrapped around his head—tied at the back, I supposed. It was one of the big net ones that widows wore.

"John?" I said again.

"I'm here," he said. "Thank God. I thought you'd broken your neck."

"No." I sat up. It took me a long time. I was still afraid to make any sudden move, and every muscle in my body felt bruised. "I ache," I said finally, "but I don't think I broke anything."

"You should hire yourself out to the movies," John said. "A stunt man who could take a fall like that and live to tell about it would make a fortune."

"Stunt person," I said.

"What?"

"Stunt *person.*"

"Oh, for God's sake." He started to hobble his way toward me.

I got up and went toward him. He could have made it to me, but his wrists would have been cut to ribbons by the ropes, and we were in enough trouble already. I stopped him mid-hobble and made him lean forward, giving me better access to the knots. They looked like they'd been tied by a child. The rope ends had been pulled together repeatedly, in no particular pattern and no particular shape.

"You're right," I said. "They are amateurs. If my Girl Scout leader ever saw this, she'd faint away."

John cleared his throat uncomfortably. "Listen," he said. "Don't get upset. I mean, don't get any more upset than you are now. But we have a problem."

"News you can use," I said irritably. "Starting with the fact that there's a dead body in the kitchen."

John's body jerked under my hands. "Whose?" He was almost shouting.

"Sit still," I told him. "I've got to get you out of here. I haven't got the faintest idea what to do in a situation like this."

"Neither do I at the moment. Kerry, who—"

"Costa Papageorgiou," I said. I got the last knot with a violent tug in a direction that shouldn't have helped, but did, and pulled the ropes away from his hands. Even in the present extremity, I couldn't help noticing what nice hands they were. He brought them to the front of his body and began flexing the pain out of them. Surgeon's hands. Safecracker's hands. Who cared?

"Agapé killed him," I went on, going to work on the ropes around his legs. He still got a pained look on his face every time he moved his fingers. "I found him on the kitchen floor and she had a knife and blood all over her." I gave him as quick a rundown as I could of what I'd thought had happened, ending with her pushing me down the stairs. "Which is the last thing I remember, because I think I got knocked out," I said.

"Of course you got knocked out."

"Of course I got knocked out," I agreed. I sat back and let him go to work on his leg ropes himself. My initial reading of him had been accurate. He was not a person who could comfortably be passive.

"We'll have to get you to a hospital as soon as we can," he said, picking at the knots. "Though when

245

that's going to be, I don't know. The nearest hospital is in Rhodes, but there's an American doctor on Malina who takes care of the consulate staff. In the meantime—" He looked into my eyes. "Kerry, don't panic, all right? But I don't know where Chas is."

I don't know what hit me first—guilt, because I'd been so relieved to find John alive and untouched by Agapé's knife that I'd forgotten all about Chas; or terror, because Chas at the hands of Marina and the rest of them was dead meat. If he wasn't dead already.

"Did they separate you?" I asked John. "Put you down here and take him—"

"They didn't take him anywhere," John said. "At least, not as far as I know. We weren't together."

"Not together?" I tried to think this through and came up with a muddle. "But you were supposed to be together," I said lamely. "You were going off together and then you were coming back together to get me. At five o'clock."

"I was trying to head you off at the pass." John picked angrily at the last of the knots, the one near his ankles. It was a mess. He'd been working on it for minutes and hadn't been able to make it budge. "We were in the village," he explained, "and we talked to this new priest, this American—"

"I heard Marina and Costa talking about him," I said. "He's only temporary."

"Very temporary," John agreed. "He's going to do the funeral, say the service Sunday, and go back to Athens. He's only doing this as a favor to somebody, to begin with. Anyway, Chas and I were at the church when we saw Pan going in and out of those little houses they build in the sides of the hills. You were right and you were wrong, Kerry. They made the gold into offerings, gold replicas of tin replicas of gold offerings, but the damn things weren't being kept in the boxes the people in the houses had."

"Then where are they?"

"I don't know."

"I don't, either. But, John, if they weren't there, it wouldn't have been dangerous for me to go, would it?"

"More dangerous than you'll ever know. It wasn't the gold they didn't want you to find. It was the boxes. You'd have gotten a kick out of the boxes."

"Why?"

"They were marked *Skoulouris Importing,* for one thing. They were dated today instead of next Tuesday, for another. They had a point of origin that said Samothraki, which is on the other side of the peninsula, for a third. And they had a brand-new destination. Zurich."

"Oh boy," I said. "Pan found a partner."

"I'd guess Marina found him. And some partner. According to my information, Skoulouris is the biggest crime lord in Greece. Not much compared to some of his competition, but not bad, either. He's been paying off half the government for years."

"And he's got connections in Zurich."

"Right. And I'm in a lot of trouble, because once that stuff is no longer destined to enter the United States, it's supposed to be none of my business."

"Oh well," I said. "They couldn't hold you to that."

"Oh yes they could. We got into a lot of trouble in this part of the world in the Nixon years. The CIA came in with *carte blanche* and they got stupid. Or worse. Mostly worse. They insulted people. They treated heads of governments like office boys. They nearly sent both Greece and Italy into the arms of the Soviets, because nobody had ever taught them any manners and nobody had ever tested them out to see if they were psychopaths. The policy right now is hands off unless we've got a damn good reason for doing otherwise. And even then, we're supposed to work under the direction of the local authorities as much as possible."

"Well, you can't do any of that now," I said. "You'd get yourself killed. You'd get us all killed."

"I know that."

"And what about Chas? Where did he go?"

"I don't *know* where he went. I was coming to get you, and he was going to take the Jeep and hide somewhere safe. Then, if I hadn't come back in an hour, he was supposed to bring in the cavalry."

"Come himself?" I asked, appalled.

"I was hoping he'd head for Agios Constantinos and get Louganis." He saw the look on my face and shrugged. "We're trying not to interfere, but that doesn't mean we're not keeping an eye on things. Louganis is on the A-list. He's as clean as Ivory Snow."

I sat back on my heels and tried to think. "Did you tell him that?" I asked. "Did you tell him to go into Agios Constantinos—"

"I suggested it, but I didn't make it hard and fast. I couldn't make it hard and fast. I didn't know what was going to happen."

"Oh, fine," I said miserably. "John, Chas is a space cadet. The only thing he's ever been able to get straight in his life is academics. He—"

"I know, I know," John soothed. He put his hand on my hair and stroked my head. The gesture was meant to be comforting, but it was mostly distracting.

I let myself be distracted. Until that moment, I don't think I realized how tense and frightened I was. I had been so busy sorting out the facts of the case, I hadn't had time to notice my feelings. I put my hand in John's free one and rubbed my thumb along the ridges of bone.

"I don't know if you realize this or not," he said after a while, "but things are even worse than they looked back at the church. This business with Agapé —she must have been the one at the bank—"

"She's nuts," I said.

"I wouldn't doubt it. The killing of the guards was a very amateurish touch. It was the first clue anyone had that whoever had pulled off that robbery hadn't been as experienced in that kind of thing as you'd have expected. It was a stupid move. A robbery that size is going to bring down enough heat. You don't need a couple of unnecessary murders to fan the flames."

"John, I think she likes killing people. I know that sounds bizarre—"

"It doesn't sound bizarre at all. It's the only explanation that could cover the available facts. The two priests, one of them right in this house. That girl, in full view of everyone in Kilithia. Costa, in the kitchen, of all places. I don't think Marina or the rest of them would have had any compunction about offing a few people, but Marina would have kept it rational if she could. Kept it quiet and far enough away so it wouldn't touch them."

I thought of the conversation I had overheard on the stairs. "I don't think Marina likes the way things have been going," I said. "I heard her tell Costa to keep Agapé under control. I mean, she didn't say Agapé, but I'm sure now that's who she meant. And when Agapé heard Marina coming into the kitchen, she was terrified."

"She's got good reason to be terrified. And not just of Marina, either. Skoulouris is in on this now, and he isn't going to tolerate a wild woman. She's lethal in more ways than one."

I had a terrible thought. "Does Skoulouris have people here? His own people?" I asked.

"I don't think so," John said. "There's no need for it. The shipment is all marked and ready to go. It would be too great a risk to bring his people here. They'd stick out. They'd be noticed. Kilithia is a very small place."

"Right," I said. "This way, if anything goes wrong, it's all Pan and Marina."

"At this end, yes."

"For a minute there, I was worried Chas was going to have to duck those people as well as the Peterises."

"Has it occurred to you we have to duck them, too?" He tugged gently on my hair. "In case it hasn't hit you yet, we are locked in the basement of Pan Peteris's house, with no way out either of us can see, while the people upstairs are harboring a homicidal maniac and trying to get close to six million dollars' worth of stolen gold out of the country."

My stomach heaved into a wave a surfer would have been gratified to see. "Thanks for reminding me," I said.

John leaned over and brushed his lips against mine, teasing me, gently and persistently, until I began to lose all sense of danger and urgency. I didn't forget about those things. The rational part of my mind cataloged them endlessly, while making disinterested comments on the power of love and attraction. Fortunately or unfortunately, the rational power of my mind didn't seem to have much control over the rest of me.

I turned on my side, pressing closer to him, feeling the shape of his strong shoulders under his jacket. It was so much nicer to think about that than it would have been to think about all those other things. I'd never been much for blood and gore. Even my favorite detective stories kept that kind of thing to a minimum.

I put my hand under his jacket and rubbed against his sweater. He wore big, heavy-weave sweaters, the kind with the nylon patches at shoulders and elbows. They suited him.

"Kerry," he said gently.

"Mmm."

"Kerry, as much as I'd like to spend the rest of the day doing this, or night, or whatever it is at the moment—"

"You're going to get scary again."

"I have to. And you know it."

"Right." I sat up again, pulling away from him. "Why is it that every time we get involved in something like this, something nasty comes up to keep us from going on with it?"

He laughed and kissed me again. "If we get out of this alive," he promised me, "I'll take you on one of those island cruises where you spend all your time eating too much and lying around in bed."

"Lying around in bed," I said. "How do you know I do things like lie around in bed?"

"I don't. I just have every confidence you'll do it for me."

"I don't think I want to hear the end of this argument."

"Good. You want to know how we're going to get out of this alive?"

I pulled all the way away this time, to the wall, where nothing could distract me. "Thank God you have a plan," I said.

He grunted. "I gave this quite a bit of thought," he said, "while you were out cold. I didn't have anything else to do. At any rate, we have two options. One is to go up and try to force our way into the kitchen. That wouldn't be too hard. I think this is one of those places they'd call a root cellar back home. It wasn't designed to be a prison. There's nothing special about that door. We could probably kick our way through it."

"Well, why don't we?" I said. "For God's sake, it would have to be better than sitting around down here—"

"Listen," John said.

I listened. There were footsteps above us, heavy ones and light ones, treading back and forth across the kitchen floor with some regularity.

"Damn. I've had so much else on my mind, I didn't even notice," I said.

"I noticed. I'm not sure, but I think what they're doing up there is moving the gold. It's the kind of thing Marina and Pan would want to keep an eye on themselves. With the stuff going through Zurich instead of New York and with Skoulouris's name on it instead of Pan's, they can put the contraband all in one place instead of dispersing it through hundreds of boxes. It would certainly be more efficient. If we went bursting through the kitchen door now, we'd be outnumbered and worse. We'd get killed."

"So what do we do?"

He gave me a big grin. "We do what any good general would do," he said. "We get them to come to us."

It took longer than I'd expected to set it up, and every minute we worked made me jumpier. It would have been different if we'd had real weapons, but all we'd been able to come up with was a disintegrating packing crate we'd taken apart to make what looked

252

to me to be very inadequate clubs. It didn't help my nerves any that we had to attempt to take that crate apart, and do everything else, in as close to complete silence as possible.

"Just remember," John said. "We want them to come down, but not before we're ready for them. Don't drop anything. Don't make any loud noises. Don't make them suspicious."

I dropped a metal ashtray and winced, hearing the echo of tin against cement far longer than I should have. We both held our breath for what seemed like an eternity. Nothing happened. The tramping upstairs was heavier now. It was possible they had (momentarily) forgotten about us entirely.

"I called Louganis," I said. "You sent Chas to him. Maybe he'll show up at the door—"

"You want to count on that?" John said.

"No."

There was a lightbulb sitting bare in a socket over the stairs, and John went after it. It was much too high for him to reach easily, but he didn't dare take part of our broken crate to break it. The sound of breaking glass might be a tipoff. Anything might be a tipoff.

I waited at the bottom of the stairs, sweat dripping down my face; I was ready to scream. This was far worse than hiding in the linen closet had been, or eavesdropping from the top of the stairs. Now I knew exactly what was going on, and the knowledge had not set me free. If anything, it had wound me up so tight I could hardly move. Whenever I thought about what we were doing, I felt ready to faint.

We stacked the debris in the basement—the pieces of wood and metal I had fallen into when I'd come down the steps—near the top of the stairs, but far enough from the door so they wouldn't be obvious when seen in the light from the kitchen. What we wanted was to make a racket and bring someone, anyone, rushing down to find out what was going on. Our best luck would be to get hold of Pan. Agapé was far more dangerous, but she was small. We could hope to outrun her or overpower her. Pan was a massive man. Once he got hold of me, I wouldn't be able to get free of him. I had no doubt that if it came down to a contest of brute strength, he'd overpower John, too.

He might already have overpowered Chas. That was what kept me working, the thought of Chas out there somewhere, vulnerable and naive.

We piled the debris on the stairs—broken pottery, discarded ashtrays, ancient warped mixing bowls—in the hope someone would fall over it. We both had the same thing in mind—me, bouncing and rolling until I came to a crash on the cement floor, knocked out.

When we were finished, we tried to stand back and survey our handiwork, but it wasn't feasible. It was too dark, and the obstruction was too far above us.

"I just hope it's this hard to see from that end," John said grimly. He peered into the darkness and shook his head. "I just can't tell. I just can't see a thing."

"Let's get this over with," I said nervously. "Let's—"

He stopped me. "We aren't going to get anything over with yet. Come back here." He grabbed my arm and pulled me farther into the shadows and to the side. "You don't want to be standing in front like that when they come down," he cautioned. "Pan or Agapé or even Marina could be dangerous. They could be armed. They could be smarter than we think they are. You want to be off to the side, so if they fire blind, you don't get hit."

"I'm off to the side now," I insisted.

He gave me the metal washtub we had found and

one of the boards from the crate. "You don't do anything until I tell you to," he said.

"Which will be when?" I demanded urgently. "I don't see—"

John pointed to the ceiling. "Footsteps," he said. "We're listening for footsteps. When we hear Pan's footsteps, the heaviest ones, going this way"—he traced a pattern in the air—"then you start banging that thing. Pan'll be heading for the kitchen door. He'll probably be carrying something heavy if we're right about what they're doing up there. You make a racket and keep making a racket. Drive him crazy. Make him lose patience. What we want him to do is drop what he's carrying and rush for that door at the top of the stairs—rush without thinking, don't you see?"

"So that he'll come rushing down the stairs and fall over the stuff we've got laid out there."

"Exactly."

I rubbed my palms against the side of the metal washtub. "I think I'm losing my nerve," I said. "You have no idea how I think I'm losing my nerve."

"You're not losing anything." John stroked my hair again. "You're the bravest person I know, and you're going to come through this beautifully."

"You're a very bad liar," I told him. "I just hope we can get this finished *fast.*"

We didn't get it finished fast. In fact, for a while I began to think we wouldn't get it finished at all. No sooner had we got the plot set up and ready to work when all sound ceased in the kitchen and all the footsteps disappeared. It was the worst moment I'd ever had: sitting there in that damp, cold basement, holding a wooden crate slat over a punctured metal washtub, living through minute after minute of absolute silence. I began to get the crazy feeling that we were all alone. There was no one upstairs. There was no danger waiting for us. There was nothing, just two deluded people in a basement playing spy.

Maybe if things had happened faster, they wouldn't have gotten as crazy as they did. By the time we heard noises in the kitchen again, even John was getting edgy. John being edgy drove me wild. He was my rock, my anchor. It was all right for me to be going crazy quietly. He was supposed to be rational and firm and confident. As long as he stayed that way, part of me believed we would get ourselves out of this.

He did not stay that way. As his mood disintegrated, so did mine. My nerves were raw and my head was pounding. The darkness around us felt solid and malevolent. Somewhere above us, the wind was screaming out of control, twisting into the worst kind of Mediterranean storm. It battered the house and whistled through the crack under the door at the top of the stairs. It probably rattled windows, too, although we couldn't hear them. I'd been in one or two of these storms. The damage they did was more emotional than physical. They might tear a few shingles off the roof or demolish a rain gutter, but their distinguishing feature was the sudden, random changes in barometric pressure. In some places, this can cause tornadoes, but Greece was too mountainous, too hemmed in by water. Here, the wildly swinging highs and lows, combined with wind that whistled and gusted and tore at the fabric of the earth, called up only cyclone emotions. Like the Santa Ana winds or the typhoon squalls of Asia, like full moon nights in otherwise calm places like Michigan and Illinois, the great winter weather fronts of the Mediterranean were crime and craziness weather.

It got to me. I would be less than honest to say it

didn't. What worried me was that it also seemed to be getting to John. He was twitching and tense, and he was getting reckless. I looked into his eyes once during that long wait, and I never looked again. There was a hard, angry light in them, evidence of an emotion I wasn't sure he had under control.

When we first heard sounds in the kitchen again, we both nearly jumped out of our skin.

"Easy," John commanded. He sounded impatient and angry at me, and I shrank away.

Somebody—Marina, I thought—let out a stream of Greek that seemed to go on for five minutes. John strained forward, trying to hear, but after a while he sat back again, disgusted. The kitchen was too far away and the acoustics were wrong. He couldn't catch anything.

He saw me looking at him and shook his head. He pointed to the ceiling.

It is remarkable what you can hear when you have to—when you seriously make yourself listen. Words were indistinguishable, but after a few moments of effort, I found movements clear as a bell. Marina's step was jerky and uneven. She was using her cane, and I could hear the hollow, wooden sound of it hitting the kitchen linoleum. Pan walked like a great lumbering beast. He made the house shake.

At the sound of the step I knew to be Pan's, I tugged excitedly on John's sleeve, ready to go. He waved me away again. Then, probably deciding he had been too abrupt, he turned to me and began pantomiming. I was to wait until Marina left the kitchen or until Pan did and came back, carrying something.

I put my head on my arms and closed my eyes. The tension went on and on, on and on, with nothing to break it. I was losing little pieces of myself to the strain.

Upstairs, Marina's gait creaked and knocked, creaked and knocked, until it was out of hearing. Pan, still for a moment, began to pace. I sat up straight, suddenly alert.

John was holding his arm in the air like the whistle man at the start of an Olympic race. I kept my eyes on his hand as ardently as a hopeful medalist waited for the signal to run. I counted seconds and half seconds and milliseconds in my head, willing the time to pass, willing the conditions to be right, willing myself into self-control. The effort went on forever, and it was nearly futile. John's arm came down as my willpower disintegrated, giving me permission to do something I would no longer have been able to stop myself from doing anyway.

In one respect, however, I was perfectly competent. I set up a racket that would have brought Ramses I out of his tomb.

22

It was dark. That's the best explanation I can give for how everything got so terribly confused, and it doesn't begin to address the issue. Everything happened so fast. First I sent up my noise, then Pan opened the kitchen door, then Pan came down the stairs. Then the plan fell apart. In one sense, we got exactly what we wanted. Pan was neither armed nor coolly in control of the situation. In another, we failed miserably. Pan fell on the stairs, but he was better at it than I had been. He curled himself into a ball as soon as he started to slip. He rolled down the stairs in perfect safety, bruising a few parts of his body (like his *golou*, as the Greeks would say), but injuring nothing important. He was wide-awake and ready to go when he hit the cement, and he was a much better fighter than either of us had expected.

Of course, I should have expected it. Even in all the noise and fighting, I had time enough to realize that. I had seen Pan drive a car. I knew he wasn't as clumsy and incompetent as he appeared to be. I simply hadn't translated that knowledge into something important enough to tell John. I had let him go into the fight with entirely erroneous beliefs about the strengths and weaknesses of his opponent. For all I knew, I was getting him killed.

I still had the crate slat in my hands. John had lost his when the fighting started. Pan had come out of his roll and leaped on top of him, dislodging the slat and pinning him to the floor. John hadn't stayed pinned long, but by the time he'd managed to get Pan off his chest, he was facing a bare-handed fight. Pan had little finesse but a lot of speed, and more muscle than I liked to think about. He didn't have much respect for the marquis of Queensberry, either. He punched and bit and kicked, blindly and indiscriminately, with little or no thought to what part of John's body he was aiming at. Once, he nearly got John in the kneecap. He came so close, I thought my heart would stop.

I got a good grip on my crate slat and tried to move in close to them. It was very hard to do. They were moving, mostly in circles, spinning so quickly I could never keep one or the other of them in sight for longer than a few seconds. I brandished my wooden stick in the air, caught in an agony of indecision and confusion. If I accidentally hit John, we would both be dead. If I didn't hit Pan, I thought we'd *still* both be dead.

I came another step closer, hesitant but determined, and as I did, John saw me.

"Run," he screamed at me. "Run, for God's sake."

I stared at him. Run? What did he mean?

The sight of me standing there like a chicken ready to be plucked gave him a little something extra. He drew back his foot, planted it squarely in the center of Pan's belt, and kicked as hard as he could. Pan went reeling backward toward the far wall, caught off balance.

John whirled on me, grabbed me by the shoulders, and shook me until my teeth felt loose in my gums.

"Run," he yelled at me again. "Go upstairs. Get to a phone. Get *out* of here."

Light dawned. Run. Of course I should be running. I should be heading for the hills, or at least for Kilithia. In that moment, a brave new plan blossomed in my head. That new priest, the American, would have nothing to do with the Peterises and their gold. He might have a car, or some way to contact Agios Constantinos. Hell, he might be willing to come up to Pan's house and help the good guys. If I could get to the church, I could give us a fighting chance.

I shook free of John's grip and wheeled, heading for the stairs. That was when I saw Pan, on his feet again and heading for us like a freight train with an open throttle.

"John," I screamed.

He turned around just in time. Pan was in the air, arms out in front of him, hands opening to grab John's throat. John caught him by the wrists, and they both went over.

I didn't stay around to see how this round came out. I ran—up the stairs, over the numerous scraps of metal and wood still littering the steps, through the kitchen door.

And right into the arms of Agapé.

I hadn't expected to see her there. It was criminally stupid, but it was true. I had forgotten all about her and about Marina. Agapé had a knife, not the shortbladed one she'd had before, but a big long kitchen knife. From where I stood, it looked like a saber.

"I hate Americans," she said, smiling as pleasantly as a hostess at a tea party. "Did I ever tell you I hate Americans?"

"No," I said. "You've never told me."

"Stupid fat women," she said. "Stupid fat men. Too rich to know what's good for them." She thrust the knife at me, through my sweater, into my skin. I felt it break through, as if I'd stabbed myself with a needle.

The sweat was coming down my face again, getting into my eyes. It was running down my back, too, making my turtleneck feel like a wet bathing suit. Behind me, the fight got louder and more violent by the second.

There is a way to handle a person with a knife, to get the knife away from him, to give yourself a chance to escape. My father had explained it to me, at length, the night we had the argument about my going to live in New York. My father might disapprove of my reluctance to enter law school, but he doesn't want to see me killed. And he doesn't believe in victims. Everybody should be prepared to take care of himself. If you are set upon by a single rapist without a gun, you should be prepared to put his eyes out—a maneuver he demonstrated that night, with nauseating attention to detail. If you are attacked by someone with a knife—

Agapé's eyes had gone into glitter mode. She was lit up like a Christmas tree, with "an inner light," as the old religious romances used to say, except that there was nothing I'd call religious going on in her head. Agapé liked blood. She liked the smell and the feel and the sight of it.

Agapé looked over my shoulder, in the general direction of the noise. *"She* says he'll never marry me now," she said. I supposed she was referring to Marina and to Pan. *"She* says he'll do what she tells him. But he won't. He'll do what I tell him. First he'll break the neck of your friend, then he'll do what I tell him."

"Of course," I said.

"She's just an old woman," Agapé said. "She doesn't move very well."

She brought the knife forward again, higher now, between my breasts. In another move, she would be at my throat and it would be too late to do anything. I could feel her stabbing against the hard square of plastic that was the front fastening of my bra, playing with it. A few more prods, and it would pop open.

"If you back up again, you'll fall," she said. "You don't want to fall again, do you?"

"No," I said. "No, I don't."

"Then don't back up. Not even a small step."

I looked down at the knife. She was pressing it against me, harder and harder. She was right. If I took another step backward, I would fall. I couldn't face that again. I stared and stared at the knife, remembering my father's instructions, wondering just how badly I was going to hurt myself.

"You can't go back," Agapé said. "But I can go *up*."

She was grinning at me, literally grinning at me. I had to do something.

I brought my hands up very slowly, not wanting to startle her with any sudden movement, not wanting her to notice what I was doing. She was holding the blade with the sharp side pointing up, so I had to curl my wrists to make it come out right. I got my hands around the blade, with the sharpened edge pressing into my finger joints, just before she saw me moving.

When she saw what I had done, she gaped. She may have done more than that, but I was in no state to notice. That blade was sharp. It went through my skin effortlessly, and it hurt like hell. I don't think I've ever been in such pain.

"Stupid," Agapé spat at me. *"Stupid."*

She flicked the knife upward, expecting it to cut and wound and knock my hands away, but I held fast. I held on more tightly than I'd ever held on to anything. I went beyond pain. The blade was longer than the haft. There was no way she could get the thing away from me unless I let go.

I wouldn't let go. It took a while for that to sink through her thick skull, long, agonizing moments when she grabbed and pulled at the knife, shredding the skin on my fingers. When it finally hit home that she wasn't going to get the thing back, she went crazy.

"Putana," she screamed at me, then more Greek, millions and millions of words of Greek pouring out of her like water through a dam sluice.

"Agapé," Marina said sharply, and I turned my head in that direction. I'd forgotten about Marina, for the second time. I had a terrible feeling it was a mistake.

Agapé, who had been so afraid of Marina during her first attack on me, now didn't even seem to hear the old woman's voice. She made another swipe at the knife. I'd tried to turn it around, to grasp it by the haft, but my fingers were too damaged. Tears were streaming down my face from the pain. The best I could do was hold on as I had been holding on.

"Putana," Agapé said again, stepping away from me and staring at the knife. *"Putana, putana, putana."*

She let out a yell like an ancient warrior going into battle and lunged at me.

I should have gone down. I should have broken my neck and my head and half the rest of the bones in my body. There was no reason at all why Agapé should have veered so far to the right, giving me just enough room to get out of the way. I watched in shock as she pitched headfirst into the stairwell. I had no emotion left to react to the sound of John's voice at the bottom of the stairs, saying "damn" and a few other things I couldn't catch, audible because all other sound had ceased. The fight was over. John was down there somewhere, whole and alive.

And there was blood on my jeans.

I looked at the knife in my hand. I had been holding it so tightly, not much blood had escaped, and what had was mostly on my sweater, where my hands were resting against my chest. The blood on my jeans was well below the knee, and there was a lot of it.

John was coming up the steps, dragging something with him. I turned away, toward Marina. John would get up without my help. If Pan hadn't been beaten, he would never have allowed himself to be dragged that way.

Marina was putting her gun down on the counter next to the washing machine and taking off her gloves. They were fine black mesh gloves, for mourning. I'd seldom seen her without them.

"I didn't hear a noise," I said.

She shrugged. "We have silencers even on the Greek islands, Miss Hansen." She made a rude gesture in the direction of the basement door. "A crazy woman. It all comes apart because of a crazy woman. And because I was weak."

She looked weak. Her progress to the kitchen table was halting and painful, her body racked by weariness as well as arthritis. She slid into one of the wooden kitchen chairs with a grunt of relief.

"I was always better than all of them," she said. "Smarter than all of them. Surer than all of them. Stronger than all of them. They'd have spent their lives here, digging in the dirt like animals, if it hadn't been for me."

"They're not *animals* here," I said, surprised to find myself indignant at this insult to Kilithia. "They want the same things you do. They just have a few scruples about the way they go about getting them."

She waved a hand languidly in the air. "You lie to yourself. They lie to themselves, too. I should have done this all years ago. I should have killed you when I had the chance—or made him fire you." She laughed bitterly. "Oh dear, how we discussed that. And I thought it would be safe. Sending you. I thought it was better to use the extra passports as seldom as possible. I thought you'd get the work done and never suspect anything. I thought you were stupid."

"As far as I'm concerned, I was a complete idiot."

"Yes?"

There was a sound behind me, and I turned. John was bringing Pan into the kitchen, dragging that massive, limp body like a sack of coal. He looked from me to Marina to the gun on the counter, too far from anyone to be a threat. Then he dumped Pan's body on the kitchen floor.

"I'm not even going to ask," he said. "I'm sure it will be explained in time." He gave the gun another look. "On the other hand," he said, "just in case—"

I stopped him before he picked it up. "She just killed Agapé with it," I said.

His hand hovered in the air above the gun. Marina laughed.

"That's the key, isn't it?" she said. She sounded delighted with herself. "I just killed Agapé with it. And I set it all up. I made all the decisions and all the mistakes. I should have killed you," she said to me. "Or at least stopped you from seeing your brother. That was the end. But it doesn't matter now. I could have killed you, too, and waited for him"—she nodded at John—"to come up the stairs. I could have gotten you all."

"Why didn't you?"

She looked amused. "Oh well," she said. "I would

have been caught then, wouldn't I? It would have been too much to explain away."

"I don't think you're going to be able to explain this away."

"No?" She pointed at Pan's body on the floor. "He's alive, I suppose."

"Yes," John said. "He's alive."

"As long as he's alive," Marina said, "I'll never be touched." She gave me a pitying smile. "There's the drawback to women's liberation," she said. "No Greek jury will ever take my son's word against mine. No Greek jury will ever believe I killed anyone—and even if you got them to believe that, you couldn't get them to believe I wasn't justified. Oh, for a mother to save her son from a truly, provably evil woman! Oh, what a mother has to suffer at the hands of her erring children!"

"You're giving motherhood a bad name," I said with revulsion.

I had been edging forward, trying to get closer to John. When her hand darted out, I was well within range. She caught my sweater and pulled me to her.

"Listen to me," she said, her breath hot and foul in my face. "They are animals here. You have to live in the dirt and the flies and the hunger and the ignorance before you realize it. You have to live where a man can beat you to death after he's had a few drinks—and get away with it—to realize it. Look at my son, in his suit from Brooks Brothers and his Philippe Patek watch. Without me he would have been another Costa Papageorgiou, a brute and a bull with dirt under his fingernails and ouzo in his head instead of brains."

She straightened suddenly, letting go of me. The fever and malice were gone. She was a frail old woman, small and bent, weighed down by the eternal black of her mourning. She looked like a hundred Greek grandmothers in a hundred Greek villages on a couple of dozen Greek islands, a harmless old woman living on memories and dreams and the progress of her children's children.

"There," she said. "That's what you've been waiting for. Your friends have arrived."

I looked uncertainly at John, and he nodded.

Then I heard it too: a car on the drive, footsteps and voices in the foyer and the living room.

Chas came through the kitchen door with Kiriou Louganis in tow, looking so proud of himself I was almost sorry all the real trouble was over.

Epilogue

THERE WERE NO cruise boats working the Greek islands that time of year. There weren't even any tourists who wanted to ride on them. The temperature was low, the seas were choppy, and rain was nearly inevitable. We had to charter a boat in Rhodes, and her captain—a pale little British expatriate John had had to do everything but threaten with sudden death to force to take us on—thought we were crazy.

We weren't, but I didn't blame Michael Torker for thinking so. He was prone to seasickness (so was Admiral Lord Nelson), and used to seeing the main deck of his three-masted, teak-hulled, custom-made extravagance littered with rich people in bathing suits. Instead, he got Chas in two sweaters and bare feet, carting around disorganized scraps of paper with what looked like hieroglyphics all over them. He got John, in jeans but sans shirt, with his ribs taped so many ways he looked like a mummy. He got me, with all those shifting bandages on my fingers. It would have been kinder to tell him who we were and what had happened, but not one of us could work up any enthusiasm for disclosure. Michael Torker didn't read newspapers. He barely opened his mail from home. He was new to Rhodes—he usually put in somewhere in Italy for the winter—so he didn't know anyone to pick up gossip from. He was the first person we'd met in a month who didn't want to restrict the conversation to what had, had not, might have, and should have happened in the case of The Government of Greece *vs.* Peteris.

The fact is, we didn't know much about what was happening in The Government of Greece *vs.* Peteris. Kiriou Louganis and his colleagues, like policemen all over the world, liked to keep their discoveries and their strategies to themselves. The fact that John and Chas—and I—had literally solved their case for them was beside the point. The only thing *they* thought we needed to know was the date we were to appear as witnesses. Kiriou Louganis promised to call us about that personally.

The gold *tiri* were in a box on the back of a truck in a stable in Upper Kilithia, which is what the government in Athens likes to call a collection of five mud and stone houses so far up Themnos Mountain they should have fallen off before the people there had finished building them. John got that out of Kiriou Louganis by threatening to make all three of us disappear right around the start of the trial. He could have gotten more, but we didn't really want to hear it. John and I had things we wanted to do. Chas was willing to come along for the ride.

What John and I wanted to do was neck. Actually, it would have gone beyond necking almost immediately, except that my fingers were all bandaged up and Pan had broken two of John's ribs in the fight. The rib situation was compounded by the fact that John hadn't *noticed* anything was broken until we had everyone down in Agios Constantinos being questioned. Then he'd passed out on Kiriou Louganis's office floor, and Robert Hobart—that little weasel of a man whose chin looked too weak to support the rest of his face—had had to airlift in an American doctor from Athens. The American doctor in Malina was drunk.

The rib situation had improved to the point where I could get my arms around John's chest and squeeze—gently—without his screaming in pain, when we had our first really good day on the water. It was by then late March, and the promises of spring were everywhere. We had sun and very little wind. It was warm enough so that John's bare back, although covered with goose pimples, was not making him shiver. We had a calm sea. John and I lay stretched out side by side on a pair of chaise longues, holding hands when we couldn't do anything else and doing other things when we could. The difficulties in fully consummating this relationship were getting me a little crazy. For years, I had considered the entire enterprise boring. Here was a man who made me feel as if said enterprise with *him* would be anything but, and I had to restrain myself constantly to ensure I didn't refracture delicately setting bones. The fact that he was very, very good at all the peripheral aspects of that activity only made the situation worse. I was dying to get my hands on him. Better yet, I was living for the day he was healed enough to get his hands on me.

He was giving me a demonstration of something called the feather technique when Chas came on deck, clumping along in his bare feet and humming to himself, oblivious to anything private he might be interrupting.

"Kerry?" he called. "John? Ker—oh." He dropped into the empty chaise longue. "At it again, I see."

"Of course we're at it again," John grumbled, disentangling himself from me and sitting up. "What do you think we hired the boat for?"

"I won't even dignify that with an answer. Are you two going to get married?"

"Chas," I said. Actually, I'd thought about that myself. A good man is hard to find, as Flannery O'Connor said, and since I'd finally found one, I didn't like the idea of letting him go. Or leaving things on an ambivalent basis, either. On the other hand, it seemed much too early to bring all that up. We'd only known each other for two and a half months.

My father had known my mother exactly six days when he proposed.

I rearranged my sweater and told myself there was no use thinking about that.

John took the offensive. "Was there something in particular you wanted to talk about," he asked Chas, "or are you just here to be entertained?"

"Oh," Chas said. He reached into the pocket of his jeans and came up with a small wad of paper. He threw it on John's lap. "Here. While you two were spending your time incommunicado, I went into Mykonos." He met our blank stares with incredulity. "Last night?" he prodded. "When we were docked?"

"Oh," John said. "Yeah. I remember something about that." He turned to me. "Why didn't we leave the ship?"

"You thought there wouldn't be any good restaurants," I said.

"I can't *believe* you two," Chas said. "Food and—" He saw my glare and grinned. "Food and love," he corrected himself. "Do you realize half the population of the United States would probably kill to do what you're doing now, if you'd only get off the boat and do it?"

"I'm doing exactly what I want to do," John said. He picked up the paper Chas had tossed into his lap. "What's this?"

"I got some newspapers in Mykonos. And don't tell me you don't want to see any newspapers. You've got to catch up with the world sometime or other."

"I don't see why," I said.

John unfolded the little scrap of paper. "If this is another paean to your unprecedented heroism—good *lord.*"

"What is it?" I said.

"What did she do, announce the engagement from jail?" John said.

"Marina's going to marry someone?" I said.

"Caliope's going to marry someone." John tossed the clipping to me. "My father was right. All Greeks are crazy."

I flattened the clipping against my knee. It was from one of the largest Greek papers, a sensationalist rag called *Ethniki,* and it was exactly like every other wedding announcement they printed. Loosely translated, it read:

Peteris-Sarantides

Marina George Peteris has announced the wedding of her daughter, Caliope John Peteris, to Mr. Stephen Sarantides of Athens. Mr. Sarantides is a feature reporter for the *Greek Progressive* and a co-editor of that paper. See page 11.

"Sarantides," I said. "Why is that name familiar?"

"You remember that picture of you, with the mud and the gun and your shirt—"

"Don't remind me," I said. "I don't have to tell you that's not one of the stories I sent to Mother."

"Well," Chas said, "he also did one of his famous treatments of the Peteris family. God, he made them sound like the Borgias. It was wonderful. Anyway, as far as I can tell from page eleven—"

"You read page eleven?" John said.

"Of course," Chas said. "I read the *Enquirer* at home, too. Anyway, as far as I can tell from page eleven, he did a hatchet job on the Peterises and in the doing he met Caliope. And so—"

"Well," I said. "It was what she always wanted. To be married, I mean."

John looked as if he thought the two of us were crazy. "Married to some guy who's busy making your family look like dirt."

"Be reasonable," I said. "The papers don't have to do a lot of work on this one. There are at least six people dead. And Marina—well, you heard Marina."

"Yes, I did," John said. "But there are ways to handle those things."

"Not in Greece," I said. "And let's face it. If the police weren't taking this tack, if they were being all upright and steadfast and British fair play, Marina would be getting just what she was looking for. Meaning off."

John still wasn't happy with it, and I loved him for it. Maybe I'd been going about things the wrong way back in New York. I'd always thought my requirements for a man ran along the lines of good-looking, upwardly mobile, well employed. Of course, John was all these things, but he was other things, too. I was beginning to see that the other things were much more important. A sense of purpose, a commitment to justice, loyalty—*character*. Who'd have thought character could be sexy?

"Kerry?" John said. "Where are you off to?"

"Personals ads," I said.

"What?"

"Give it up," Chas said. "She does this kind of thing all the time."

I patted John's hand. "It's nothing," I said. "I was

just off on a tangent. I know the way the Greek courts run is appalling, and I know I shouldn't approve of it, but I just can't stand the idea of that woman sticking it all on Pan and getting off scot-free. It wouldn't be fair. No matter how big a jerk Pan is."

"Well, don't get too mushy over Pan Peteris. He's the one who shot at you."

"And missed," I reminded John. "Not by much, I know, but still. We know now he was a very good shot—" This had come out in the papers. Apparently, Marina had been training her crew for this operation for years. Pan's job had been to learn how to handle a rifle, and he'd done a bang-up job. He could outshoot the Greek National Rifle Team. Being Pan, he'd been too vain and too unintelligent to hide it. When the police had asked for a demonstration, he had given it to them. *That* piece of news had made the front page of every paper in Greece for three days running, until everybody remembered that the only people who'd been shot were the guards at the bank, and there was a videotape of Agapé doing that. "So," I said, "we have to assume he could have hit me if he'd wanted to, and he didn't want to. I don't think Pan ever had the killer instinct."

Chas stretched comfortably in the chaise longue, apparently having decided the conversation had gone far enough so he was no longer interrupting. "The person I always feel sorry for," he said, "is Caliope. Her mother has no use for her. Her brother treated her like a doll he could dress up to let everyone know how much money he was making. They didn't even bother to tell her what was going on, at least not in detail. And she's getting slammed with this almost as badly as everyone else involved."

"She's not going to jail," John pointed out. "She's not even being prosecuted."

"And she's getting married," I said. "She'll be thrilled."

"She's getting married to a Greek," Chas said. "She always wanted so badly to be a New Yorker. A *real* New Yorker, as she put it."

"And she did know what was going on," I said, "no matter what she's saying now. Now that I know what was going on, I can look back at a dozen conversations in that house and see the reactions—the way people looked, the things they said, the way they ran away from certain topics. They all knew."

"Still," Chas said stubbornly, "Caliope got a raw deal. I just hope this marriage makes up for it."

John stretched luxuriously on his chaise longue. "You amaze me," he said. "Two months ago, you were ready to kill these people. In fact, if I remember correctly, you were getting very creative about the way you wanted to kill them. Now you're mooning around feeling sorry for them. They nearly got you put away in a federal penitentiary."

"Yeah," Chas said. "Well—"

"Space cadet," I said. "Have I ever told you you take after Mother?"

"Once a week since I was eight."

John put an arm around my shoulder and began to caress the side of my face farthest from Chas, using his thumb in a soft, circular motion that made me feel very floaty. I nuzzled against him, feeling self-satisfied. Yes, there was definitely something different about my response to John Borden. He also proved a point—my mother's, unfortunately: it *is* different with the right person.

I turned on my side, propping my head on my arm, and began to run my hand over his chest. He had a very hairy chest—blond-hairy and soft, but hairy nonetheless. It was unexpected. I'd always assumed (for no good reason) that pale men would be smooth-chested. The sight of all that golden down kept giving me ideas.

John leaned over—stiff and slow, because of the bandages and the vestiges of pain—and began to kiss me on my nose. Being kissed on the nose turned out to be a very pleasant experience. I wouldn't have expected that, either.

"Why don't we go downstairs," John whispered in my ear. "We haven't tried anything in two days."

"You're still creaking," I said doubtfully, referring to the sound his chest made when he made any sudden or violent move.

"I'm going to be creaking the rest of my life," he said. "I can't wait that long."

"Neither can I," I said.

"Ahem," Chas said.

It was like being hit over the head with a bucket of cold water. John and I looked up simultaneously, equally annoyed.

"Don't you have work to do?" John asked Chas. "Aren't you supposed to have your dissertation outlined by the time you get back to New York?"

"I got an extension," Chas said blandly. "They've read all about me in the newspapers. They don't want me to ruin my health."

"Damn." John wrenched himself up, wincing at the sharp movement. "You know, Hansen, you and I are going to have to have a long talk."

"I don't want a long talk," Chas said. "It's just that if you two are going to get married, I want to know now, because if you two are going to get married, I'm going to have to go to Tiffany's, and going to Tiffany's is expensive. If you see what I mean."

"I see what you mean," John said. "You can stop worrying. My intentions are entirely honorable. My intentions are always honorable."

"I know that," Chas said. "But I'm a poor graduate student. I just can't pop off and buy a silver something—"

I cleared my throat painfully. "Chas?" I said.

"What?"

"Yes you can."

"Yes I can what?"

"Pop off to Tiffany's and buy a silver something." I sat up and grinned sheepishly at the two of them. "I've—um, I've been writing letters."

"You've been writing letters," Chas repeated. The look on his face was murderous.

"Now, Chas," I said. "This couldn't go on forever. As it is, it's been going on longer than it should have. And he's really very reasonable when—"

"Reasonable?" Chas shouted. "Our father? The last time our father was reasonable, hell was a very cold place. What in the name of all that's holy did you tell him to get him to answer you?"

"Well," I said, bracing myself for the worst, "I sent him your press clippings."

Murderous would have been a euphemism to describe the look Chas gave me *that* time. I didn't dare let Chas open his mouth.

"I know the stories were inaccurate," I said, "but that really doesn't matter, because you really were very brave throughout the whole thing—"

"I nearly had a nervous breakdown during the whole thing," Chas said coldly. "And you know it."

"I mean at the end," I said.

Chas sighed. "Kerry, I can't do this. I can't be the person he wants me to be. I can't even want to be that person anymore. And I don't want to spend my life pretending and lying to him and feeling inadequate."

"I know," I said. "But I think it's all right. I don't think he's been any happier about this situation than we've been. He just needed an excuse. So I gave it to him."

"And he wrote you back?"

"He sent a telegram when we were in Rhodes last time. It's down on my bed in my cabin. I was reading it over this morning. You'll like it, Chas. It must have cost him five hundred dollars. I'm not kidding—it's that long."

"I hope you know what you're doing," he said.

"Trust me," I said.

"I never want to hear anyone ask me to trust them again." Chas got off his chaise longue. "I'll leave you two to your diversions. I want to go read that telegram."

John and I watched him go, a tall, lanky figure with just a little anger in his step—and just a little apprehension. I sympathized. Our father can be a tiger when he wants to be. Fortunately, this time I wasn't worried. Our father can also be a pussycat when he wants to be, and he was in a distinctly domestic mood at the moment.

I turned back to John and put my hands in his hair. He has very thick, very smooth hair. It feels like silk.

"I've been trying to reconcile those two for five years," I said. "It's nice to have it done."

"It would be nice to have a lot of things done," John said, nuzzling my neck.

"Did you really mean it," I asked him, "about your intentions being honorable?"

He started to trace the contours of my face with his fingers. "I'm an old man," he said. "Over thirty and

279

all grown-up. I'm past the stage where quantity and mobility are the prime considerations."

"I've met men of forty who still think quantity and mobility are the prime considerations," I said.

"Cases of retarded development." He started nibbling my ear. "Do you think we could get to the details later? There's sort of this other subject that keeps coming up and I—"

I slid down in my chaise longue, turned sideways, and folded myself in his arms. "I *know* how that subject keeps coming up," I said.

His laugh, when it came, was very deep in his throat.